P9-DXZ-476

It Happened One Knife

IT HAPPENED ONE KNIFE

JEFFREY COHEN

THORNDIKE
CHIVERS

This Large Print edition is published by Thorndike Press, Waterville, Maine, USA and by BBC Audiobooks Ltd, Bath, England.
Thorndike Press, a part of Gale, Cengage Learning.
Copyright © 2008 by Jeffrey Cohen.
The moral right of the author has been asserted.
A Double Feature Mystery.
The Edgar® name is a registered service mark of the Mystery Writers of America, Inc.

The text of this Large Print edition is unabridged.
Other aspects of the book may vary from the original edition.
Set in 16 pt. Plantin.
Printed on permanent paper.

LIBRARY OF CONGRESS CATALOGING-IN-PUBLICATION DATA

Cohen, Jeffrey, 1957–
  It happened one knife / By Jeffrey Cohen.
    p. cm. — (Double feature mystery) (Thorndike Press large print mystery)
  ISBN-13: 978-1-4104-1081-8 (hardcover : alk. paper)
  ISBN-10: 1-4104-1081-1 (hardcover : alk. paper)
  1. Comedians—Fiction. 2. Motion picture theaters—Fiction.
3. Large type books. I. Title. II. Series.
PS3603.O358I82 2008
813'.6—dc22   2008029209

BRITISH LIBRARY CATALOGUING-IN-PUBLICATION DATA AVAILABLE

Published in 2008 in the U.S. by arrangement with The Berkley Publishing Group, a member of Penguin Group (USA) Inc.
Published in 2009 in the U.K. by arrangement with The Berkley Publishing Group, a member of Penguin Group (USA) Inc.

U.K. Hardcover: 978 1 408 42141 3 (Chivers Large Print)
U.K. Softcover: 978 1 408 42142 0 (Camden Large Print)

Printed in the United States of America
1 2 3 4 5 6 7 12 11 10 09 08

Something appealing;
something appalling;
Something for everyone:
a comedy tonight!
— STEPHEN SONDHEIM,
*A Funny Thing Happened
on the Way to the Forum*

This book is dedicated to the memory of Etta Sanders.
The real crime is that she's not here to read it.
Don't believe politicians when they say you're safe.

PROLOGUE

This wasn't just another DVD: this was life or death. Or life *and* death. I was hoping for life; there had already been enough death.

I sat down in front of my own television with a great deal of trepidation. For other people, this wouldn't be an unduly tense moment, but I think it's been noted more than once, I'm not exactly other people. For a classic comedy fanatic like me, this was a very scary moment.

What if this movie wasn't funny for me anymore? What if *no* movie was funny for me anymore? I've spent so much of my time, my energy, my *life* on the idea that comedy is therapeutic; suppose I was about to discover that it not only couldn't heal my wounds, but had actually caused them?

A man sitting alone in his postdivorce, furniture-challenged home in the wee hours of the morning is never entirely rational.

In this case, though, I had logical reasons

for being a little nuts. When you spend most of your life idolizing people, and then get to meet them, it's something of a disappointment when they end up dead.

It's even more of a problem when you feel you had a hand in killing them.

I turned on the TV, reached for the remote control, and literally held my breath. The next few minutes would tell the tale: either I'd laugh, or —

Well, I didn't want to think about the alternative . . .

1

If you can do comedy, you must do comedy.

— BILL MURRAY

Without heroes, we're all plain people and don't know how far we can go.
— BERNARD MALAMUD, *THE NATURAL*

Thursday
Killin' Time
A SPECIAL ATTRACTION

"Is he dead?" Vic Testalone asked me.

"They're all dead," I said. "He didn't leave any of them alive."

"How can that *be?*" he asked. "Does this kid know what he's done?"

Vic, a sales rep from one of the film distribution companies I work with, was probably born smoking a cigar; he had one in his mouth now, but knew better than to light it in the lobby of my theatre. Comedy

11

Tonight, like all New Jersey movie theatres, has a strict no-smoking policy, but I would have insisted on it even if the state didn't. I hadn't spent the past four months getting this place repaired just to have Vic impose the smell of a cheap stogie on my new carpet.

I shook my head. "Anthony just thinks it's cool," I answered him. "He's not considering the moral implications of his actions."

"I'm not concerned with moral implications," Vic answered, snarling. "He's killing the sequel possibilities."

That threw me for a loop. I'd only agreed to let Anthony Pagliarulo, the theatre's projectionist/ticket taker, show his first film — an ultraviolent pseudo-Western called *Killin' Time* — as a one-time-only break from our all-comedies-and-nothing-but-comedies policy because he'd caught me at a vulnerable time. Suffice it to say that four months earlier, when I agreed to show the film, my theatre had looked like one of the cowboys in Anthony's "Western" *after* the branding-iron scene. I'd made good on my promise after the renovation because I couldn't think of a graceful way to pull the plug. But now Vic was treating this glorified (if relatively high-budget) student film as if it were something *real*.

"What the hell do you mean by 'sequel possibilities'?" I asked him. "You think someone would to want to distribute that thing?"

"It's got blood." Vic held up a finger. "It's got cursing." Another finger. "Killing, sex, cruelty, characters nobody could possibly like." Finger, finger, finger, thumb on the other hand. "It can't miss."

Vic and I had left the auditorium when the credits started to roll (but long after heads had started to roll, which made it too late for me), and now the rest of the "crowd" was spilling into the lobby. "This was a movie in which we saw a bullet enter a man's head *from inside*," I told him quietly. No sense giving the rest of the invited audience a chance to voice their displeasure as well. "We saw intestines being pulled out. We saw a man's tongue put through a meat grinder."

"Now you're catching on," Vic said. "Oh, and before I forget, are we set for the next month?"

Vic's a sales rep for Klassic Komedy Distributors (they think the "K"s make it funny), which handles many of the vintage comedies I show each week in conjunction with a contemporary comedy. He doesn't really need to come down to Comedy

Tonight to get his order; we could complete our business in three minutes on the phone. But he says I'm "the only schmuck who knows movies so obscure Leonard Maltin's never heard of them." Vic likes to visit.

"Yeah," I told him. "We've got *The Ghost Breakers, Never Give a Sucker an Even Break,* and *Back to the Future.*"

"I still say *Back to the Future* is too new," Vic protested. "It's less than twenty-five years old."

"By what, twenty minutes?" I asked. "I need a time-travel comedy to go with the new Adam Sandler. What do you think I should run?"

"How about *Where Do We Go From Here?*"

"Fred MacMurray is funny? Anyway, that's a musical," I told him. Vic waved a hand at me.

"You should show this thing from tonight," he said. "You'll have an exclusive before the kid makes a deal somewhere."

I spied my ex-wife across the room. "I don't want to talk to you anymore," I told Vic, and walked toward Sharon. Vic had the nerve to look surprised.

Before I reached my ex, however, I was waylaid by Leo Munson, a former merchant marine who is Comedy Tonight's one and

14

only regular customer. Leo, a trim man in his sixties who looks to be a head-to-toe callus, comes to the theatre every night it's open, and is as obsessed with classic comedy as I am, but with broader taste. He keeps asking me for Three Stooges shorts. I keep playing Bugs Bunny cartoons.

"That was really something," Leo said, tilting his head in the direction of the auditorium.

I'd been dreading this moment. "I warned you not to come tonight, Leo," I told him. "I know it's not your thing, but you insisted . . ."

"It was terrific!" he said, breaking into an eerie grin. "The kid has a wild sense of humor, doesn't he?"

"Um, yeah," I nodded, unable to blink. *Yeah, that amputation scene was a laugh riot.*

"I spent four months watching Turner Classic Movies because you were closed for repairs," Leo said. "That's four months of *Mildred Pierce* twice a week. Gives a man perspective."

"Perspective? Four months of Joan Crawford makes you appreciate an artistic sensibility that includes a man being pulled apart by buffalo?"

"Your projectionist is gonna be a big deal director, Elliot," Leo said. "You're lucky to have him now, before he gets famous."

"Uh-huh." It was the best I could do. "Yeah. You're right, Leo. Gotta go now." I headed for Sharon again, but Sophie, our ticket seller/snack bar attendant, was beckoning me toward her. I sighed, and changed course for the new refreshment stand.

It was, I had to admit, a vast improvement over the previous one, which had been essentially a glass-topped table with some candy boxes on it, next to a card table for napkins, straws, and popcorn salt. This one was gleaming, lit from within, and tastefully and skillfully displayed all the varieties of chocolate-coated self-destruction we sold. It was even refrigerated to keep the candy from melting. It was, for snacks, a better home than the one I lived in. My insurance company, upon being informed of the refreshment case's price tag, had helpfully offered to recommend another agency for any future business insurance needs I might have, but had ponied up nonetheless.

In the four months Comedy Tonight had been under reconstruction, I hadn't seen either Sophie or Anthony. But I'd continued to pay both of my young employees, as I'd decided it wasn't their fault the theatre couldn't open. So it had been a shock this afternoon when Sophie had shown up for

16

work in something other than the funereal teenage Goth wardrobe I'd been accustomed to her wearing. Until recently, Sophie had resembled Christina Ricci in *The Addams Family*. Now she was wearing a loose-fitting gray sweatshirt emblazoned with the slogan "A woman needs a man like a fish needs a bicycle" and black sweatpants over high-top sneakers. She looked like a figure from *The Life of Gloria Steinem,* as performed by the enrolled class roster of Feminism 101.

"Should I keep selling candy after the movie's over?" Sophie asked me when I got there.

"If people want to keep buying it, yeah," I said. "Why not?"

"Because continuing to sell these high-calorie, sugarcoated products simply perpetuates the cycle of control, the corporate patriarchy keeping women docile and distracted," she said.

"Yeah. Because we all know men don't buy candy or popcorn."

"Men aren't subject to the same unreasonable standards of 'beauty' as women," Sophie said, miming the quotes.

"Try to stick to one argument," I advised. "What did you think of Anthony's movie?" I'd seen her watching through the rear auditorium doors.

"The objectification of women was deplorable," Sophie said. "I was appalled by the sexism."

Finally, someone who had seen the same movie as I had. Well okay, not the *same* movie, but at least an objectionable one. "I understand exactly where you're coming from," I told Sophie.

"Other than that," she continued, "it was awesome."

I fled to Sharon, allowing no one to get in my way.

She looked great, of course, and was standing by herself. Sharon's second husband, Gregory the Anesthesiologist, had not accompanied her, which livened up the proceedings by roughly 20 percent. Gregory had moved back into their house recently, despite Sharon telling me they'd separated. I considered this latest move a bad thing, but that's just an opinion.

Given the reactions I'd gotten about the film so far, I was almost afraid to ask Sharon (after all, it was possible the rest of the gathering was right, and I was wrong — maybe *Killin' Time* really was the next step in the progress of the cinema, and I would have to kill myself), but I plunged ahead. "What'd you think?"

18

Sharon is a lovely woman, slim and just tall enough not to be considered short, but now her eyes were open about a quarter inch wider than normal, which gave her a somewhat stunned expression, like Carol Channing circa 1962. "What *was* that?" she said.

"You didn't like it?" I had to be sure; my confidence was shaken.

"*Like* it? I'm amazed I kept my dinner down!" Thank god, someone who hadn't drunk the Kool-Aid. "What the hell *was* that?"

"It was *She Wore a Yellow Ribbon,* as it might have been seen by Torquemada, the Grand Inquisitor," I told her. "What did you expect?"

"A story would have been nice."

"I'm starting to remember why I fell in love with you," I told her.

"That's funny," she told me. "I'm remembering other things."

I was about to comment on her flattering turn of phrase when applause broke out from my right. Anthony was descending the stairs from the balcony, and his Rutgers University friends — most of whom hadn't become his friends until word had gotten around that he'd managed to get a movie made — began to salaam before him and prostrate themselves on the carpet. I thought of mentioning what the carpet had cost, but decided it wouldn't impress them. College kids.

I'd offered to man the projector so Anthony could be in the auditorium while *Killin' Time* was running, but he'd refused to turn over custody of his baby (the film, that is, not the projector) to anyone, particularly given the cantankerous nature of our ancient projector, a contraption only Anthony truly understands. So he'd run the movie himself, rewound it, and was now walking down to the level of his adoring public.

And by god, they *were* adoring. The fifty or so Rutgers students Anthony had invited for this special closed-to-the-public event did everything but throw rose petals in his path. Even some of the "adults" whom I had invited, like Sharon, Leo (well, actually I'd tried to dissuade Leo, but I still get credit for his presence), and Bobo Kaminsky, the owner of the local bike shop I practically keep in business single-handedly, were shouting *bravo.* I think Sharon's *bravos* were strictly out of politeness, though. Tall, thin, and positively wan, Anthony looked more amazed than proud as the Rutgers crowd declared him Lord of All He Surveyed. In short, it was the most enthusiastic response any film had ever gotten from an audience at Comedy Tonight, and yes, I resented it, but hey, give the kid his night. I nodded to Sophie, who began to pass out plastic flutes of fake champagne (some in the room were underage, and I don't have a liquor license). I'd poured them right after the second decapitation, though, so the "wine" was probably flat as a piece of paper by now.

Anthony's semi-girlfriend (she thinks so; he's not sure) Carla Singelese appeared from somewhere and gave him a huge kiss to much *woooooo*-ing from the crowd. Anthony, who's usually as serious as a triple bypass, even smiled.

I noticed Anthony's roommate Danton up the stairs a few steps, looking down on the main event, without a drink in his hand (the only such person in the room), and I tried to get Sophie's attention, but she was back at the snack bar and away from the tray of "wine." I took a flute from the tray and handed it to Danton, then walked back to Sharon's side. When all the "champagne" had been distributed, I called for quiet. Then I called for quiet again, because no one had heard me the first time. When I was about to try an unprecedented third time, I heard a piercing whistle come from my immediate left. As the crowd fell into a sudden hush, I saw Sharon taking her thumb and index finger out of her mouth. She grinned at me sheepishly.

"Well, *somebody* had to do it," she said.

I raised my glass in Anthony's direction. "To Anthony," I said, "who wowed us all with his talent tonight, and who will no doubt grow as a filmmaker as he learns his craft at school. This is indeed a fine beginning. Congratulations."

Anthony's eyes narrowed a bit, as if that wasn't effusive enough praise, but he sipped from his glass (okay, his *plastic*) and turned his head toward Carla, who was holding her drink up for the next toast.

"Um . . . I've never made a toast before, but this is such a special night . . . I'm so proud of Anthony, and the amazing film he just showed us!" (This may be the place to note that Carla said it with at least three exclamation points, but I'm including only one at a time out of a sense of restraint.) "I'm sure he's going to become a big director, like, right away, and I'm just glad to be right here by his side, now and forever! I love you, Anthony!"

There was a large ovation for that one, and Anthony reached over and kissed Carla, even though he looked a little taken aback by her toast. Anthony isn't much given to public displays of . . . anything, really. He's not a cold person, but he always seems to be thinking about something else.

A few more toasts were made, largely by people I didn't know (and who seemed to know Anthony only peripherally). I took Sharon to one side, near my office door, where the din was a little lower, and where I couldn't see people spilling cheap, fake bubbly on my new carpet before the paying public even got a chance to walk on it.

Bobo rumbled by on his way out of the theatre. Bobo doesn't spend much time doing anything other than selling bicycles — certainly not *riding* one. If it were possible, he would keep the cycle shop open 24/7. But he's a large man, in every direction, and needs to maintain his largeness by ingesting titanic amounts of carbohydrates, which takes time out of the day. He gave me a thumbs-up on the movie and kept walking, probably to go home and dream about gearshifts and fried chicken.

"How are you doing?" Sharon asked me.

"What do you mean?"

"I mean, you've been out of business for four months, you spent most of that time watching this place get rebuilt, and you've been driving me out of my mind with your impatience. So I'm saying, now that it's over and you can get back to your mission in life, how does that feel?"

I looked at her. "Don't hold back, baby. Tell me what you *really* think."

"Elliot. No matter what's happened between us, we've always been able to talk to each other." She saw the look I was starting to give her, and said, "Okay, except right before you filed for divorce. But still, I'm proud that we managed to split up and stay friendly. Now, you're going through a big moment in your life, and I want to know how you're doing."

"I'm doing fine," I said.

She waited. "That's it?"

I shrugged. "I'm doing fine, *ma'am?*"

Sharon's lips twisted into the shape of Yosemite Sam's moustache. "Look, Elliot, if you don't want to talk about it . . ."

"It's not that I don't want to talk. It's that I have nothing to say."

She was about to prove me wrong — one of her favorite activities — when Vic appeared out of the crowd, rushed toward us, and grabbed me by the arm. "Elliot," he said. "Where can we talk?"

"Pretty much anywhere we have vocal cords," I told him.

"Privately," he said.

Sharon gave me a look that said, "To be continued . . ." and excused herself for the ladies' room. I opened my office door and ushered Vic inside. "Okay," I said. "What's so urgent?"

I sat in my creaky, understuffed swivel chair, which had not been replaced in the renovation, damn it, and looked at Vic. He held up his cell phone. I waited a moment, then picked up a stapler to show him, figuring this was a new game.

Turned out it wasn't. "I've been on the phone," Vic said. "Got in touch with a few guys I know in the city."

"Organizing a poker game?" I asked. It was worth a shot.

"Guys from film distributors. Indie studios," he said.

It took me a moment. A long moment. "Oh Vic, don't tell me . . ."

"Yeah. I think I can set the kid up with a deal. Get the movie distributed."

"You're a classic comedy distributor. What does your company want with *Hannibal Lecter at the O.K. Corral?*"

Vic sneered. No, really. "It's not for the *company*," he said. "We don't make prints and book theatres like a studio; we handle a catalogue. You know that." I did, but he was confusing me with this talk of distributing

Killin' Time. "I think I can work out a deal for the kid with a real studio, or at least an indie."

"And pocket a tidy finder's fee for yourself?" I asked.

"If they think I deserve it," Vic grinned.

"You sincerely believe that the festival of disembowelment we just saw could be attractive to a real movie studio, and be shown in actual theatres?" I'd seen more complicated stories told in books with titles like *Pat the Bunny.*

He grinned, and almost bit through his unlit cigar. "I think I've got him set up at Monitor Films," Vic said.

I stood up and closed the door behind him. Considering the size of my office, Vic might have thought I was trying to get a little more intimate than he considered comfortable, because he said, "Hey, Elliot . . ."

"You've got to do me a favor, Vic. Don't tell Anthony about Monitor yet."

You might have thought I'd asked him to set his pants on fire and sing "In-A-Gadda-Da-Vida." "Are you crazy?"

"Vic, Anthony's a twenty-year-old kid who's riding high on the rush of showing his movie to an audience that loves him and was going to say it was great no matter what. He'll be stupid tonight and do anything that feels good. Let him have some time to think, some time to realize this isn't *Citizen Kane* he's got on his hands here. Just give him a week, okay?"

"Elliot," Vic said, "there are many fine decaffeinated brands on the market."

"I'm serious."

"That's what worries me. Nobody's even offering him a deal, for crissakes. We're talking about him taking a *meeting.*" Vic sneered at me with the exact expression he'd use on someone who told him *Plan 9 from Outer Space* was a better movie than *Duck Soup.*

"What's worse — he takes the meeting and gets a small-time deal that'll push him out of the nest way before he's ready, or he takes the meeting and gets shot down, and blows his self-esteem all to hell? Show me how this plays out well."

"What are you, jealous?"

"Oh, please. I did the Hollywood thing, and didn't like it," I told him, remembering *Split Personality,* the movie made from my one-and-only novel, despite it not having even a shred of resemblance to the original story. "Besides, where do you get contacts outside a catalog of fifty-year-old comedies?"

"What, I can't have friends?"

"I'm your friend," I told him. "And I'm asking you as a friend, don't tell Anthony about the Monitor thing, just for a week or two."

"No chance, Elliot. I'm not going to ruin my credibility with Monitor because you're worried the kid is 'too happy' tonight." Vic scowled, and turned to push open the door; which would be a cute trick, since the door opens in, and it is, as I might have mentioned, a very small room.

My mind raced, and I had to catch up with it in a hurry. There had to be some way to get Vic off this obsession for a minute. I figured that if I changed the subject to business, Vic would be distracted, but the first thing it occurred to me to say was: "You guys don't have *Cracked Ice,* do you?"

It was a desperation move. *Cracked Ice* (1956), the crowning achievement of the comedy team of Harry Lillis and Les Townes, was a rarity in 35mm prints. It was a favorite of mine, but not something that there could be much demand for, even in comparison to the vintage movies I usually order from Vic and his company.

The ploy had the effect I'd hoped for; Vic's hand slipped off the doorknob, and he turned to me with a major grin on his face.

"Sure, we have it," he said, without having to check his BlackBerry. That's why I like Vic. "But that's not the half of it."

I knew that tone. "Okay, what's the half of it?"

"You're a Lillis and Townes fan?" he asked.

That was a question? Harry Lillis and Les Townes were the bright shining light in one of comedy's most bleak periods, the mid-1950s to early 1960s. In reality, Lillis himself was the comedic genius, while Townes was an unparalleled straight man, a decent singer (his recording of "Rainy Day Love" was a number one hit for six weeks in 1954), and the romantic lead in their movies, or at least the ones that had romantic leads. Townes wasn't the most handsome man who ever lived, but he had great charm, absolutely perfect timing, and he knew a good thing when he saw it.

And Lillis — well, Lillis was a force of nature.

Combining Groucho's rapid-fire wit with Harpo's brilliant physical comedy, Harry Lillis was the Marx Brother who *should* have been, if Zeppo hadn't been selfish about being born into the family. Not to mention that Lillis was a good thirty years younger than the youngest Marx *frere.*

29

Was I a Lillis and Townes fan?

"You could say that," I told Vic. "My mother threatened to disown me in high school if I didn't stop talking like Harry Lillis. So, spill. What's the big story?"

Vic's grin was all the more smug. "I *met* Harry Lillis," he said.

"When you were a kid?"

He shook his head. "Last Wednesday."

I can be cool when I put my mind to it. This wasn't one of those times. My mouth dropped open a couple of feet, and I stammered "Wha . . . wha . . . wha" for a few moments. *"Where?"* I managed to croak.

"He's living in Englewood, at the Actors' Home." Vic was so in control now that he could have lit his cigar with the deed to my theatre and I wouldn't have stopped him. "Guy's gotta be pushing eighty, from one side or another. But if you squint and imagine a little, it's like being on the set of *Cracked Ice*."

"What were you doing in Englewood?"

"I went up to the home. They want to have a little entertainment for the residents, you know, and there aren't a lot of distributors have the catalog we do, so they asked about a few films. They can't get everything they want on DVD. I went up to talk to the guy in charge, and sitting there in the dining room, large as life, was Harry Lillis."

I wanted to simultaneously touch Vic's hand, the one that must have shook Lillis's, and strangle him for living out my fantasy. "What's he like?" I asked.

"Just like you'd imagine. You know, they didn't get those nicknames for nothing." In the trade press, Lillis and Townes were known as "Arsenic and Old Lace," because Lillis would never compromise and was constantly at war with whatever studio the team was contracted to, while Townes was the peacemaker, smoothing out the rough spots in negotiations and relations with the press.

"A little acerbic?" I guessed.

"He told me I looked like a beach ball smoking a cigar," Vic said.

"Wow! An insult from Harry Lillis! You're so lucky!"

"I know," he said, too cool to exist in my universe. "Told some great stories, too. Did you know he dated Vivian Reynolds before she married Townes?"

I waved a hand. "Everybody knows that."

"Yeah, well here's something everybody *doesn't* know: Lillis and Townes are planning a comeback."

That salvo did some damage. I sat, stunned, for what seemed like an hour.

"Lillis and Townes are coming back? At their age?"

Vic nodded, and rotated his cigar. "He's got some idea for a movie about two old guys robbing a bank, and he says Townes is interested."

I couldn't believe it: either Lillis had one masterstroke left in him, or this would be the most embarrassing coda to a brilliant career since Ethel Merman recorded a disco album. Oh yes, she did.

But the wheels in my head were turning. "Cancel *Back to the Future,* Vic," I told him. "Get me *Cracked Ice.* I've got an idea. And think about what I said regarding Anthony." And before he could protest, I maneuvered my way around him and out into the lobby.

Most of the guests had left. Sharon approached when I entered the lobby. "I was wondering where you'd gotten to," she said, and then saw my expression. "What's up?"

"I'll tell you tomorrow," I said. "Lunch at C'est Moi!?" She nodded.

Anthony was still near the staircase to the balcony, talking to a man I recognized as his father, Michael. The conversation didn't appear to be a happy one, despite the occasion.

"All I'm saying is, take some time and think," Pagliarulo the elder told his son as I approached. "Don't do something rash."

"I'm not being rash; I'm seizing the moment," Anthony said, a contemptuous tone in his voice that the young reserve only for their parents.

"Ant'ny . . ." his father began.

"It's *Anthony*!" my projectionist hollered. "You gave me my name; pronounce all the letters in it!"

Michael shook his head sadly and walked toward the outside door. I stood next to Anthony and spoke quietly. "He's your father," I said.

"He wants me to deny who I am," Anthony said.

"Really? Who are you?"

"I'm a filmmaker," said my employee. "Not a student."

"Anthony. You're not thinking of leaving school, are you?"

Anthony looked away. "John Ford never got a degree," he said.

"Neither did Charles Manson, and look how well *he* did. Look, it's a big night for you," I told him. "Don't let it be the night you fought with your father. Go make up with him."

"I can't. I have to close up the projection booth. I rewound the film, but it's not in the cans yet."

33

I sputtered. "I'll do it. Go."

Anthony started to answer (I'm convinced he was worried about leaving his baby in the care of a philistine like me), thought better of it, and I watched as he walked quickly toward the door to the theatre. I could see Carla waiting for him at the front, and then the two of them hurried toward where Michael Pagliarulo must have been.

Sophie was closing up the snack bar when I walked over. She'd never admit it, but she took great pride in her high-caloric domain, and was very fussy about where everything was kept. I watched for a moment while she wiped down the top of the counter, where a bit of popcorn butter had left tiny smears. When it was spotless, she smiled a private smile.

"You like the new snack bar, Sophie?" I asked.

Her face froze in an expression of indifference, the official emotion of high school seniors. "It's just a glass box," she said.

"Were there any stains on the rug from the wine-substitute?"

"You wish. Just what a man would want to see, the woman on her knees cleaning stains off the rug. You're all alike." She huffed, and walked away. I was glad to have made her so happy.

Sharon must have left, and Vic was gone, so I was alone in the theatre, tired from this dress rehearsal and ready for tomorrow's opening night. One last thing to do.

I went into the office and picked up the key to the projection booth, which I was sure Anthony would have locked behind him. I climbed up the stairs to the balcony, where the smell of fresh wood, fresh paint, and fresh carpet were still scenting the air. But I was too weary to enjoy the newness. I unlocked the door to the projection booth and walked in.

The projector was shut down, as it should be, and the audio system was turned off. I looked for the rewound reels and stopped dead in my tracks.

There was nothing on the projector. The empty film cans were not on the floor next to the control table. There was no sign at all that a movie had been projected here tonight.

Anthony's one and only copy of *Killin' Time* was gone.

2

Barry Dutton is the chief of police in Midland Heights, New Jersey, so I was surprised when he personally responded to the call about a routine burglary. Even in jeans and a sweatshirt, he looked like an African-American version of the Chrysler Building.

"I didn't expect to see you, Chief," I said.

Dutton looked around the projection booth and nodded. "I was off-duty, but when I heard the radio call, I had to see for myself," he said. "You haven't even re-opened for real yet, and you already have another crime. Nice work, Elliot."

"I'm a businessman," I told him. "I'll do anything necessary to keep you coming back."

"So what's missing, exactly?" Dutton asked. "The call said it was cans of film. What does that mean?"

"We still call them 'cans' of film, even

though they don't really come in cans anymore," I told him. "In the old days, the film reels came to theatres from the distributors in metal cans. Now, the reels come here in plastic boxes with locks on them to prevent piracy." We exchanged a look. "You remember film piracy," I said.

"I remember." Dutton grimaced, which made him look like a grizzly bear fretting over fluctuations in the stock market.

"Anthony got his print from the duplicator, and it was in three of the locked plastic containers when he brought it in. He told me he'd left the film, rewound, on the reels, but hadn't put them back into the boxes yet. Now both the film and the boxes are gone."

Dutton's eyes narrowed; he was thinking. "Have you called Anthony?"

"Before I called you, actually," I answered. "He's, let's say, not pleased. He's on his way."

Dutton strolled casually around the room, taking in everything there was to see. "So the amateur film is missing. What are these?" He pointed at the boxes of film reels I had placed on the floor.

"Our reopening program for tomorrow night."

"Did you look to see if the movie from

tonight is all that's gone?" Dutton asked.

"I did check. Strangely, it is the only thing missing."

"Why strangely?"

"Because we're reopening for real tomorrow night," I said. "I got the films today from the distributor, the new Will Ferrell movie and a copy of *My Man Godfrey.* They're both here, and they'd definitely be a more attractive target for film pirates."

"Maybe they took the wrong film," Dutton said. "Did you check the boxes?"

"Yes, and they're the right films in the right boxes, all marked," I told him. "Besides, once you've broken in, why not take all the films? Why just that one? It's not even of any value to pirates — it's not a 'real' movie."

Dutton sat down in the projectionist's chair, which creaked under his weight. I started to wonder why we hadn't replaced any of the chairs other than those in the auditorium, and then remembered it was because the insurance paid only for actual damages, and not all the improvements I wanted to make in the theatre. Silly insurance.

"It's a good question," he said. "Maybe someone thinks they can hold it for ransom. Is the movie any good?"

I made a face. "If you're a fan of surgery without anesthesia, you'd really love it."

Dutton winced. "Not exactly *The Sound of Music*, then?"

The Sound of Music? What the heck kind of cop is this guy? "No."

Chief Dutton sat back and closed his eyes. "So we have a crime in which someone broke into the booth, but we don't know how. Was the door locked?"

"Yes," I said, "and only Anthony and I have keys."

"Okay," he rumbled, eyes still closed. "They broke in without signs of physical damage, and stole what was probably the least valuable thing in the room. Have I got that about right?"

"Yeah. The projector, the equipment, the other films would probably each get more on any kind of black market than Anthony's movie. In fact . . ." It had just struck me.

Dutton opened his eyes. "In fact, what?" he asked.

"The only person who would have considered that movie the most valuable thing in the room was . . ."

"Mr. Freed!" Anthony was standing in the doorway, leaning on his arms, which were propped up on ninety-degree angles on the jambs. "What did you do?"

39

I knit my brow, because I didn't know anything else I could do with my brow. "What did *I* do? What do you mean, what did I do?"

"I know you didn't like my film," he said, breathing hard. "But that's no reason to stand in my way. Why did you steal it?"

3

Friday
My Man Godfrey **(1936)** AND *Butt-ler* (THIS
WEEK)

"So Anthony thinks *you* stole his movie?"
my father asked.

Driving through the unfamiliar streets of
Englewood, New Jersey, Arthur Freed
(home redecoration expert — that is, paint
and wallpaper retailer — retired) still knew
exactly how to cut to the chase and make
me feel uncomfortable, even as he scanned
street signs for a clue to our location. It was
a good hour from my New Brunswick town
house and another forty minutes from
Dad's door, in a part of the state I don't
know like the back of my hand.

"He knows I didn't think it was the next
Dr. Strangelove, and he knows I'm the only
other person with a key to the projection
booth," I said. "Anthony thinks I'm trying
to sabotage his budding directorial career

41

because I need him to run my projector."

"Well, are you?" Dad asked. Parents always think so highly of their children.

It was my own fault that I had to put up with this abuse. I am the last New Jerseyan over the age of seventeen who doesn't own a car, because I believe in decreasing our use of oil (foreign and domestic) and cutting back on greenhouse gases (except after I have a heavy lunch). So my usual mode of transportation is a bicycle.

Unfortunately, the state of New Jersey is constructed specifically to deter anyone who doesn't want to drive a car from living here, and there is precious little public transportation between New Brunswick to Englewood that wouldn't take about a day and a half in the journey. So, as I often do on such occasions, I had prevailed upon one of the many drivers I know to give me a ride.

Sharon was busy with her practice (as if keeping the populace healthy were more important than driving her ex-husband around; really!), so I'd called Dad. When he heard where we were going, and whom we'd be meeting, I'd barely had time to hang up the phone before he showed up at my door. I didn't come by my love of classic comedians by chance; it's a genetic thing.

"No, I'm not trying to sabotage Anthony's career," I answered him. "I don't even think Anthony's going to *have* a career if he drops out of school, but I wouldn't stand in his way. I'm not his father."

"I've noticed we don't have grand-children," Dad said.

I exhaled. "Let's stick to one neurosis at a time, okay? Take a right here."

He pulled the car into the driveway of the Lillian Booth (no relation to John Wilkes, we're pretty sure) Actors' Home, set on a hill overlooking a wooded area and seeming quite serene indeed. Dad parked the car at the top of the hill, about ten yards from the front door of the Home.

I'd called the Actors Fund and arranged the visit through the administrator, an astonishingly young man named Walter Lee. Walt, as we'd been instructed to address him, looked to be about twelve on a good day, but assured me he was in his late twenties.

He took us through the Ed Herlihy Foyer (Ed had done a lot of commercials for Kraft Foods in the 1960s, and apparently they paid well), and inside, explaining that there were actually two homes on the premises: "One is an assisted living facility, for residents who don't have health issues that demand more extensive care, and the other is a nursing home, where we provide more complete health care."

At the moment, Harry Lillis was one of forty-two residents in assisted living, Walt said. There were sixty-seven others on the nursing home side. While the Home's residents were predominantly from the New York stage scene, mostly actors, dancers, writers, technicians, and others, anyone who had spent at least twenty years in the entertainment industry was eligible for a room in the Home, when there was an opening.

"Of course, Mr. Lillis is best known for his film work, and he would have been welcome here because of that alone," Walt said as we walked through a hallway that I believe was dedicated to Colleen Dewhurst. "But he and Mr. Townes also worked on the stage in New York before they started making movies." It was true; Lillis and Townes had headlined a Broadway revue in 1950 called *You're Making It Up.*

Dad was a few steps ahead of us, which was interesting, seeing as how he had no idea where he was going. I'd rarely seen him this excited. "Why don't we step into the dining room?" Walt suggested.

At eleven in the morning, there were barely any people in the dining room, but the only thing that mattered to us was that one of them was Harry Lillis.

Slightly less tall than (his official-studio-bio-inflated) six foot three, Lillis was leaning against a post in the center of the room, and I knew immediately that Vic had been right: with the sun hitting him the right way, from far enough away, and making allowances for hair color, that was the same Harry Lillis I'd seen play Waldo Krunsacker in the classic *Peace and Quiet* (1957).

He was talking to a small woman, who had surely been very attractive in her day, since today she still looked good, and she had to be in her midseventies. She was seated on a sofa facing away from the large-screen television, and laughing at whatever Lillis said.

"That's Harry Lillis," my father said, not to anyone in particular.

Walt nodded, and walked to Lillis. He spoke quietly to the legend of my childhood, who looked in our direction. He must have been reminding Lillis that he'd agreed to meet us today. Harry Lillis nodded, and Walt beckoned to Dad and me.

We stood rooted to the spot. So rooted I wouldn't have been surprised if leaves sprouted from our arms and heads. I couldn't move, and I knew Dad felt the same way.

That was Harry Lillis!

After an eternity or two, it was obvious we wouldn't be able to traverse the fifteen feet to the great man, so Lillis stood up straight and walked toward us. I had now regressed to the age of eight, and he kept getting taller as he approached.

I'm told that some men have a strong reaction when they meet boyhood idols from the ball field or the gridiron. I like to watch a baseball game now and again, but my heroes have always been comedians. I wasn't sure I'd be able to speak. Ever again.

However, I was able to move my arms, which I know because I held out a hand for Lillis to take. He didn't.

"I'm the decrepit old man," he said. "You're supposed to walk to *me.*"

Walt, trying to keep the peace, chuckled, as if we didn't know Lillis would make jokes, likely at our expense. "Now, Mr. Lillis," he said. "You don't have any trouble walking, and you know it. It's good for you."

"Yeah, so is broccoli, but you're not going to find me eating that," Lillis responded. He looked at Dad. "You're no kid," he said. "The younger one clearly thinks I live in a television set. What's your excuse?"

Dad, always more resourceful than I am,

had recovered. "I think you live on a movie screen," he told Lillis. "I'm still awestruck. Mr. Lillis, I'm a big fan." He stuck out his hand, and Lillis took it.

"It's a warm day," Lillis said. "I could use a big fan. I'd prefer an air conditioner, but you'll do. You got a name?"

Dad grinned and nodded. "Arthur Freed."

"I thought you did a great job on *Singin' in the Rain*," he said.

My father has the same name as a legendary producer of musicals who worked at MGM in the 1940s and 50s, and Lillis probably didn't expect us to know that. "Thanks," Dad said. "Although that Debbie Reynolds was a pain in the ass."

Lillis laughed loudly and put his arm around my father's shoulder. Together, they looked like the cast of *Laurel and Hardy Celebrate Rosh Hashanah*. Lillis started to lead my father out of the room.

"I understand you want to show some of my pictures in your theatre, Arthur," he started. "That shows incredibly good taste on your part."

They were almost to the door, and I was still feeling like my shoes had been nailed to the floor. I couldn't even turn to face them.

"Not me," I heard Dad say. "It's my son who owns the theatre." He must have turned toward me. "Elliot!"

I gathered all of my strength and I concentrated on moving my legs. Finally, after a disgusting amount of time, I turned and walked to the door of the dining room, where my father was standing with a comedy legend. I stuck out my hand again.

"Mr. Lillis," I said very slowly. "I'm very honored, and I'm very nervous."

This time, Lillis took my hand, and spoke softly. "Don't worry, son," he said. "You're right to be."

"Honored, or nervous?"

"Both."

We accompanied Lillis to his room, where Walt said we could have more privacy, and "Mr. Lillis can be more comfortable." (Lillis responded, "If I were more comfortable, I'd be living in a place with better carpets.") Then Walt excused himself, and we sat down. Lillis sat on his bed, of which he said, "A single, damn it," and Dad and I took the chairs that were next to his desk. For all the world, you would have thought Lillis was living in a dorm room at some slightly upscale college.

"This place is as much fun as a mortuary," Lillis began, unprompted. "They all sit around all day and tell me about" — and here, he affected an upper-crust accent that would have fooled Thurston Howell III — "*the thea-tah,* and how grand it all was, you know. Nobody from my business, the picture business, no comics, just *ac-tors.* I'm glad to see a couple of guys who appreciate the art of it." And then, just because he couldn't resist, "Even if it has to be the two of you."

"I think you'd appreciate Comedy Tonight," I told Lillis. I had regained the power of thought during the walk to his room. "I show a classic comedy, and a new one, every week. Laurel and Hardy, W. C. Fields, the Marx Brothers . . ."

"The Marx Brothers were the ones who knew how to do it right," Lillis said. "They didn't ask you to feel sorry for them. They did what they wanted, and dared you to say they shouldn't. You never see comedy like that anymore."

"You did it," I told him. "You and Mr. Townes."

Lillis suddenly affected a very interesting, if hard to identify, expression. His eyes got a little dreamy, but his mouth twisted into a sneer. It was as if he were remembering an unusually happy moment in which he was horribly insulted.

"*Mr. Townes,*" he said, "doesn't get the respect he deserves. Les wasn't just a great

49

straight man. He could do the joke. He could fall on the banana peel and land the right way. I got the headlines because I was the goofy-looking Jew and I had all the smart remarks, but Les . . . Les was a genius."

"I'm told you guys might be making a comeback." I sent out a trial balloon.

Lillis's eyes focused in a nanosecond. "Who told you that?"

"Vic Testalone," I reminded him. "The man who came up to talk about renting some older movies here."

"Testalone . . . Testalone . . ." Lillis said, trying to place the name. He snapped his fingers. "I got it: Short? Not so thin? Looks like a beach ball smoking a cigar?"

I grinned, and Dad nodded. "That's him."

"Yeah, I told him about it. Don't know why. When you get old, you don't feel like you have time to keep a secret."

"I wouldn't know," Dad piped up.

"Neither would I," Lillis agreed.

"The comeback," I interjected.

"Comeback," Lillis sneered. "Where was I? Was I away? *I* knew where I was."

"Where?" I asked.

"Mostly Cleveland," he said. "I would have said 'Philadelphia,' but that had too many syllables for the joke."

I decided to be more direct, if such a thing was possible. "Are you and Mr. Townes going to make another movie?"

"Another movement?" Lillis feigned horror. "I'll thank you not to inquire about my bowels, young man."

"Another *movie*."

"Ah. A different question, although there are those who think otherwise. Well, we've discussed it. I think it could happen." Lillis was watching my eyes, gauging my interest. He probably saw more interest there than in his bank account, which (contrary to his "more comfortable" remark) was rumored to be quite impressive.

"That would be amazing," I gushed. It slipped out.

"That remains to be seen. But that's not why you came up here today, is it?"

I was caught off guard by his question. "No. I mean, yes, but, no. See, I was hoping . . . that is, I wonder if you'd consider . . ."

"Is that the way you always talk, or do you actually know about sentences?" Lillis asked me. I repeated the question in my mind a few times so I could tell my grandchildren how the brilliant comedian had torn me down.

"He knows sentences," my father de-

51

fended me. "And I don't mean like 'seven to ten years for armed robbery,' either."

Lillis smiled. Dad could establish a genial rapport with a crocodile; it's why he had been a brilliant salesman for four decades. "It's nice to see *you* can keep up, anyway," Lillis told him. "Was he just an off day for you, or do you think your wife had a thing going with the mailman?"

If anyone else had said it, Dad would have picked up the table lamp and crowned him with it. But from Lillis, you knew it was the part of his image that he could still control. It must have been a terrific burden to have to insult everyone you meet, and make them enjoy it at the same time.

"Mom didn't like the mailman," I told him. "She said he only brought bills. But I do look a little like the dry cleaner."

Dad looked a little shocked, but Lillis laughed. "Welcome to the same conversation, kid," he said. Then he gave me a very careful look and said, "Okay. You didn't drive up here today just to appall your father. What is it you came here to ask?"

4

"Harry Lillis is coming to your theatre?" Sharon asked.

"What did I ask you?" I reminded her.

We sat in the late September sunshine, in the outdoor section of C'est Moi!, a misnamed restaurant that served burgers and sandwiches (although wraps and salads had recently made their way to the menu) on Edison Avenue, the main drag of Midland Heights. The temperature was in the low seventies, probably the last time we'd see that this year, and Sharon had suggested we take our weekly luncheon al fresco.

"Not to call it 'your theatre,' " she recited. "But do I have to say Comedy Tonight every time?"

"No, sometimes you can refer to it as 'The State's Only All-Comedy Movie Theatre,' but only if you say it loudly, and with a couple of exclamation points," I answered. "I can use all the publicity I can get. And yes, Harry Lillis will be there a week from today."

"To get you publicity." Sharon bit into a turkey club. Mayonnaise would have squirted out on anyone else's lip, but it knew better than to try that with my ex-wife. She emits a frequency that keeps dirt off her body through sheer intimidation.

"To celebrate his distinguished career," I countered. "The poor man almost never leaves the Home anymore. This will show him that people still love his work." I speared a piece of celery from my garden salad — I'm trying to get back to where my waistline once belonged — and ranch dressing practically leapt off the fork onto my shirt. Had to make it past the hand holding the napkin, too. It was very persistent ranch dressing.

"And it will get you publicity."

I dabbed at the spot on my shirt. "Is that such a crime? The theatre hasn't exactly turned central New Jersey on its ear with popularity. What's wrong with drawing a little attention?" I asked.

Sharon stared off into space as she droned, "Nothing." Then she sat and stared some more. I knew that meant something was coming out of left field, and I braced myself for it.

But then Sharon sighed, and now I knew it was *serious.* This was the way she'd acted just before she told me that she and Gregory were, let's say, more than professional acquaintances.

"We've never talked about The Kiss," she said. The capital letters were implicit in the way she said it.

I exhaled. "You had me worried for a minute," I said. "I thought you were going to say you're moving to Anchorage, Alaska, and couldn't decide how to tell me."

Her eyes narrowed a little. I put down my fork. "Well, we've never talked about it," she reiterated.

I decided to act casual, and went back to spearing green things that used to be in the earth. "So we haven't talked about it," I said. "We kissed in my office, once, four months ago. It hasn't happened again. What is it you want to say?"

She glared at me for a time. "You're being impossible."

"I'm not, you know. If I were impossible, by definition you'd be eating alone."

When you've known someone for ten years, and were married to her for six of them, you get to know her expressions. Sharon's look repeated her last sentence.

"Okay," I said. "Let's talk about the kiss."

"No. It's obvious you don't want to."
There were reasons we got divorced that
had nothing to do with Gregory. Well, very
little to do with Gregory.

"Come on," I said, now begging to partici-
pate in a conversation I'd rather have
avoided. "I want to hear what you have to
say."

Clearly, she had been rehearsing in her
mind, because she dove right in: "I think
the kiss meant something. I think we've
both been trying to deny that it did, but the
fact that we haven't talked about it for all
these months means it was significant. If it
were casual, one of us would have mentioned it in passing. I know us; I think we
need to talk about why we did that."

"Okay. We were in a small office, standing
very close to each other, and I still find you
very attractive," I said. "We've been apart
for almost two years. Longer, if you count
the time we were still married but not talking to each other. So I slipped for a moment."

Sharon's face said, "Oh, please," while her
voice said, "Come on, Elliot. It's obvious.
Both of us are trying to deflect our emo-
tions and not dealing with the possibility
that we might still have feelings for each
other. We're in classic avoidance mode."

I looked at her for a moment. "You and Gregory are in couples therapy, aren't you?" I asked.

She actually avoided my eyes. "Yes," she said.

"How's that going?"

"I'm not seeing a lot of effort on Gregory's part to deal with his . . . jealousy." Sharon's second husband had behaved badly — okay, *very* badly — after he'd inadvertently witnessed The Kiss. He had, in fact, tried to commit violence on my person.

"He's blaming you," I guessed.

"And it's *so* unfair," Sharon nodded. "Okay, so maybe I reacted to some friction in our marriage by coming back to you for a *minute,* but come on! If he'd done the same thing, I wouldn't have tried to kill the woman he'd kissed."

"I would have vaccinated her and given her a Purple Heart," I said. That was probably a miscalculation.

Sharon gave me a curdling stare. "You know, our marriage wasn't exactly a Disneyland attraction, either."

"I don't know. Mr. Toad's Wild Ride?"

She laughed, in spite of herself. "Peter Pan's Flight, I think."

"Star Tours."

Sharon laughed again, her giggle picking

up speed now. It took her a moment or two to croak out, "Haunted Mansion."

"Oh, thanks a lot!"

Sharon inexplicably dissolved into hysterics, and to be honest, I laughed for a while, too. Nothing either of us had said had been that funny, but it was one of those moments between couples. Ex-couples. People who used to be couples. You know.

When she had recovered, Sharon put her hand over mine. "This is what I mean. We're still good together."

I raised an eyebrow. "I never said we weren't. You know, the divorce wasn't my idea."

"You filed the papers," she reminded me.

"I was convinced you'd be happier . . . elsewhere. Was I wrong?"

"I don't know anymore," Sharon said, and suddenly, I didn't know, either.

I headed back to the theatre to get ready for the night's showings, and to interview a kid about joining our cockeyed team of optimists at Comedy Tonight. I'd been meaning to hire an extra person for some time, and with the reopening, this seemed like the logical moment. I had run a help wanted ad in the *Press-Tribune,* and got one call from a kid named Jonathan Goodwin.

Sophie and Anthony were fine at what they did, but by definition, there were only two of them. Anthony was already in college; he'd be around a couple more years at most, and Sophie, now a high school senior, would be going off to college next September, most likely an all-female one, in the mood she was currently exhibiting. And unless she followed Anthony to Rutgers, it would probably prohibit commuting to work at Comedy Tonight. As if her education were more important than her part-time job.

As it stood, both Sophie and Anthony worked five nights a week, including weekends. That meant I had three days (Friday to Sunday) with both of them in the theatre, and four days when the "staff" consisted of myself and one other person. Even in an operation as small as Comedy Tonight, that was too small a crew. I needed a swing person, and if the interview worked out, that would be Jonathan Goodwin.

Jonathan, a sixteen-year-old sophomore at Midland Heights High School, had sounded so breathless on the phone (after I'd seen his e-mail application) that I worried for his level of excitement at the interview. He showed up a half hour early, a tall, skinny kid with a neck like a giraffe, dressed in a

Monty Python shirt and a pair of shorts that hung down almost to his ankles, making me wonder if they still qualified as shorts. He also wore a pair of flip-flops normally associated with the area we Jerseyans call "down the shore."

"You always get this dressed up for business situations?" I asked him.

"I don't know," Jonathan said, head down. "This is my first job interview."

Oh, geez. Now the kid's whole life of employment expectations was riding on my reaction. I'd have to be nice to him, something that usually makes me break out in a rash. "So, you've never had a job before?"

He looked up with some anxiety, and shook his head. "Raking leaves for my mom," he said. "Mowing the lawn."

"Guess that doesn't really count, huh?"

Jonathan hung his head again. "I guess not."

"You really need the money?" Maybe the kid's mom was pushing him to get a job and he really didn't want to, so he was acting like someone who'd rather be in front of his PlayStation.

"No," he said.

A heck of a conversationalist, too.

Finally, I couldn't stand it anymore. "Why do you want the job, Jonathan?" I asked.

He didn't hesitate. "I love comedy," he said without inflection.

My eyes narrowed. "You mean like *Old School*? *Knocked Up*? Stuff like that?"

Jonathan looked startled. "Well, yeah, I guess," he said. "But really I like the Marx Brothers, Laurel and Hardy, Jerry Lewis." He pointed to his shirt. "Monty Python."

Uh-oh. "Do you know who Ernst Lubitsch was?" I asked Jonathan.

He nodded enthusiastically. "He directed *Ninotchka*," he said. *"The Shop Around the Corner. To Be or Not to Be."*

Damn! "Preston Sturges?"

"The Miracle of Morgan's Creek, Hail the Conquering Hero, The Lady Eve."

I threw out a name he couldn't possibly know. "Frank Tashlin?" I asked.

"Son of Paleface, The Girl Can't Help It, Cinderfella. He was also uncredited on *The Lemon-Drop Kid,* and did a lot of Warner Brothers cartoons."

I was defeated. "When can you start, Jonathan?" I asked, and he actually looked me in the eye. He grinned.

We filled out the necessary paperwork, agreed he'd start the next night, and the minute Jonathan was out the door, Vic Testalone walked in. He wore the same expression Edgar Kennedy, famed "slow-burn" artist in Hal Roach comedies, had whenever someone would drop a piano on his foot or hit him in the face with a dead fish. That Hal Roach was a subtle guy.

"Someone run over your pet ferret, Vic?" I asked.

He looked around, as he always did, for a second seat in my office. As always, there wasn't one. I barely had room for the one I was sitting on. "Yeah, you," he said. "It wasn't enough you tried to appeal to my good nature — despite the fact that I don't have one — about the kid's movie. You didn't trust me to do the right thing . . ."

"Should I have?"

"Of course not," he answered. "But it's the lack of trust that hurts. Then you go and steal the kid's movie so I can't even tell him about Monitor Films and how they may be interested. What's the point, if there's no movie to show them?"

Another nut job. "I didn't steal the movie, Vic," I told him.

"Sure you didn't. I suppose it was the work of the Sprocket Hole in the Wall Gang, riding willy-nilly around the country pilfering movies that could make some money for struggling distributor reps. Who else would have taken it, Elliot, seriously?"

"Willy-nilly?"

"I was under pressure," Vic said.

"How come I'm guilty until proven innocent? How come everybody comes in here assuming I stole the movie, and then dares me to prove I didn't?"

"Everybody?"

"Anthony thinks I took it, too," I told him. "What kind of insane do-gooder would I have to be to commit a felony in the name of saving Anthony from himself? What am I, his fairy godfather?"

Vic leaned against my desk. "I don't know. Is there something you want to tell me?"

"Yes. I'm looking for another distribution company."

He guffawed. No, really. "Another one with a thirty-five-millimeter copy of *Cracked Ice*?" Vic asked.

Okay, so he had me. "Where is it?" I asked, my pulse racing just a little.

"Where's *Killin' Time*?" Vic asked.

"How the hell would I know?"

"Well then," he said, "I guess I don't know where *Cracked Ice* is, either."

5

Friday

Cracked Ice (1956)
A *Very* SPECIAL ATTRACTION

Standing in front of the glass doors to my theatre in a rented tuxedo, I was mostly wishing the butterflies in my stomach would be captured by a tiny net wielded, perhaps, by the half of a turkey sandwich I'd had for lunch. We were waiting for Harry Lillis to arrive, and everyone who works at Comedy Tonight was excited (except Sophie, who wouldn't work up any genuine enthusiasm unless Betty Friedan was bringing Gertrude Stein by to watch *Diary of a Mad Housewife* and *An Unmarried Woman* on a double bill. Maybe when her birthday came around, I'd book *9 to 5* for her, but I knew she wouldn't appreciate the gesture).

I was *not,* however, worried about our feature film arriving. Vic had caved in quickly about my booking a copy of *Cracked*

Ice when I noted that I could easily call his boss and mention that a representative of Klassic Komedy Distributors was refusing to rent a film to the firm's best customer. And who was Vic kidding, anyway: he wanted to see that movie on the big screen as much as I did.

I'd held an inspection of the troops as soon as everyone was in the house, and found them attentive, impressed with their mission, and none wearing clothing that compared with that of the boss (that's me): a tux that Fred Astaire himself would look upon with envy.

Sophie had shown up in a power suit with lapels sharp enough to cause deep wounds if touched. Anthony — well, Anthony was upstairs in the projection booth, though he was wearing Dockers and a T-shirt with the poster from *Amarcord* on it, but our newest employee, Jonathan Goodwin . . . let's just say that Jonathan was not exactly reflecting the elegance of the evening in his chosen attire.

One of the reasons I'd hired Jonathan was because he'd worn a Monty Python T-shirt to the interview, and that had to count for something. The problem right now was that he was wearing the same T-shirt again; in fact, he'd been wearing it almost every day since he started a week ago, and I wasn't sure it had been washed since I'd hired him. It created a contrast to my tuxedo that I felt was not optimal for the paying customers.

The other problem was that Harry Lillis hadn't shown up yet, and therefore the tuxedo would soon begin to show sweat stains.

"I thought I made it clear that tonight was special," I told Jonathan, who seemed uncomfortable and was avoiding eye contact.

"You did," he said, bewildered. "Why?"

There was no point in arguing it: I don't make my staff wear uniforms, mostly because I don't want to pay for uniforms (and okay, because I think uniforms are dumb), and it wasn't as if Jonathan had spare clothing at the theatre. Anyway, it would have taken me an hour to explain to him why his attire was less than appropriate for an occasion of this magnitude.

Besides, when I'd told Jonathan (on his first day of work) that we'd be expecting Harry Lillis less than a week later, he had almost wet himself. Turned out he was at least as big a Lillis and Townes fan as I was, so Jonathan was probably more nervous tonight than I was, and that was saying something.

I decided to go up to the projection booth, even though I knew Anthony was perhaps a tad distracted by another issue. Another issue we'd discussed at least twice a day for a good number of days, now.

"Why did you steal my film?"

"I'm tired of saying it, Anthony: I *didn't* steal your movie. I only told you it was missing. Don't shoot the messenger."

"You were against my starting my career now, weren't you, Mr. Freed?"

"Anthony. I'm only the guy who gave you a job. I like you, but I'm not so caught up in your life that I'd perform a felony because I thought you needed a life lesson. You're aware I don't have any children. It's by design."

"You got divorced."

"Don't change the subject."

"Why did you steal my film?"

"I'm going to tell you this one more time: I have *no idea* where your movie is. I never saw the reels of film after you carried them up to the projection booth. I walked in after the showing, and they were gone. *I didn't steal your movie, Anthony.*"

"You didn't like *Killin' Time,* did you?"

"No, I didn't. I didn't care much for *Hostel,* either. But I didn't drive from theatre to theatre, pilfering prints. I'm not a

67

thief, Anthony, and I'm starting to get just a little insulted by your constant insinuations that I am. I think you're a nice kid. I'm glad you got to make your movie. I was happy to screen it here in the theatre for you. I have absolutely no motivation to take it away from you, and if I knew where it was, I would gladly go get it and deliver it safely into your hands. If you want to quit your education and plunge headlong into a business that offers a .000001 percent chance of success, I would disagree, but I wouldn't stand in your way. Listen carefully, Anthony: I didn't steal your movie."

"You didn't like *Hostel*? Really?"

"Get the trailers spliced." There was no sense in discussing this further, and besides, I was still nervous, so I went back downstairs and found Jonathan unmoved from his lookout post at the front door.

I checked my watch again. "Where is he?" I said aloud.

"I don't know," Jonathan answered in all earnestness.

"Go help Sophie with the snack bar," I said. Jonathan glanced longingly at the front door, but walked toward the snack bar as told. Sophie would probably bounce him to Anthony after a minute, and then he'd be back with me, watching the door for signs

68

of Harry Lillis.

Tonight, though, Jonathan was the least of my worries. I was wearing a rented tuxedo (something that comes as naturally to me as advanced trigonometry comes to your average plankton) and the guest of honor was now officially twenty minutes late. I walked out the front door, no doubt looking like a displaced maitre d', and looked up both sides of Edison Avenue. There was no limousine. I went back inside before someone in a wedding dress could run down the street and stand me on top of a huge cake.

The local papers had promised to send reporters, who also weren't here yet, and News 12 New Jersey, the local cable access TV channel, had sounded interested about sending a crew if there wasn't a fire in Middlesex County that night. Harry Lillis was a god to people like me, and a vague memory to everyone else. The publicity would be negligible, at best, and I had no idea if a crowd would show up or not. Hence, the butterflies in my digestive system.

It was still forty minutes until the advertised time for his appearance, ten minutes before I'd open the doors to the public, but Lillis wasn't here yet, and that couldn't be good. Traffic at this hour on a Friday night could be to blame — which would explain why my father and Vic Testalone hadn't shown up yet, either — but I'd told the limo company to get to the Lillian Booth Actors' Home in plenty of time. I reached for my cell phone.

Before I could dial, Jonathan came ambling back over to me from the stairs. He stopped in front of me, ignored the fact that I was dialing my cell phone, and said, "Anthony says the limo company just called and said Harry Lillis told them not to come." Anthony was using Jonathan to send me a message, rather than talk directly to the man he had decided had stolen his film. This message had come through loud and clear.

"What?"

Jonathan nodded. "They said Mr. Lillis had told them he didn't need it."

"Does that mean he's not coming?"

Jonathan shrugged.

My breathing was starting to get heavy. "What do you want me to do?" Jonathan asked.

"Go sweep up the auditorium."

"I did that already." Maybe I didn't *need* the extra help after all.

"Go outside and make sure the marquee is lit up," I said. I just needed a moment to think. Jonathan looked at me like I had told him to do something insane — which I had — but he went outside.

As he swung the door open to go out, Sharon came in. She was dressed to the nines, or at the very least the eight-and-a-halves, but tastefully, showing nothing she didn't want you to see. Her eyes widened when she saw me, and she made a show of looking me up and down.

"Well, we're looking dapper," Sharon said. She walked to me and picked a thread off my shoulder, then brushed it. I have dandruff. Now you know.

I heard a siren in the distance and actually found myself envying the poor soul being driven to the hospital. At least someone was trying to help *him.*

"Us looking dapper might have to be the entertainment," I said. "Lillis isn't here, and it sounds like he's not coming." I told her about the phone call.

Sharon's upper lip vanished into her mouth as I talked. "Oh my," she said. "What are you going to do?"

"Depends. Did you bring your hara-kiri knife?"

"Left it in my other pants," my ex-wife said.

The siren got louder as Jonathan opened

71

the front door and walked toward us. He gave me his usual puzzled look when he reached Sharon and me. "The marquee lights are turned on," Jonathan said.

Sharon gave me a glance that said, "Shame on you for making fun of that boy," and I countered with one that said, "I gave him a job, and mind your own business." We have very expressive glances.

"Oh yeah," Jonathan continued. "And there's an ambulance pulling up in front of the theatre."

I stood there, absorbing that information for a few seconds, then I ran for the front door, Sharon only a step or two ahead of me.

At the curb of Edison Avenue, in front of Comedy Tonight, was a private ambulance bearing the logo JERSEY MEDICAL TRANSPORT, with its rear doors open. And being lowered to the sidewalk was Harry Lillis. In a tuxedo.

And in a wheelchair.

6

"It's nothing," Lillis said. "I'm fine."

"You don't *look* fine," I answered. "Last time I saw you, you could stand up."

"I can still stand up," he said as a burly looking African-American male nurse named Mitchell (according to his embroidered white coat) rolled him into the theatre. "It's walking that presents a problem."

"Mr. Lillis had what you might call an unfortunate occurrence," Mitchell said in tones that spoke of an upbringing in Coney Island. "He slipped in the common room and did some damage to his hip."

"Mr. Lillis!" I moaned.

"Harry," he corrected. "Or I get Man Mountain Dean here to put me back in the ambulance."

"Okay, *Harry.* Are you all right?"

"Of course I'm all right," Lillis snapped. "I could get up and dance the merengue, if I felt like it. I just like having someone push me around." He looked up at Mitchell. "My luck it couldn't be the little blonde from the nursing home side."

"You're not sick enough for her," Mitchell deadpanned.

"No, I'm not healthy enough for her," Lillis shot back. Then he looked at Sharon and said, "You're a doctor?" I'd introduced them at curbside.

"Yes, Mr. Lillis."

"I'm healthy enough for *you*." He did an eyebrow wiggle Groucho himself would have envied. "And did you miss the part about calling me Harry?"

Jonathan had yet to speak. His mouth opened and closed every once in a while, but no sound came out. I could empathize.

We reached the auditorium doors, and I was careful to get in front of the wheelchair so I could open them ahead of Mitchell. He nodded as he wheeled Lillis into the theatre.

"Are you sure you can go on tonight, Harry?" I asked.

"I tried to convince him he shouldn't," Mitchell said, clucking like a mother hen. "But you don't think anybody but you knows anything, do you, Harry?"

Harry wasn't listening. He looked around the theatre as he rode down the center aisle toward the stage, taking in the miraculous

74

work done to restore the balcony, the massive amount of restoration Dad and I (mostly Dad) had supervised, the new seats, the old seats, the plaster gargoyles over the auditorium exits, the cupola with the enormous chandelier, and the painting above it. I had to admit, it was quite a sight.

"What a dump!" Lillis spouted, in a perfect Bette Davis impression. I had to admire his technique: Lillis was one of the few impressionists who didn't exaggerate the voice he was doing — he went for accuracy. In the Lillis and Townes films, he had spoken lines as Cary Grant, Humphrey Bogart, Dean Martin, Dwight D. Eisenhower, and on one occasion, his partner. He was so good that there were many who argued that Townes had dubbed the line later on, but both comedians had always insisted it was Lillis who did the voice.

"It's still under restoration," I said meekly.

"It looks like it's still under condemnation," Lillis replied when Mitchell had successfully navigated him to the base of the stage. He must have seen my look, because he added, "But our picture will class up the joint, kid. Don't you worry."

"Harry," Sharon admonished.

He looked surprised. "What?"

Jonathan broke in, finally able to speak, as

75

long as he didn't have to speak to Lillis: "How are we going to get him up on the stage?" he asked Mitchell.

We looked at each other for a moment, and then Lillis simply lifted his arms, and Mitchell picked him up out of the chair like a large bag of charcoal, threw him over his shoulder, and walked up onstage. Jonathan carried the chair, and once both were on the same plane, they were reunited.

"Now you know why they didn't send the little blonde," I told Lillis.

"I don't know if she could have lifted me," he said, "but it would have been fun to let her try."

When Jonathan opened the theatre doors precisely at seven, there were already people waiting. Miraculously, Lillis and Townes weren't quite the forgotten antiques I had feared. The theatre filled quickly, and even the balcony was packed. Normally, that would make me nervous, but the sight of a full house — a *really* full house — was enough to dispel fears of a structural collapse; besides, the construction crew had done a really thorough job. By seven thirty, Sophie had sold a week's worth of snacks, despite her scowling at every male who ordered anything (I'd have to talk to her about the five-year-old boys, who shouldn't have to share the blame), and Jonathan had torn more tickets than we'd ever sold before. This was the first time we'd sold out every single seat, balcony and all. A few hearty souls even bought tickets to stand in the back. It was a good thing the Midland Heights fire chief hadn't shown up, or he'd have seen we were exceeding our legal capacity.

Clearly, I'd have to find a way to get a comedy legend to show up every night.

I stood behind the screen with Lillis, Mitchell, Sharon, and Vic, who had shown up just a few minutes earlier. We spoke quietly, despite the fact that the crowd couldn't hear us over their own conversations. Out of the corner of my eye, I saw my father approaching from the wings of the stage.

Vic looked at me with something resembling distaste and asked, "So, what are you doing about the missing film?"

Missing film? Did our copy of Cracked Ice *go . . . oh yeah,* that *missing film!*

"Anthony's movie? I told the cops, and they're investigating. What do you mean, what am I doing about it?"

"You know the kid can't afford to make another print," Vic countered. "You know this means I can't make a deal with a studio.

You don't seem too concerned."

"When did I get the responsibility for this? I'm not his father, or his agent." I almost took the cigar out of Vic's mouth just out of spite.

"Two people you know well could profit from recovering that film, and you could care less," he said.

"If you want to get technical," I told him, "that expression should be 'you *couldn't* care less.' If I could care less, that would indicate that I care."

"I don't want to get technical," Vic said with great finality. We stood quietly for a few moments, and I refocused my attention on the evening at hand. But Vic, while not physically resembling a Jewish mother in any way, had nonetheless managed to make me feel just a tad guilty.

"I'll go out and do a short introduction, and then I'll call for you, Harry," I said to Lillis. "Do you want me to come back and get you?"

Lillis shook his head. "No, this guy can do it." He tilted his head in Mitchell's direction. "If I keel over from the exertion, he's more qualified to carry me to the ambulance." Then he turned to Sharon. "Unless the doctor would be willing. If I went into cardiac arrest, she could take off her shirt and examine me."

Sharon had spent enough years married to me to know when she was needed as a straight man. "If you go into cardiac arrest, Harry, what good would it do for me to take off *my* shirt?"

Lillis smiled. "At least I'd die happy," he said.

I stepped out in front of the screen and Anthony, up in the booth, turned on a spotlight we have for just such occasions. We'd also found an old podium in the basement when I'd bought the place, and we'd wheeled it out to use for the introductions. This was the first time we'd ever used it.

"Good evening," I said, and the crowd immediately quieted. Sharon didn't have to whistle like a construction worker this time. "Welcome to Comedy Tonight. We're very excited to have you all here for a very special evening. Tonight, we are being visited by a legend of film comedy whose work is unparalleled, a man who clearly stands among Groucho Marx, W. C. Fields, Charlie Chaplin, and Gene Wilder as a master in his field."

"Larry the Cable Guy!" a teenager called from the crowd, and there was laughter.

"Yeah, him, too," I said, plowing on. "Just a quick explanation. Mr. Lillis will come

79

out and speak for a few minutes, and then we'll have the first New Jersey showing of *Cracked Ice* in twenty years . . ." There was applause from the crowd. "And at the end of the evening, Mr. Lillis will appear again for a Q-and-A session. So please save your questions. We'll send around cards for you to write them down during the film."

I couldn't see a thing beyond the first row with the spotlight in my face. Leo Munson, wearing his captain's hat, which meant it was a formal occasion, was seated next to the woman who'd been laughing at Lillis's jokes when I first met him at the Booth Actors' Home, with a corsage pinned to her very tasteful lapel. I wondered if she was Harry's date for the evening, but before I had the chance to speculate further, I heard the voice of an older man call out, "Why do we need cards? Can't he *hear?*"

There was a murmur from the area of the shout. I thought I'd recognized the voice, but couldn't place it. Trying to avoid an ugly scene, I turned toward the wings and shouted, "Ladies and gentlemen, a true comedy legend: Harry Lillis!"

The audience broke into loud applause, and Mitchell wheeled Lillis onto the stage. The audience, or at least those that I could see clearly, leapt to their feet, and Lillis, positively beaming, waved to them. The ovation went on for a good number of minutes; I wasn't counting, but the thrill I got from that moment was enough to keep me grinning for a long time.

Or more to the point, it *would* have kept me grinning for a long time if, as soon as the din died down and the audience took their seats, that same voice hadn't screamed out, "My god; he's in a *wheelchair!*"

Lillis's eyes narrowed, and he put a hand up to shield his eyes from the spotlight. If I hadn't been standing immediately to his left, I wouldn't have heard him mutter, "Son of a bitch."

"You sick, Lillis, or are you just old?"

I tried to step forward to address the voice, but Lillis reached out and grabbed my right arm. "Don't," he said. "You know who that is, don't you?"

And, suddenly, I did. I reached out my left arm, and shouted to the crowd, "Ladies and gentlemen, *Les Townes*!"

Sure enough, Townes, dressed in a blazer and slacks and looking fit, walked up to the skirt of the stage, where we had built two small steps, and I helped him onto the stage. The audience, aware of the entertainment history they were witnessing, stood and applauded some more. Townes took a deep bow.

If I was speechless when I met Lillis, I was mortified when I met Townes. Here was yet another of my boyhood idols, and I'd almost exploded at him a moment before. It flashed on me at that moment that I should have sought Townes out when I'd found Lillis, and asked him to the screening tonight. But, given his reputation for being a gentleman, I hoped Townes would let me off the hook. He took a second bow, and then as he stood, gestured that I should lean in; he wanted to tell me something

"What's the matter," he asked. "I'm not a legend?"

7

Watching *Cracked Ice* with the two men who made it was an education. The small elite group of us: Sharon, Dad (Mom had seen enough of Harry Lillis during my teenage years, but sent her regrets, along with a batch of cookies guaranteed to cause heartburn if used as anything but coasters), Vic, Anthony (when he wasn't changing reels), Mitchell, and I, sat silently while the two old pros watched their crowning work, their pinnacle of achievement, the highlight of their careers . . . and trashed it mercilessly.

It took me a shorter while to get over my awe at being in the same room with Les Townes, mostly because he and Lillis were busy taking verbal shots at each other that were as funny as they were pointed. Not that I wasn't amazed at listening to the team, but after a while, you started to feel like part of the club. I almost felt like taking a couple of shots at the movie myself, but it was one of my all-time favorites, and I couldn't bring myself to criticize it.

In case you haven't seen it (and I strongly suggest you do), *Cracked Ice* is a brilliant comedy based on the idea that a prehistoric man — shown in a brief opening sequence fleeing a rear-projection brontosaurus left over from *King Dinosaur* (1955) — falls into one of the many glaciers that were available at the time, only to be discovered, and thawed, in 1956 (otherwise known as "modern times"). He is examined and taken in by an eccentric doctor, and eventually learns to become a smooth, Brylcreemed playboy who does well with the ladies.

The genius evident in the handling of this rather pedestrian plotline (beaten to a bloody pulp, for example, by Pauly Shore in *Encino Man*) was that any other comedy team in history would have had the stronger comic presence — in this case, Harry Lillis — play the caveman. Lillis and Townes knew better. The caveman would spend much of the movie grunting, and that would rob Lillis of his verbal wit, perhaps his greatest comic weapon. And after "evolving," the caveman (eventually named Bob) would be a charming, if oily, ladies' man, something that would again keep Lillis from cutting loose.

They reversed the roles, and the result was classic. Or so I thought, until I heard Lillis and Townes rip it to pieces before my very ears.

"Look at that lighting," Townes grumbled from his seat behind the screen (you can actually see very well back there, although the image is naturally backward). "Who directed this turkey, anyway?"

"I did," Lillis reminded him.

"Oh, yeah." Townes grinned.

Lillis pointed at the screen, as if we might be watching something else. "You see that? My tie's inside the doctor coat in one shot, then outside, then back inside. And I knew it from the first dailies, but they wouldn't let me go back and reshoot it. Cheap bastards. They said nobody'd ever notice."

"I've seen this movie fifty times, Harry," I told him quietly, "and I never noticed until you said something just now."

He gave me a look that shut me up for twenty minutes.

They proceeded like that for some time, noticing every tiny continuity error, groaning at some of the jokes that I'd always thought were brilliant, despairing at how each of them looked on-screen. But when they got to the examination scene, they both stopped talking.

Perhaps the most well-remembered of any comedy scene the team ever performed, the scene halfway through *Cracked Ice,* in which Harry Lillis, playing Dr. Horatio X. Ledbetter, decides to perform a thorough examination of his prehistoric subject (Townes), is a seamless grafting of sophisticated verbal wit onto relentless slapstick that has never been equaled on film. Entire theses have been written in postgraduate film programs on the scene, and even those haven't blunted its delirious momentum.

At one point, Dr. Ledbetter slips on a bar of soap (don't ask how a bar of soap ends up on the floor; just trust me, and go rent the movie), and the caveman, having been told to follow his doctor's lead, deliberately slips on the floor, too. The camera stays on the empty room — a static shot — for forty-two seconds, and the grunting and groaning (and Lillis's offscreen remarks, which he has insisted were ad-libbed) is all we have to go on for the longest time. When the two men finally stand up, the caveman is in the doctor's coat, and the doctor is wearing a leopard skin. It defies explanation, but it is hilarious.

Tonight, neither Lillis nor Townes spoke during that scene — despite the raucous laughter coming from the audience — but they restarted the acid commentary immediately after. I didn't dare open my mouth, and neither did anyone else in our small group. We listened, and we learned.

The question-and-answer period after the film was priceless: even relatively innocent questions like, "When you were shooting that scene, did you have a cold?" were met with less-than-innocent answers ("A cold *what?*"). Anthony, with his digital video setup on a tripod, recorded the event, and never looked happier. Even when he looked at me, the alleged destroyer of his dreams, he couldn't stop smiling.

It went on for over an hour, far longer than Mitchell — who seemed terribly protective of Lillis — was comfortable with, but the two old pros showed no sign of flagging. When I finally ended the session, to groans from the audience followed by a long standing ovation, it was with the same feeling one has after any big (and enjoyable) moment in one's life: *Wow, that was great* coupled with *Is that it?*

After the audience left, we sat in the lobby of Comedy Tonight as Lillis and Townes continued to hold court. Townes, almost as tall as his partner (and better preserved, at least to the untrained eye), sat with his long legs stretched out in front of him. Sophie was still putting the snack bar back together, although there was precious little left; almost everything we'd had in stock had been sold. I'd have to call our candy distributor early tomorrow morning to get replacement snacks in time for the next evening's showing.

Sharon, Vic, Anthony, Jonathan, and I sat on the steps to the balcony, while Harry Lillis, in his wheelchair, and Les Townes, in my desk chair (the most luxurious seat I owned that wasn't bolted to the auditorium floor), bantered themselves silly for an hour and a half. The woman from the Booth Actors' Home, whom Harry introduced as Marion Borello, "a dame from way back when," sat next to Lillis and rarely took her eyes off him, giving Harry looks I think he saw but chose not to return. Mitchell, glancing impatiently at his watch, hovered nearby, leaning on the snack bar and getting dirty looks from Sophie, who had just polished it to a mirrorlike finish. Dad sat in a folding chair I'd dusted off and set near the two guests of honor.

"How did you come up with all that stuff when they're on the floor?" I asked Lillis about the examination scene.

Townes jumped in ahead of him. "Would you believe the studio wanted us to cut that?" he asked. "They said it was a shot of the wall for forty seconds, and nobody would want to watch it. Harry had to fight with them for a week over it, and to the day he died, H. R. Mowbrey insisted we were crazy."

Lillis grinned at his partner's admiration for his work and his tenacity. "I threatened to walk off the lot and never come back," he said. "I think Mowbrey wanted to take me up on it." Lillis's battles with the studio owner were the stuff of legend; while they were negotiating a contract extension in 1955, Lillis once actually sent a man in a gorilla costume to Mowbrey's office with instructions to follow the poor man around all day and, well, ape every move Mowbrey made.

"Whenever we got too deep into it, we sent Vivian in to talk to him," Townes said. There was a moment after hearing the name of Townes's late wife, and their on-screen leading lady, that the two men both grew quiet, but Dad, sitting on a folding chair to one side, broke the silence.

"She could talk the studio into letting you guys have your way?" he asked. That's it, Dad, rub in the sad memories a little bit. I love the man, but he sometimes has the sensitivity of cast iron.

89

"Ah, Vivian," Townes said. "The best straight man a comic ever had." It didn't answer Dad's question, but that didn't seem important.

"Straight man?" Sharon, who was standing to my left, asked. "Why wasn't she a straight woman?"

Townes shook his head. "No such thing," he said. "Margaret Dumont was Groucho's straight man. Dorothy Lamour was Hope and Crosby's straight man. If you weren't a comic, you were the straight man, setting up the jokes. And nobody did it better than Vivian."

"Yeah, and you had to go screw it up and marry her," Lillis replied. The group laughed, but I noticed a look passing between the two comedians that would indicate the humor wasn't necessarily intentional. They were glaring into each other's eyes like a pair of dogs trying to determine which was the alpha male. It wasn't pretty. Marion Borello stopped beaming at Lillis long enough to look annoyed. At Les Townes.

Dad broke the moment after the laugh died down. "How did you get to direct, Harry?" And the look between the two partners ended as Lillis began his story. Sometimes, my father is exactly the guy you want around.

After another few questions, Mitchell announced his intention to cold-bloodedly murder anyone who stood between Harry Lillis and the door, and the little group broke up. I walked over to Les Townes first, and held out my hand. "I'm so glad you came," I told him.

He didn't take my hand. "Then how come you didn't invite me?" he asked.

I was stunned for a few seconds, not sure if Townes was joking. "Mr. Townes, you have no idea how sorry I am about that. I didn't know how to get in touch with you," I said.

"Harry knew. Did you ask?"

"No," I admitted. "It never occurred to me that you were around here, or that you'd come if we invited you. But I'm glad you did."

Townes thought for a moment, then shook my hand. "Apology accepted," he said.

Out on the sidewalk, we all hugged and tried to extend our time by just another few seconds, but Mitchell was adamant, and started readying the van to raise Lillis's wheelchair. After Vic and Dad said good night and left, Sharon and I watched as Townes approached Lillis and bent over to take his hands. Marion stood to one side, waiting to ride back in the ambulance with

Lillis. It turned out she'd taken two buses and a train (then a taxi from the New Brunswick station) to get here tonight. "I don't like to drive at night," she explained.

"That's dedication," I told her.

Marion smiled. "Not just that," she said.

Les Townes held Harry Lillis's hands in his own two for a long moment. The look exchanged between the two partners was affectionate, and sad.

"Stay warm, Harry," he said. "Just stay warm."

"You're the best there is, Les," Lillis told him. "Don't let anybody tell you otherwise. The *best.*"

Townes turned away and nodded toward Sharon and me, then walked to his car, and drove off. I walked to Lillis just as Mitchell was attaching his chair to the lift apparatus.

"That was very touching, Harry," I told him. "I'm glad you guys got together tonight."

Lillis appeared to be wiping a tear from his eye. "Thanks for setting it up, Elliot," he said. "It's nice to remind myself after all these years what a dear, dear man Les Townes really is."

Mitchell started the motor on the lift, and Lillis (and the chair) rose up into the back of the ambulance. And just as Harry Lillis settled into the vehicle, he looked down at me again.

"He murdered his wife, you know," Lillis said. "Les killed Vivian, and then burned the house down."

And Mitchell closed the back doors of the ambulance.

8

If you can keep your head when all about you are losing theirs, it's just possible you haven't grasped the situation.
— JEAN KERR, *PLEASE DON'T EAT THE DAISIES*

Saturday

I spent the morning at my bedroom computer, scouring the Internet for information about Vivian Reynolds's death. I hadn't actually done much Internet research before, other than to look up a defunct comedian on the Internet Movie Database every once in a while, but I dove in now.

The volume and breadth of information available was amazing, and somewhat frightening. There were entire websites devoted to Vivian's memory, which was rather astounding, considering that she never really became a huge star. Her IMDb listing showed only three films before she began working with Lillis and Townes, and after that, she always played second fiddle (third fiddle) to the team. (I also discovered that there was a male actor named E. Vivian Reynolds, who appeared in five films between 1917 and 1934, ending his career playing "Butler" in *Love at Second Sight*.)

A number of the Vivian Reynolds sites referred to her "tragic death," but only one, www.whokilledviv.com, suggested the death was anything but an accident. Citing "sources within the LAPD at the time of the fire," the (anonymous, like the "sources") writer of the site tried to make the case that Reynolds was dead before her bungalow caught fire, and while no names were mentioned, it's clear from references throughout the site that the person hosting it believed Reynolds's marriage to Les Townes was less than idyllic.

The facts I could confirm on multiple sites were these: On November 10, 1958, while Lillis and Townes were working on a film (*Step This Way*, which had no female lead), Vivian Reynolds spent the afternoon at the Hillcrest Country Club, across from 20th Century Fox on Pico Boulevard. She spent a few hours in the bar, but didn't drink to excess, according to the bartender. She then left by herself.

She must have gone home to Bel Air, because three hours later, the Los Angeles Fire Department responded to reports of a fire, and found the Townes/Reynolds home in flames. By the time Vivian's body was found, it was identifiable only through dental records.

The official record listed the fire as electrical in nature, and did not classify it as suspicious. Townes, at least outwardly inconsolable, didn't return to the set of *Step This Way* for eight weeks, a very long time during the reign of the studio system (Clark Gable, for example, was back on the set of *Somewhere I'll Find You* only thirty-eight days after Carole Lombard's death in a plane crash). It was up to Harry Lillis, who was also grieving for a lost love, to shoot around his partner and eventually to cover Townes's absence by claiming that he, Lillis, had pneumonia and couldn't film. When they finally managed to finish the movie, it was hardly the team's best effort (understandable, under the circumstances), and although they worked together for another five years, the seeds for Lillis and Townes's split were planted the day Vivian Reynolds died.

Still, the LAPD had been quick to declare the fire one of the accidental, electrical variety, and Vivian Reynolds's death an awful consequence of that accident. No foul play was determined in the case. Clearly, it was up to me to bring in the experts.

"So let me get this straight," said Chief Barry Dutton. "You want me to investigate a death that was ruled an accident."

"Yes," I agreed. It was chilly in his office. You'd think the town would spring for a better heating system for their top law enforcement official. I'd brought coffee and doughnuts. You learn stuff when you hang around with cops.

"And it took place in California," Dutton continued.

I nodded. "Bel Air, to be exact."

"In 1958." Dutton, who was standing over me to better emphasize his intimidating physique, glared into my eyes.

"That's right," I told him. It had seemed a better idea a few moments ago.

Dutton sat down heavily. "I have three assaults to investigate," he said. "Five domestic disputes, any number of traffic violations, and two burglaries, one of which, you might recall, took place at your theatre. So tell me, Elliot, why am I sitting here talking to you about a Hollywood murder from the early days of Cinemascope?"

"It was Vivian Reynolds, Chief. She was married to Les Townes, and Harry Lillis himself told me her husband murdered her." This, too, had sounded much more convincing while inside my head.

"It was fifty years ago. I'm sure the cops who issued the report on the fire are dead, or at least retired for the past three decades. The crime scene is probably a Wal-Mart by now." Dutton's voice was soothing, like he was talking to a dangerous maniac holding an AK-47.

"It's Bel Air," I said. "At the very worst, the crime scene is now a Versace outlet." He didn't look convinced, and I had to admit, I was on shaky ground myself. "Look, I'm not asking you to take it up professionally; you're three thousand miles and half a century removed from the investigation. But I'm asking: if *I* were going to look into it, what would I do?"

Dutton reached into the box of doughnuts and pulled out an especially chocolate one, which he eyed like a lion going after a freshly killed antelope. "Oh, no," he said. "I'm not going down *that* road again. I'm not helping you get involved in digging up information on a violent crime. I'm not encouraging you to annoy people who are better left unannoyed, just because you've decided you're Philip Marlowe. Not happening, Elliot. Not this time."

"Okay, so how goes the investigation of Anthony's missing film?" My face was, I assure you, all innocence.

"That's it? You're dropping the Case of the Well-Done Starlet?" Dutton, for reasons I can't fathom, appeared skeptical.

"Sure," I answered. "You convinced me. It was a long time ago, in a city far away."

"Stop talking like Luke Skywalker; you're scaring me. You're saying I've convinced you to be rational? Just like that? It hardly seems characteristic."

I took a doughnut, too. What the hell; I'd paid for them. So I'd do a few extra sit-ups . . . as soon as I started exercising. "Look. It was something an old man said about a woman he probably loved before his best friend married her. It was obvious the memory of her was painful for both of them. He was just babbling; it had been an emotional night. You should have been there, Chief."

"I *was* there," Dutton said. "At least, at the public part. I'm an old Lillis and Townes fan myself. I was in the balcony."

"You're a brave man." I still didn't trust the balcony, no matter how many thousands I'd spent rebuilding it.

"You don't get to be chief of police based solely on good looks," Dutton said without the hint of a smile.

"Anthony's movie," I changed the subject back again. "What's going on?"

"It's an ongoing investigation. Why should I tell you anything?"

I studied him. "Because I'm the owner of the business that was burglarized."

"True, but until I have a suspect . . ."

"Because you've shared information with me before . . ."

Dutton nodded. "*There's* an experience I'd want to repeat."

"How about this: because I bought the doughnuts, and if you want that last double chocolate, you're going to have to tell me something."

His hand, in mid-grab for the pastry in question, stopped dead in the air. He considered. "All right, fine. I took the list of invitees you gave me and interviewed a number of those who might have some reason to take the film." Then he snatched the doughnut before I could have completed an entire blink.

I offered, "Such as Anthony's father, who doesn't want him to quit school; Carla, his girlfriend, who doesn't want him to get too famous too fast; and Leo Munson, whose odd taste in films might be hiding a deep-seated obsession with bad movies?" I considered adding myself and Sharon, who might have been trying to spare the world the sight of *Killin' Time,* but I think anything that might add the word "suspect" to my name on a police file is best left unsaid.

"Yes, and a few of Anthony's classmates," Dutton said. "I'm not sure it wasn't a frat prank or something. I even considered the idea that Anthony had stolen it himself to collect the insurance . . ."

". . . until you discovered he had no insurance on the film," I finished for him.

"Precisely." Dutton didn't say, "Precisely, *Holmes,*" but he could have.

"Is there anything I can do to help?" I asked. "People have been accusing me of being too blasé about this. I'd like to at least *look* like I'm doing something."

Dutton's brows lowered, which I took to be a sign that he was thinking, or trying to determine how to get the rest of my doughnut out of my hand. "There's really nothing I can think of," he said.

That was, actually, the answer I was hoping for. I smiled. "Good enough," I told him. "Now, about this murder in Hollywood . . ."

"Okay, okay," Dutton said, as if I'd been

browbeating him. "You can question Anthony's roommate, Danton, or your ex-wife."

That was, actually, *not* the answer I'd been hoping for. "Sharon?" I said. "Why do you think Sharon stole the film?"

"I don't, or I wouldn't be suggesting it to you," Chief Dutton said. "We've already talked to both of them, and you could never say publicly that I even suggested you walk by their houses. But if it'll make you happy to show Anthony you're doing something, this will create that appearance."

"I really would rather look into the murder . . ."

"You can go to any library you like and look up the press clippings from 1958," Dutton said with real gravity in his voice. "I'll bet there's stuff you can Google. But you won't get one hint of cooperation from me or any of my officers."

I figured I'd send up a trial balloon. "Do you think Anthony's girlfriend, Carla, took the movie, to keep him from moving to Hollywood and out of her life?" I asked.

Dutton shrugged. He wasn't giving anything else away.

I sat and looked at him for a moment, then sipped my coffee. If *that* was the way he was going to be about it . . . "Danton," I said. "Is that his first name, or his last name?"

"You're the sleuth," Chief Dutton said. "Go find out."

9

Since Dutton had been adamant about my not persevering with the Vivian Reynolds investigation, I decided to concentrate on that. It wasn't that I didn't respect him; I do. But I'm a contrary cuss, and I generally do what people tell me not to do. I didn't say it was rational.

I rode my bike back to the town house and got right on the phone to Sergeant Margaret Vidal of the Camden Police Department's homicide division.

I'd partially financed Comedy Tonight with the money I'd made selling my first (and only) novel, *Woman at Risk,* to a Hollywood production company. The producers promptly changed everything except the color of the police officers' uniforms and made a movie called *Split Personality,* which resembled the book in that all the people had feet and hands, and things like that.

But in researching the novel, I had spent a good deal of time with the Camden homicide detectives, chiefly (because no one else wanted to talk to the idiot writer) Meg Vidal. She and I had gotten close but not intimate for a short period of time, and then not, as soon as the book was written. But now when I called her, she still answered the phone, and I appreciated that.

"Elliot Freed. Don't tell me: you're working on a new book."

"As a matter of fact, I am," I lied. "But not a novel. I'm writing about a murder that took place in Bel Air, California, in 1958. I got some stuff off the Internet, but I don't know anybody out there except the perpetrators of that movie they made from my book, and let's just say I'm not on their speed dial. Who can I call?"

"You once told me that if you called and said you were writing another book, I should come up and shoot you," Meg reminded me.

"I said another *novel*," I told her. "This is nonfiction. I'm just reporting the facts."

"I thought you owned a movie theatre."

"A man can't have a hobby?"

"Elliot." Meg's voice sounded less than enthralled. "You're lying to me."

"How can you tell?"

105

"I'm a trained investigator," she said. "And you're a really bad liar. What's really going on?"

I explained the situation and told Meg I'd like to do some research into Vivian Reynolds's death. "I really don't see how I could screw up an investigation that was closed in the last century," I told her.

"Neither do I, but I'm sure you'll find a way," she answered. "Still, I can put you in touch with a guy who was on the LAPD then. Friend of my dad's. You give him a call, and tell him Magpie said hello."

"Magpie?"

"You want help, or not?"

She gave me the name of her father's friend, we got up-to-date on the sorry state of our lives, and I hung up. Maybe someday I'll actually be in a room with Meg again; she's good people.

Talking to Meg had bolstered my resolve. Vivian Reynolds was calling to me; I had to discover the truth about her death. It was back to the World Wide Web.

Research has never been my specialty, but I'm fascinated by the amount of information — true and otherwise — available through search engines these days. I spent three hours moving from site to site, gathering bits of data here and there, finding things I knew were completely incorrect (*Peace and Quiet* was *not* filmed at the Sarasota racetrack — they actually went to Santa Anita because it was cheaper), discounting some sites, and moving on to others. Most of the facts about Vivian Reynolds's death were duplicated over and over again; there was little fluctuation, and in many cases, the same newspaper accounts and documents were cited on multiple pages.

In other words, I wasn't getting very far, and there was almost no hint that Les Townes might have had anything to do with his wife's death; it certainly seemed like the fire was an accident.

Until, tucked away on whokilledviv.com, I noticed a copy of a studio sign-in sheet from the day of the fire: on a full day of shooting, Les Townes had signed out from the Paramount lot at 1:30 p.m. — and didn't return for eight weeks.

He'd been off the soundstage, unaccounted for, at the time the fire started in his home. And according to the call sheet for *Step This Way* (also provided by the website), Townes was supposed to have been onstage for the entire afternoon, shooting scene 78, on "the dancing school" set. This excited me more than anything else on the

Internet.

There had never been a dancing school scene in *Step This Way:* was the scene shot and excised, or was it not filmed after Vivian's death? Lillis, who was directing, would know. I was sure if I got in touch with him and asked . . .

But perhaps that was beside the point.

The fact was, Les Townes was not on the set when he was called for, and his whereabouts were not known at the time Vivian Reynolds died. Wouldn't the cops have known all this stuff? It was enough to justify calling Meg's police source, so I reached for the phone.

But the doorbell rang, and stopped me in my tracks, assuming one can have tracks when sitting down and reaching for the telephone. My doorbell *never* rings; I don't know that many people, and I almost never invite anyone to the town house. I'm still working on making it feel like someplace *I* want to be, let alone someplace other people would like to be.

Mystified, I walked to the door. I'd have looked to see who was waiting on my doorstep, but the builder had neglected to equip me with either a peephole or a window near the door, which I assume means that the builder doesn't care if I'm ambushed by a serial killer masquerading as a pizza delivery guy. That wouldn't work anyway, because I always go to get my own pizza. New Brunswick is a town where you can walk to stuff.

I decided to throw caution to the wind and open my front door, and there was Sharon, hand on one hip and an expression on her face that said there could be no arguing with her.

"Gregory and I have separated," she said. "Legally. I'm filing for divorce."

That was quite a step, and I was impressed. "Did he move out?" I asked.

"No." The tone was evasive. There was more to this than met the ear.

I tried the obvious next tactic. "Did *you* move out?"

"No." Defiant this time. "If I move out, he can get the house."

"And if he moves out, you can," I ventured.

"That's right."

"So you've separated, but you're living in the same house. Do you want to come inside?" I gestured into the town house.

She walked into the hallway. Sharon doesn't love being in the town house — it makes her feel like her leaving me left me in a hollow, sad existence, which, let's face it, is true — so she didn't walk all the way in, but the rush of excitement from her news was driving her. Her voice was a half tone higher than usual, and she was talking fast. If it had been 1987 and I didn't know her well, I'd have sworn she was using cocaine.

"I have this sense of freedom I haven't felt in a long time," she said. "Not like I've thrown off a heavy weight, but more like I have all these possibilities. I'm not tied to Gregory anymore. I'm a free agent. Elliot! It's like buying a new car. You can have your choice of any one you want."

"How romantic," I noted.

"Don't knock it," she said. "I was feeling this way when I met you the first time."

"Walk into the house," I tried. "It doesn't bite."

Sharon made a face at me and walked into the living room. She'd been here before, but not since I'd added the floor-to-ceiling shelves for the massive video collection I'd inherited, sort of, a while back. She stood, awed by its enormity.

"I'm back in the dating pool, I guess," she went on. Maybe the videos weren't getting to her as much as I thought. "I'm available."

That sounded like far too good an opening for me to ignore. I'd been hoping for such a statement for a long time. I sucked

110

in a deep breath.

"Well then," I said. "How about having dinner with me one night this week?"

Sharon stopped and turned to make eye contact with me. She realized my invitation wasn't simply for another let's-be-pals lunch at C'est Moi! like we'd been doing for more than a year now. I was asking her on a date.

It took a long moment, but then she said, "I'd love to."

10

Sunday

Cracked Ice **(1956)** AND *Time Traveler: The Story of Wendell Ludicke* (LAST FRIDAY)

On the bicycle ride to the theatre for an afternoon showing, I considered the size of the step I'd taken with Sharon. Most men have a best friend, someone with whom they discuss taking such a risk ahead of time, but I hadn't known I was going to ask that question before it came out of my mouth, and besides, my best friend was the woman I was asking on a date.

I supposed I could talk to my father about it, but that would have been remarkably weird.

For the few of us who are divorced but not in the majority of ex-couples who would prefer to duel to the death rather than reconcile, there is always a lingering doubt: Maybe we could have stuck it out. Maybe we didn't give the marriage enough of a chance.

Maybe we still love each other.

On my side, I knew how I felt. I'd loved Sharon when she was my girlfriend. I'd loved her when she was my wife. Even when she came home one night to tell me she preferred to be married to Gregory, I felt betrayed, hurt, and disoriented . . . but I loved her.

Yesterday, she had seemed to offer me the chance to start again, to go back to the place we'd started and see if there was still ground to explore. And the moment she'd said it, the moment she'd held out the possibility that we could do exactly what I'd wanted to do for the two years we'd been living apart, I had jumped in and suggested a major step in a major direction.

But had I pushed too hard, too soon? That would be my style, based on past experience. Sharon was in a strange emotional place right now, and I might be taking advantage of that.

On the other hand, I couldn't let some imaginary other guy, someone I hadn't met, find out Sharon was back "on the market" and ask her out ahead of me. Call me old-fashioned, but I think the ex-husband has the first right of refusal on a newly separated ex-wife.

Perhaps this was a rule no one had considered before.

We'd made a tentative "date" to go out for dinner at somewhere other than C'est Moi! the following Thursday, a night that was usually slow at the theatre and when Sharon's practice did not have late hours.

That gave me four days to sort out in my mind whether this was a door opening wide to a second chance, or the offered embrace of a straitjacket just before they put you in the padded cell.

Today, although we offered an early show of the new Will Ferrell comedy, business was slow. Six other theatres in the area were showing the same movie, and they had stadium seating, video games in the lobby, and larger newspaper ads than I did. I felt like I was starring in *The Little Movie Theatre Around the Corner,* and was being forced out of business by a heartless chain of movie houses — like, all the other ones.

Normally, I'd be hovering over Anthony in the projection booth, but the icy breeze coming off his demeanor meant I'd have to put on an extra sweater, and I wasn't in the mood. Jonathan was watching the house, such as it was, from the back of the auditorium, and Sophie, on the pretense of selling snacks, sat behind the counter reading *The Feminine Mystique.*

There didn't seem to be any need for my presence, so I retreated to my office. Standing outside the door was Carla Singelese, Anthony's girlfriend, looking like a street urchin selling flowers. I said hello and invited her into the office. Carla looked surprised, but came in. She sat in the desk chair, so I stood.

"Why aren't you up in the booth with Anthony?" I asked.

"I don't like to distract him when he's working," Carla answered, staring at my Harpo Marx screen saver. "We'll go out afterward, and he can wind down." Anthony could make running a movie projector sound like a marathon event. Come to think of it, running my projector was enough to tire out the average triathlete.

"So how are you and Anthony doing?" Why do people ask such stupid questions of vague acquaintances? I wouldn't ask someone I knew well about their personal relationship to start a conversation. If I knew anyone well.

"It's been hard since . . . well, you know." Carla looked away, and I wondered what the hell she was talking about.

"I don't know," I said. "Since what?"

Carla looked astonished. "Since you took his movie," she said.

I shook my head, trying to loosen the cobwebs. "I didn't take anything, Carla. I don't know why Anthony thinks that, but I didn't steal *Killin' Time.*"

Her mouth opened. "Are you sure?"

"Of course I'm sure," I answered. "I was there when I didn't do it. In fact, I sort of thought *you* might be trying to separate Anthony from the rival for his affections."

Carla stood up in a blatantly melodramatic gesture she'd probably seen in an old Jean Arthur movie that Anthony had forced her to watch. "Me? Why would I want to do that?"

"Because if Anthony starts a Hollywood career now, he might not take you with him," I suggested.

"Of course he would," Carla said, defiance in her eyes. "Anthony loves me."

"I'm sure he does. But success does funny things to people. If you thought . . ."

"Well, I *didn't* think," Carla cut me off. "I wouldn't ever get in the way of Anthony's film career, Mr. Freed, and I'm sorry you think I would." She started for the door, which isn't a long walk, but it's an awkward one if someone is in your way.

"I'm sorry, Carla, I didn't mean to upset you. It's just that I'm offended that everyone seems to simply assume I took Anthony's movie, and I guess I took it out on you. Please forgive me."

Since I was actually being sincere, I was glad Carla stopped and considered, then smiled at me. "I understand," she said. "You were using reverse psychology."

"I was?"

"Sure. You wanted me to know how it felt to be suspected, so you pretended to suspect me. Now I know what you're going through." Carla reached up and kissed me on the cheek. "Don't worry, Mr. Freed. I'll talk to Anthony for you." And she squeezed past me and walked out into the lobby to talk to Sophie.

Yeah, that was it.

It took a while, but I regained my senses and found the piece of paper on which I'd written the phone number Meg Vidal had given me. I dialed carefully, as it was long distance, and our budget is, for lack of a better metaphor, stretched to the limit.

I expected the voice that answered to be crusty. Ex-cops are supposed to be crusty, especially those who used to be big-city homicide detectives. But this voice was soft and patient, almost cozy. You wanted to crawl up inside it and wrap it around you.

"Sergeant Robert Newman?" I asked, figuring this was his roommate, his manservant, or his nurse.

"That's who I used to be," he answered. "And who exactly is this, calling me thirty years after I left the force?"

I told him who I was, and dropped Meg's name — and her father's — early in my explanation. In fact, I dropped the "Magpie" reference, and got a chuckle from the other end. Sergeant Newman listened quietly, until I brought up the reason for my call.

"I wasn't the primary on the case," he explained. "It was investigated by the fire department first, then the arson squad, but there was never any evidence that the fire had been set. It was electrical; started in a wall in the kitchen, if I recall correctly."

"If you *recall* correctly?" I marveled. "I wish I could remember something that happened to me last week as well as you remember what happened to you fifty years ago."

"So do I," Newman said.

"So there was nothing suspicious about the fire at all?" I asked. "Why did they call in Arson?"

"I never found out," Newman told me. "But I heard kind of behind the scenes that

118

there'd been a tip. Somebody had seen the victim's husband in the area of the house before the fire started."

I sat up a little bit in my chair. I'd have sat up a lot in my chair, but then, you'd have to know my chair; it's just not possible. "Was it suspicious that Les Townes would be in the vicinity of his own house?" I asked Newman.

He took a while before answering. "You understand I can't verify any of this. It was just something I heard around the station house."

"I understand."

"Well," Newman said, "whoever saw the husband said that he was carrying things *out* of the house. Awards, pictures in frames, things like that. As if he was leaving."

"Or cleaning out the things he didn't want to lose in the fire," I said.

"Yeah," Newman agreed. "Like that. Allegedly."

"Did Townes report anything like that — awards, photos, posters — lost in the fire afterward?"

"That I don't know," Newman told me. "You'd have to check the insurance records, if they still exist."

"It doesn't seem to add up," I said, half to Newman, half to myself. "There appears to be all this evidence that the fire might have been set deliberately, and that Townes would be a great suspect, but no one ever followed up."

"Hey, I was just a cop," Newman said. "I wasn't a detective and I wasn't the primary."

"I'm not blaming you, Sergeant," I told him. "I just find it strange."

"In those days? The studios could have covered up World War Two if they wanted to."

I thanked Newman and called the Booth Actors' Home in Englewood to ask Harry Lillis for Townes's phone number. After a few minutes of complaining ("What, I'm not enough of a celebrity for you now?"), he gave me a number in Queens, New York, about an hour's drive from where I was sitting.

I walked out into the lobby and looked around. Rarely had such a hive of inactivity been recorded in modern life: Sophie was still reading, Jonathan standing around. Carla must have gone up to the booth on inside the theatre. There was hardly a sound from inside the auditorium, other than that of the movie itself. I walked to the snack bar.

"Hey, Sophie," I began, "how'd you like to give me a ride?"

She looked up from her book and rolled her eyes in time-honored teenager fashion. "Typical male," she said. "Need, need, need."

11

After Staten Island, Queens is probably the least understood borough of New York City. Everyone knows Manhattan — they see it on TV every New Year's Eve. They *think* they understand Brooklyn, because they've seen lots of World War II movies where one of the "earthy" characters is named "Brooklyn," and there are reruns of *Welcome Back, Kotter* on TV every once in a while. They've heard of the Bronx, because Yankee Stadium is there. But Queens? Since the World's Fair moved on in 1965, not many people outside the tristate area have given it much thought. Except when they watch *King of Queens,* which was shot in Culver City, California.

The fact is, Queens encompasses a lot of space, and runs the gamut. There are parts of it that constitute the most suburban areas within New York City limits, and the directions Les Townes had given me on the phone indicated he lived in one of them.

Sophie, hands clenched tightly at ten and two on the wheel, her two-month-old driver's license no doubt burning a hole in her pocket, watched the road intently as I navigated through the streets. So far, we seemed to be doing all right. Everything was right where the paper in my hands said it would be.

"Why don't you drive yourself?" Sophie asked me through clenched teeth. "Why are you always making women drive you around?"

"First of all, I *do* drive; I just don't own a car," I answered. "And I don't *only* get women to drive me; sometimes men drive me, instead."

"Why?"

"Because I don't believe in destroying our environment strictly for our own convenience," I told her. I figured the political conviction in my voice would impress her.

"So how is *me* driving you better than *you* driving you?"

"I'm still working on that."

We rode in silence for a few minutes, other than my reading out directions when appropriate. Sophie hadn't blinked since the Queens Midtown Tunnel. The obvious lightning bolt finally hit me in the head. "This is your first time driving in New York, isn't it?" I asked her.

Her silence told me I was right.

"Do you want to pull over and let me drive?" I asked.

Sophie's eyes narrowed. "So you think the little lady can't handle it, is that it, Elliot? You think the big, strong man has to step in and save the day every time . . ."

Women (or in Sophie's case, girls) were making less sense than usual to me lately. But instead of saying "shut up and drive," like I wanted to, I said, "I think this is it." Because I thought it was.

Sophie pulled her car (a year-old Prius her parents had bought her) over in front of a respectable, if not wildly impressive, brick detached row house that had been expanded in the back. Not the kind of home where you'd expect to find a legend, but hey, Louis Armstrong lived in a house like that in Queens for decades after he became a star — until he died, after which living there would have been impractical.

It was Les Townes in that house, a guy I'd spent my twenties trying to be as cool as. Never at a loss for the right thing to say to a lady. Never unable to smile his way into your heart. Always able to hit the high notes without breaking a sweat. Nothing *ever* bothered him.

At the screening Friday night, I hadn't been prepared to meet Townes the way I was when Dad drove me to Englewood to meet Lillis. And he'd gotten the best of me in every conversation we'd had so far, because I didn't know how to react to him. I had no sense of what the man was like offscreen.

I got out of the car, but Sophie demurred, saying she'd prefer not to "be introduced as your chauffeur," and stayed in the car. As I walked up the steps, she put iPod buds into her ears. I guess car stereo is for the Male Establishment.

It wasn't like I hadn't met Les Townes just a few nights before, but now, I was barging in on him to ask whether he'd murdered his wife fifty years earlier. It's not a social situation in which I'm particularly well practiced, nor comfortable. I didn't *want* Townes to have killed Vivian Reynolds; I wanted him to be smooth and dashing and swilling a martini with a carnation in his lapel. That probably wasn't going to happen, though. I stood there for a moment, gathering my thoughts.

Sophie lowered the power window on the passenger's side and yelled up at me, "If you push that button, a bell will ring." I gave her a look that emphasized my position as a

Patriarch of Society and turned away from her. For a moment, I felt like I should check under my arms or try to smell my own breath.

There wasn't anything else to do, so I rang the doorbell.

I heard a good deal of clatter behind the door, and two voices — both male — speaking to each other loudly, but not in anger. I couldn't quite make out what they were saying. After a few moments, the door opened, and standing in front of me was a large man.

Okay, a *very* large man. A man whose build might bring other men (like, say, me) to their knees if it decided to do so. He was tall, and probably would have been thin, but he'd clearly been spending the past twenty years working out on very serious exercise equipment. This effect was emphasized by the tight gray T-shirt that advertised said brand of very serious exercise equipment. In case I'd missed the point.

But around the eyes and the forehead, especially, there was something eerily familiar: he had a face very reminiscent of his mother. Vivian Reynolds. I did some quick math, and realized that despite being constructed something like the Space Needle, the Hulk would have to be in his early fifties. Which meant he could still kill me, but there was a chance I could run faster than he could.

I must have stood staring at the structure in front of me for some time, because it looked at me and said, "What?"

Startled out of my heightened state of intimidation, I answered with surprising lucidity, although my voice seemed a full tone higher than usual. "Does Les Townes live here?" I asked.

The Sears Tower turned and called into the house, "Dad! There's some dude here to see you!"

From inside, I heard Townes's voice ask, "Is that Elliot Freed?"

"How the hell should I know?" Mr. Kong answered.

"There's this new thing just invented," Townes called back, his voice getting louder as he approached the front door. "It's called 'asking.' You could try that. Besides, he called and said he was coming."

"I never saw him before," said the ogre.

"That's because you couldn't be bothered to go to the theatre Friday night," his father answered.

Townes's large son turned back toward me and asked, "You Elliot Freed?"

I had little to gain by lying, so I admitted it. By now, Les Townes had made it into the front hallway and was peering around his son's superstructure to identify me.

"Mr. Freed," he said. "Back to ask for a return performance so soon."

"You were a big enough hit, Mr. Townes," I said. Might as well butter up the subject before you go in for the kill. Especially when there's a guy standing between you who could tear you in half by looking at you the right way.

Like Lillis, Townes's the face was older, wrinkled, with less hair on top, but you didn't have to squint to see Les Townes in there. He'd been a handsome man, reportedly a ladies' man until he got married, but after Vivian's death . . . there'd been no talk of another woman after that. Ever.

"Come in," Townes said, and the Colossus of Rhodes moved to one side so I could enter the room. It was less a living room than a sitting room, where a few overstuffed chairs and one sofa were framed by bookshelves and a fireplace on one side. It was a considerably grander room than I had thought when standing on the outside looking in. I complimented Townes on his home. His son eyed me from his high perch, and didn't seem impressed. The old Freed charm wasn't working on *anybody* these days.

Maybe there was no "old Freed charm." I'd have to give that some thought.

Townes nodded in the direction of the giant redwood and said, "This is my son, Wilson."

I said hello to Wilson, which was similar to saying hello to the Great Wall of China, but then, the Wall might have given a more animated reply. I'm not sure what it was about me that was annoying the comedian's offspring, but Wilson sure didn't care for me being around.

"What can I do for you, Mr. Freed?" Townes asked.

"The first thing you can do is call me Elliot," I told him, and Townes smiled and nodded. "But I'm also here because since the show Friday night, I've been getting a lot of questions about your career, and some of them I couldn't answer."

Townes feigned looking surprised. "Even you?" he asked. "From the way you were talking to the crowd the other night, I thought you knew more about us than we did." He gestured that I should sit in one of the easy chairs, and I did. Townes walked slowly to the other, and Wilson loomed in the archway to the dining room. He did not sit.

"I'm a pretty enthusiastic fan," I said, "but

I've only read what's been printed. You were the guy who did it."

"*One* of the guys," Townes replied with diplomacy.

"Granted, but you were *there*. I wasn't."

"You should be happy you weren't. Then you'd be as old as me. So, okay," Townes said, "what do your customers want to know?"

I spent about twenty minutes drinking decaffeinated coffee (what's the point?) and making up questions that nobody had asked me, but that I found interesting: How did they film the *Cracked Ice* sequence in which it appears that everyone is talking backward? (By filming it forward and projecting it in reverse.) Why was the billing Lillis and Townes, and not Townes and Lillis? (They flipped a coin.) How had the team met? (Townes was playing piano at a whorehouse Lillis visited.)

"I hear there's a possibility you two might be planning a comeback," I said to Townes.

He looked puzzled; he squinted at me as if my image required focus. "A comeback?" he asked.

"Yes." I persevered despite all indicators. "Mr. Lillis mentioned something about a script involving two older men who rob a bank . . ."

Townes's lip curled with resignation and exasperation. "Mr. Lillis," he said. "Mr. Lillis is delusional, and thinks two ridiculously old men could be a hit at the box office. He wanted me to come to the nursing home where he's living and *rehearse.* Can you imagine? He has an *idea,* not even a script, and he wants an eighty-year-old man to come up and *rehearse.* We didn't improvise; we had scripts and we stuck to them. Except when Harry had something to add. Mr. Lillis." Townes waved a hand in dismissal. I got off the subject.

"What about your titles? Who came up with those?" I knew, but it was an easy question, and we went on for a few more minutes.

Having warmed up my subject, I felt it was possible now to enter into less neutral territory. "How did you meet Vivian Reynolds?" I asked Townes.

At the mention of his mother's name, Wilson tensed visibly, but Townes, the consummate professional, showed no reaction. "I met Viv through Harry, actually," he said. "Harry knew her from a party at Jack Benny's house, and I knew he'd gone out with Viv a couple of times. But he said he wasn't interested. He also said he thought she'd be good for the picture we were making."

"*Bargain Basement*?" I asked, and Townes nodded.

"We needed a girl who looked good, but who could also keep up with Harry's patter," he explained. "In Hollywood, you couldn't walk to the telephone without tripping over a girl who looked good, but the other part was difficult." His eyes got a little glassy. "Viv was the best I'd ever seen."

"And you fell in love with her," I pressed on.

"I married her," Townes said, his voice upping the ante. "I had a son with her." He nodded toward Wilson. "I worked with her, I lived with her, and I buried her when she died."

My ears must have pricked up when he opened that door for me. "The fire in your house," I said. "Were you at the studio when you found out?"

Townes's eyes narrowed. "Yes," was all he said.

"It started in the kitchen?"

"What am I, the fire commissioner? It was fifty years ago." Townes seemed amazed that I'd broach the subject.

"I'm just trying to understand," I tried to soothe him. "There were rumors . . ." Maybe that wasn't the most soothing thing I could say.

Townes never looked upset; he merely glanced over at his son and said, "Wilson, go load the shotgun." Comedians. Always playing the moment.

Wilson, deadpan, left the room.

"Mr. Townes, I didn't mean to imply anything," I told him.

"No offense taken, Elliot. But Wilson gets sensitive about his mother. Never really knew her. If he hadn't been at his grandmother's house that day, I wouldn't have him, either. So do me a favor, now, and go home, okay?" Townes stood.

I had just started asking the questions I'd come here to ask, and thought there might still be a way to repair the interview. "I'm really sorry," I said. "Couldn't we just talk a few more minutes?"

"It only takes Wilson a minute or so to load that shotgun, Elliot. I don't think we have very long."

I stood.

"You weren't kidding?" I asked Townes. He shook his head very slowly and deliberately: No.

"Go home. Don't worry about offending me, and don't ask me about Viv anymore. I don't think that's too much to ask, is it?"

I heard Wilson coming from somewhere inside the house. His impact tremors would put a T. rex to shame. I started for the door.

"I'm very sorry, Mr. Townes."

"Go, Elliot."

I hit the door as Wilson appeared in the archway. He was, indeed, carrying a shotgun.

Panic will make you do a lot of funny things. I barreled out of Townes's house like John Belushi leaving the dean's office in *Animal House,* yelling, "Sophie! Start the car!" I ran down the steps to the street, hearing Wilson's woolly mammoth footsteps behind me. At street level, still not seeing the parking lights come on, I ducked my head to see inside the car as I ran.

Sophie still had the iPod buds in her ears, and hadn't heard me. Her head bopped in rhythm to the music.

At full speed, it's hard to look behind you, but I felt it was necessary. And I was right.

Wilson stood at the first landing, about six feet above my level, and he aimed the shotgun right in my direction. He looked serious.

But I had reached the passenger door to Sophie's car, and grabbed for the handle.

Which was locked, naturally.

I started to bang on the window with both fists. "Sophie!" I screamed. "Open the door!"

She noticed me in the window, looked annoyed, and hit a button on her side of the car. I heard the door lock click, or maybe that was the shotgun's pump being worked. I couldn't tell.

I wrenched the door open as fast as I could, and as I dove into the car, I heard the blast from the shotgun. Something whizzed past me; a lot of somethings. I couldn't tell where they were headed. Then I saw a number of tiny holes appear on the inside of the car door as I pulled it shut.

"What are you doing to my car?" Sophie asked.

"Start the car!" I yelled. "We've got to get out of here!"

Sophie began going through all the steps new drivers go through. She checked her mirrors, released the parking break, made sure the transmission was in park before turning the key . . .

I checked the side mirror in front of me, saw it had been blown to bits by the last blast, and I didn't want to wait for the next one. *"Drive!"* I yelled.

Sophie started the car and drove. I think we might have nicked the fender on the car in front of us, but we kept going. I never heard another blast from the shotgun, but I didn't exhale until we were at least three blocks away.

At that point, I finally relaxed enough to reach back and get the shoulder harness. I pulled it around me, and was somewhat surprised when the hand that snapped it into place came back with blood on two fingers.

"Hey," Sophie said. "Are you getting that on my seats?"

12

"I realize we agreed to date again," Sharon said, "but I wasn't planning on seeing your naked butt this soon."

I lay facedown on what I call "the massage table," the one with the hole in it for your face. It doesn't stop you from talking — at least, it doesn't stop *me* from talking — but it's a weird sensation to be staring at the floor and having a conversation with a woman who is picking buckshot out of your ass.

"Wasn't exactly what I had in mind, either," I told her.

"You realize I'm required to report this," she said. "It's a gunshot wound."

"You can't fudge it? Say it was a really bad case of poison ivy or something?"

"No," she said in a voice that left no room for argument.

"How bad is it, Doc?" I asked.

"Not so bad that you couldn't sit through

an hour's drive back from Queens to see me, instead of going to an emergency room. Honestly, Elliot, what were you thinking?"

My face was starting to melt into that table. When I wanted to stand, would the table go with me? "I was thinking that it wasn't bleeding very badly, and I wanted a friendly doctor to take a look at it, and not some hotshot intern on his first ER shift." With women, flattery will get you everywhere.

"Did you really think that line was going to work?" Sharon asked. Okay, maybe not *everywhere.*

"I thought the 'friendly doctor' thing might," I admitted.

"I'm a medical professional, and I'm here to tell you that if this had been bad, you could have bled to death on your way to the friendly doctor," she said. "You probably scared poor Sophie half to death."

"She was only worried about what her parents would think when they saw the holes in her Prius."

"What did you tell her?" Sharon asked.

"That I'd pay for the work at Moe's with no questions asked. Can I get up soon? All the blood is rushing to my face."

"Not *all* of it," she answered. "You're almost done. You know, Moe's going to have

138

to report the gunshot holes in the car, too."

"Moe's been through it before," I said. "You never answered my question: How bad is it back there?"

Sharon considered for a moment. "You'll sit again," she said.

13

My behind was sore, but not very, and Sharon gave me an antibiotic to take for a week in case any of the buckshot Wilson had peppered into my butt was rusty. She'd then contacted Barry Dutton, who'd rolled his eyes (I'm imagining) and called the NYPD to report the shooting. The sergeant who called me sounded wildly uninterested, asked a few questions, and hung up. In New York City, a shooting is worrisome, but nothing to get upset about.

Dutton came by the theatre the next day to check on me, and found me in my office, sitting on a pillow and eating a turkey sandwich. "Didn't I specifically urge you *not* to get involved in the Hollywood murder?" he asked, scanning the room for another place to sit, which didn't exist.

"I already have a pain in the butt, Chief," I told him. "You didn't have to come by just for that."

"That's very amusing," Dutton said. "I'll have to try to remember that." He leaned on my desk, in his efforts to appear casual. "I'm concerned that you went out to ask about this Hollywood case when I advised you not to, and got yourself shot."

"Wasn't my plan."

"Funny how things often work out that way, though, isn't it?" Dutton did his best to look serious, considering how I looked leaning on a bed pillow in sweatpants that must have shown quite the bulge from the gauze my ex-wife had used on my rear. "Elliot, you're tearing at old scars. The cops in L.A. ruled it an accidental death fifty years ago. Why can't you?"

"Something's not right about it, Chief. If it was such an obvious accident, why did Townes pull out a shotgun the second I started asking about it? How come he was signed out at the studio when the fire started, when he was on the schedule for filming that afternoon? Why did an eyewitness see him hauling his belongings out of the house *before* the fire started?"

Dutton rubbed his eyes with his thumb and forefinger. I seem to inspire that particular move in a lot of people. "I don't know. Maybe he's sick of the insinuation and reacts violently. How can I say? It was fifty years ago and three thousand miles away. Most of the people involved then are dead now. What possible good can you do after all this time?"

"Maybe I can help Vivian Reynolds rest in a little more peace. Maybe there isn't anyone else who'll speak for her. Isn't that a noble enough cause?" Okay, I was reaching, but detectives love to say stuff like that, and I thought it would resonate with Dutton.

"Give me a break," he said. "She'll be just as dead if you find out she was murdered as she is now from an accidental fire." I clearly have resonation problems. Perhaps I need to take myself into the shop for some fine-tuning.

"All right, so it intrigues me. I'm a classic comedy film fanatic. This is as close as I'm going to get to being involved with the movies I spend my life watching."

"Won't it take the fun out of the movies if you find out one of your heroes killed her?"

I hadn't thought of that. It stopped me dead in my tracks. I stared up at Dutton for a few seconds, trying to think of something to say.

He misunderstood, and said, "I guess I can't dissuade you. But I do hope you'll do the rest of your interrogations on the phone, where it's harder to shoot at a person."

Dutton stood up, and just so I wouldn't have to respond to the question he'd asked me before, I said, "What's going on with the search for Anthony's movie?"

He nodded. "That's why I'm here. I'd like to take another look at the projection booth, if you'll give me the key," Dutton said.

"I won't give you the key, but I'll take you up there, Chief," I told him.

Dutton looked positively offended. "Do you think I'm going to steal something?" he asked.

"No, but I've seen you up there before. You like to push buttons, and you think you're C. Francis Jenkins. I'll stand in the corner and watch you."

"Who the heck is C. Francis Jenkins?" I don't know if I've ever heard Dutton swear. He's the only cop I've ever met who would say "who the heck."

"When you can answer that question," I said, "maybe I'll let you go up to the projection booth by yourself."

I got the key and led the way upstairs, despite my somewhat barky backside. Walking wasn't that bad, but the stairs were not my best friend. Until you get shot in it, you don't realize how much you use your butt. His amusement badly concealed, Dutton stayed behind me. I let him into the booth, and stood in the corner, as promised.

"I don't understand what you expect to find here now," I told Dutton. "Anthony and I have both been up here dozens of times since the film was taken, and the place was even cleaned once."

Dutton looked up from under the control console. "Once?" he asked.

I shrugged. "I have a service that comes in once a week."

"It's been more than a week."

"They don't always come up here."

Dutton nodded, then stopped in his motion. "Could the cleaning crew . . . ?"

I shook my head. "They weren't up here the night of the screening. In fact, they had been through here the day before, but not on that day. And no, they don't have a spare key."

Chief Dutton's mouth curled in disappointment, and then he went back to his examination. "Not that I have to explain myself to you, but I'm just testing a very unlikely theory," he said.

"What's the theory?"

Dutton knocked on the floor under the console. "What's under here?" he asked. "It sounds hollow." He pointed to a wooden panel with four screws attaching it to the floor.

"It is hollow," I answered. "That's where we store the tools that I hope I never have to use on the projector."

Dutton reached into his pocket for a Swiss Army knife, which he opened to the screwdriver attachment. He started undoing the screws that held the panel down.

"Chief, nobody could have gotten into the booth through there; it's much too small," I said.

Dutton continued with the screws, but had some trouble using his knife attachment. I reached over to the table and picked up a Phillips head screwdriver, which I handed down to him.

"This'll be faster," I said, filling the silence. Dutton was intent on what he was doing, and didn't even thank me for the screwdriver. "No, no," I said. "It was nothing. Really."

The screwdriver did work faster, and in less than a minute, he could lift the piece of plywood up off the floor. The space underneath, maybe five feet by five feet, was dark, and there was no light under the console. Before he could ask, I handed Dutton a flashlight. Again, there was no response.

"Stop it. You're too kind."

He lay down on the floor to get a better angle, and shone the flashlight into the storage space, moving it from side to side. After a few seconds, he stopped.

"Uh-oh," Dutton said.

"What-oh?" I asked.

He reached into his pocket and took out a plastic bag, which he put over his hand. Then the chief of police from my little town stuck his hand into my storage space, and pulled out a large plastic case containing reels of film. Then another.

They were very clearly marked, KILLIN' TIME.

"Maybe my theory wasn't so unlikely after all," Dutton said.

14

I stared for what felt like a long time. Dutton stood up and put the cans on a table next to the control console. He opened them, still with the plastic bag on his hand.

Sure enough, there were reels of film inside.

"Is there a way you can tell without touching them whether this is the right film?" Dutton asked me.

Slowly regaining the power of speech, I said, "Not really. I could check the first reel to see if it's Anthony's film, but I'd have to touch it."

"Do you have any plastic bags?"

I reached into a cabinet on the wall and came out with a pair of Playtex rubber gloves. "Will these work?" I asked.

Dutton shook his head. "The kind you use in a kitchen leave marks. Just put some bags over your hands. That's the best we can do under the circumstances."

"You're not calling in more cops?" I asked.

"Not yet. Please, just check the film."

I had a box of sandwich bags (Ziplock) in the snack bar area, so after I hobbled downstairs, got them, and then hobbled back up, I slipped two over my hands and took the first reel (they're numbered) from the film can on the table. I didn't want to put it on the projector, so I picked up a thick marker from the counter, ran it through the center hole on the reel, and unspooled the first several feet of film, until an image showed on the print.

It was a title — white on black, of course — that read, "A Film by Anthony Pagliarulo."

"That's it," I told Dutton. "It's Anthony's movie. How did you know it was down there?"

"I didn't," Dutton told me. "I thought it was . . ."

"Unlikely."

"Yeah. But it struck me that something this size couldn't be carried out of here in a crowd, even one that was dwindling, without somebody seeing it. It's not the kind of thing you stick in a backpack and sneak out." Dutton sat down on one of the stools.

"So if it hadn't been carried out, it had to still be here somewhere. But why would someone want to *hide* Anthony's film?" I would have sat down, too, but the stools didn't have nice soft pillows on them.

"For the same reason they'd want to steal Anthony's film," Dutton said. "So Anthony couldn't have it."

"None of it makes any sense," I told him. "The only people who have keys to this booth are Anthony and me. I know *I* didn't stash the film in there, and there's no reason under the sun why Anthony would deprive himself of his baby."

Dutton nodded. "I know. I'm not any closer to figuring out who did this, but now I know where the film is."

"I'm starting to think you did it," I told him.

"Nah. I'm more likely to steal *The Sound of Music*." He gave me a look that dared me to make fun of him, so of course I didn't. I'm a coward, but an honest coward. "Anyway, there's only one thing to do now." He put the reel back in the film can, still wearing the bag on his hand, and then closed the case, making sure it was securely fastened. "You don't have rats in there, do you?" he asked, pointing to the storage space.

"If I do, I'd rather not know about it. Why?"

Dutton did the last thing I'd have predicted: he took the film cans, got down on the floor, and put them back into the storage space. Then he went about replacing the screws that held the plywood panel in place.

"What are you doing?" I asked.

"I can't be sure, but I think I'm putting the cover back on your storage area," Dutton said. "It's possible I'm making a pastrami sandwich, but I've never seen one that looked like this before."

My mouth opened and closed a few times. "Why?" I managed to croak out.

"Ah! A much more pertinent question," Dutton chuckled. Large men chuckling can be an interesting sound. In this case, it was less ominous than annoying. "The one advantage I have right now, assuming that you didn't stash the film when you were in a delusional state, is that I know where the film is, and the person who put it there doesn't know I'm aware of it."

"He doesn't know that you know."

"Right," Dutton agreed, finishing the last screw. "So if I remove the film now and whoever stole it comes back to check, I'll lose that advantage."

"He'll know that you know."

"Uh-huh," Dutton nodded. "And then he

— or she — would have an advantage on me."

"You wouldn't know that he knew you knew."

Dutton's eyes narrowed. "Okay, you want to stop doing that? Yes. In an investigation, it's always best to exploit any advantage you have. So I'm not going to concede the upper hand if I don't have to."

"Well, is it even a crime now that you know the film wasn't stolen?"

The chief thought about that. "Let's say for a moment that Anthony hid this himself."

I sputtered. "Why . . . ?"

Dutton held up a hand. "If there really *is* insurance, but he's saying there isn't, he could be trying to hold the company up for the cost of the film. If Anthony *didn't* hide the film, someone else could be blackmailing him to return it. Until I know, I have to assume it's a crime, and I can't let the information out."

It took me a while to digest that, and I grudgingly nodded. "But aren't you going to get the film cans dusted for fingerprints? Wouldn't that tell you who took the film?"

"Suppose the only prints on there are yours and Anthony's," Dutton said. "What will that tell me? Besides, I can get them dusted here, when I'm sure no one is around, rather than have to take them away. You'll cooperate with me on that, won't you?"

It took a second, but I nodded. "Sure."

"Then I'll still have my advantage." He stood, handed me the screwdriver and flashlight, and brushed himself off. "Better that way."

"You're putting an awful lot of time and effort into a simple break-in, Chief," I said.

He shrugged. "I have strange interests."

"I appreciate it. Is there anything I can do to help?"

Chief Dutton looked me directly in the eye with great purpose and said, "Yes. Run a movie theatre and don't get shot. Leave the investigation to us."

That was certainly my plan. Except for that last part.

15

"What the hell happened to this thing?" Moe Baxter assessed the perforated passenger door of Sophie's Toyota Prius with a twisted grin. "It looks like somebody shot it with a bird gun."

"Don't be melodramatic, Moe," I told him. "Just tell me how long it'll take to fix, and how much it's going to cost."

Moe, a mechanic and auto body repairman of considerable repute, dropped his eyebrows and thought, examining the door and the destroyed side mirror with a more professional attitude. "Sorry, Elliot," he said. "What happened to it?"

"Somebody shot it with a bird gun," I said.

He gave me a look that was eloquent and long-winded. I made a "so what" face and gestured back toward the car door. Moe decided to shorten the banter and return to business. Especially since I, in an unusual turn of events, was paying.

"I can do it in a week," he said. "Look good as new."

"A week!" I lamented. "The kid told her parents she ran into a freak hailstorm."

"And they bought that?" Moe was stunned.

"You should meet these parents," I said. "But I can't keep Sophie out of her car for a week. Come on, Moe. This is for me."

"For you, ten days."

"You can do it in two, and you know it," I countered.

Moe's eyes rounded to perfect circles. "Two days! I'm lucky if I get the replacement panel for the inside of the door in two days!"

"Three," I offered.

"Six," Moe said.

"Three."

"Five."

"Three," I said.

"Four."

"Three."

"Okay, three," Moe sighed. "But I'm gonna clip you on the price."

"Fair enough. Now. What have you got for me?" Moe and I have an arrangement — okay, *I* have an arrangement, and Moe wishes I would forget about it, but it works: when I really need a car for a day or so, I test-drive some of his trickier completed repairs and make sure they've been done to his exacting standards. I've never run into one that hasn't, because Moe and his troops do amazing work, but it serves a purpose. Mostly, it serves the purpose of getting me a car for the day without having to pay for it.

As is part of the ritual, Moe rolled his eyes and wailed in my direction. "Don't start with me, Elliot. Buy yourself a nice used car. I'll help you find one."

"I don't want to own a car, Moe. I don't want to contribute to global warming."

"I give you an SUV to drive that's the size of Montana, and you tell me how you're not contributing to global warming. Do you sense a flaw in your logic?"

"Not in the least," I said. "Come on. I know you're going to loan me something, and you know you're going to loan me something. Now, which one is it going to be?"

"I've got a Hyundai Sonata that had radiator problems," he said. "With any luck at all, we didn't fix it right, and you'll get stuck on the side of the road. How far are you going?"

"Englewood," I said.

■ ■ ■ ■

I know I could have called Harry Lillis on the phone and asked him the same questions, but I needed to see his face when he answered them. The man was an actor, and a good one (comedians are rarely acknowledged as such, unless they take on a "serious" role to show off), but I hoped I could tell if he was lying to me. Dutton had asked me to do interviews on the phone, but I didn't find the chief that intimidating. When he wasn't around.

Having been there before, I felt I knew the Booth Actors' Home well enough to get by without a guide, but I was required to sign in at the entrance, and was told that Mr. Lillis was in his room. The woman at the desk called on the phone, and Lillis must have said it was all right for me to be sent in, because she nodded at me, so I went.

He was fully dressed, sitting on his bed with an acoustic guitar to one side when I walked in. Lillis had occasionally played the guitar in his movies, but never seriously. I was surprised to see he was keeping up with it, and after the inevitable joke about my padded posterior ("You look like Ethel

Merman"), I told him so.

"It's one of the few things you can still do at my age," he said. "You have to fill the hours that sex used to take up."

"There's Viagra," I suggested.

Lillis waved a hand. "I don't believe in performance-enhancing drugs," he said. "Babe Ruth was a better hitter than Barry Bonds, and he used performance-*decreasing* drugs."

I told him about my visit to Les Townes's home, and Lillis listened carefully, raising his bushy eyebrows when I got to the part about the shotgun. When I mentioned Wilson, his eyes half closed and he said, "Oh yeah, the son." That was all.

"Why do you think Mr. Townes was so upset by a simple question?" I asked Lillis.

"Let me ask *you* something," he countered. "Why did you go there to begin with?"

Well, that was confusing. "You told me that Townes killed his wife," I said. "You were practically asking me to look into it, weren't you?"

"How was I asking you?" Lillis's eyes were clear and looking through me. "Why would I ask the owner of a movie theatre to look into a murder that took place fifty years ago? Who are you, Mr. Moto? Besides, I already know who did it."

I didn't have a coherent answer for that other than, "Well I *thought* . . ." So instead, I asked him, "If you weren't asking me to investigate, why did you even mention it?"

"It was an interesting fact; we'd spent the night talking about interesting facts," Lillis answered. "I don't know. I wanted you to know the kind of guy Les really is. An amazing comedian, a decent singer, a real professional . . ."

"And a cold-blooded killer," I suggested.

"Well . . . yeah."

"How do you know he killed Vivian Reynolds?" I asked Lillis.

"I know because he wasn't where he was supposed to be when the fire started," he answered. "Come on. Take me for a walk outside, and I'll tell you the whole story." He pointed toward the wheelchair, which sat folded in a corner next to the bed. I pulled it out and got it into shape, then rolled it to the bedside. Lillis managed to get himself into it without needing me to hold him up, but clearly it wasn't easy.

"What are they doing for that hip?" I asked him as I secured the footrests and took off the brake.

"Physical therapy," he said with a curt tone. "Pull this, push that, and how come it's not better yet?"

I pushed Lillis out the door, which he made sure was locked behind him, and through the corridors toward the main entrance of the Booth Actors' Home. Seeing the residents, all of whom were show people of some sort, talking and laughing made me think about how deep down in the DNA entertaining must be. These people hadn't worked in decades, in many cases, and yet they still knew how to make others feel good.

"They do much in the way of shows around here, Harry?" I asked Lillis as we reached the front door.

"Yeah, they bring people in, you know, a guy with an accordion or something equally torturous," he said. "Sometimes the *alte kakkers* here do something themselves. You'd think it was the Ziegfeld Follies, the way they're rehearsing."

"You ever do anything?" I asked.

Lillis gave me a look to indicate that I'd taken leave of what few senses I had left. "I haven't worked for free since I was seven years old," he said. "And even then, it was only because my father couldn't afford me."

"Don't you think the laughter would do you good?"

"I think an enema would do me good.

Laughter is a financial commodity." Okay, there went *that* topic of conversation.

Luckily, it was a warm October day, so we could stroll the grounds (well, *I* could stroll, and Lillis rode) with no worries. I took Lillis around the back of the main building, where there was a path, a field situated so that the surrounding streets were not visible, and a gazebo, with some benches nearby. I parked him near one of the benches, and sat down.

"That's as much as you're gonna walk?" Lillis asked. "For a young man, you're in diabolical condition."

"I'm in fine condition," I protested. "I stopped because I wanted to talk to you."

"Talk about what?" he asked, and I started to worry.

"You said you'd tell me the whole story. About Les Townes and Vivian Reynolds. About the fire. About why you think he killed her."

"I know what I said," Lillis shot back, annoyed. "I'm not here for dementia, you know. I'm here because I don't get around as well as I used to. Too many pratfalls."

I did my best to focus his attention on my face. "So, tell," I said.

Lillis's face changed. That's the only way I can describe it. He was thinking hard, remembering, and remembering something

160

that wasn't pleasant, so his eyebrows dropped, his mouth flattened out, and his eyes took on a faraway quality indicating that he was looking at me, but seeing something else entirely.

"I remember it was a Monday," he began. "I don't know why I remember that, but I'm sure of it. We had a pretty tight shooting schedule, and both Les and I had to be on the set almost all the time. I was directing, but we were both in almost every scene. I take it you're familiar with the movie."

I nodded. *Step This Way,* I said, and without thinking, added, "Not your best."

If Lillis was insulted, he didn't show it. "No kidding," he said. "Try making a movie when your partner is worried about his wife cheating on him for half the filming, and mourning her death for the rest."

I shook my head to get my senses back. "Townes thought Vivian Reynolds was cheating on him?" I asked.

"Worse than that," he answered. "He thought she was cheating on him with me."

"Was she?" So another year goes by that I don't win the Mr. Tact Award.

Lillis's eyes focused back on me again, and this time, he *was* offended. "No!" he emphasized. "Once Les married her, she was off-limits, and that was it."

161

"But you were still in love with her, weren't you?"

"I knew how it was. Les wanted to marry her, and I didn't. She made the right choice."

"You didn't answer the question."

"I know."

I tried to watch his eyes, but they weren't telling me much. "Why didn't you tell him you weren't sleeping with his wife?"

"I did!" Lillis shouted. "But why would he believe me? If I *were* shtupping her, would I *tell* him?"

"Okay, so what happened that day?" I could dig for gossip, or investigate a really old crime. Doing both was too tiring.

"Well, we were getting ready to shoot this scene in a dancing school. I screw up all the dances because I want to show up Les, and Les is the teacher, so he does them right, just to annoy me. It wasn't one of the big set pieces, but it would have played pretty well." Lillis was still tinkering with the movie, more than a half century since he'd had a hand in scripting it.

"I don't remember that scene in the movie," I said, my face radiating innocence.

"That's because it isn't there," Lillis said. "We never shot it. I spent the morning with the cameraman working out the moves, he

162

lit it, and when we were ready to shoot, Les wasn't on the lot."

"He knew he was in the scene, right?" Sometimes you ask a question just to see how the other person will react. Of *course* Townes knew he was in the scene.

"Of *course* he knew he was in the scene," Lillis said, disgusted. "That was the weird part. Les was *never* late for a shoot. I was the one they usually had to go searching for."

"How did you find him?" I asked.

"We didn't," Lillis said. "I got the sign-in sheet and saw that he'd signed out at one thirty, just when we were supposed to be shooting. The next time I heard from him, it was when he was at the morgue, identifying Viv's body." Lillis's eyes misted over, but he ignored them.

"He was going to kill his wife and he signed out?" I asked. "Why leave a trail?"

"He couldn't get out of the studio if he didn't sign out," Lillis said. "They used to check."

"And you've been walking around with this for fifty years? Why didn't you tell the cops?"

"And break up the act?"

I thought he was kidding, but Lillis's face was dead serious. "You didn't report the murder of a woman you loved because you didn't want to break up your partnership?" I asked him. "What kind of a man are you?"

He looked at me, now dry-eyed. "A comedian," he said. "Don't you know? We're the coldest people on earth."

"Did you ask him about it? What makes you think he killed her?"

"I don't think it; I *know* it. I know it because he told me he did it. Said he'd strangled her and then set the house on fire to cover it up."

He wouldn't talk anymore about the fire or Vivian Reynolds after that, so I wheeled him back to his room, helped him out of the chair and onto his bed, and said goodbye to Harry Lillis.

On the way out of the Booth Actors' Home, I passed the room where we'd first met, and where a group of the residents were playing cards and others were watching *General Hospital* with varying degrees of interest.

One of the card players was Marion Borello. I ventured in and sat directly behind her as she played. She didn't appear to notice me when I walked in, as she was staring rather intently at her cards.

The other three players, all men, stared at each other, but Marion never took her gaze off her own hand. Based on the way I'd seen her staring at Harry Lillis during the *Cracked Ice* event, I could confidently say concentration wasn't a problem for Marion.

"Go ahead," one of the men said. "Bet's to you, Marion."

"Don't rush me," she said testily. "You don't have anywhere you need to be."

That drew a light chuckle from the other men, and one or two residents within earshot.

Marion let the moment build. I assumed she'd had her mind made up long before the bet came to her, but was using the pause to create doubt in her opponents' minds. Finally, she said, "I'll see you and raise you five," and moved some chips delicately onto the pile.

I didn't move a facial muscle (or any other), but I'd been looking over her shoulder, and Marion Borello had a hand that stunk worse than *Love Happy* (1949), the Marx Brothers' last movie.

"Five?" another of the men asked. "Isn't the limit . . . ?"

"You want to talk limits, or you want to play cards?" Marion asked, eyes wide with innocence.

They grumbled and the argument continued for a minute or two, but the three men all eventually decided the pot was too rich for them, and threw in their cards. Marion took the chips and pulled them to her, not gloating but letting them see her stack them ever so carefully.

Finally, the three men walked away, and as I was about to get her attention, Marion, without turning around to look at me, said, "Mr. Freed. Thank you for not giving my bluff away."

I walked around to sit next to her. "My pleasure. But weren't you concerned that someone would call it?"

She waved a hand. "They're old-fashioned. Think a girl can't play poker. I beat them three times a week, and they still think I don't understand the game."

"You're a smart woman, Mrs. Borello."

"Marion, and I'm not as smart as they're dumb. But you're not here to talk about poker, are you, Mr. Freed?"

"Elliot, like I told you the other night. No, Marion, I was here to see Harry Lillis."

Her eyes grew concerned. "Is Harry all right?" she asked.

"Yes, he's fine. How do you know him? Back at Comedy Tonight, he said you were 'a dame from way back,' but I don't know what that means."

Marion smiled and cocked her head to

166

the right. "I worked with Harry and Les on a couple of their pictures," she said. "I used to be a script girl, what they'd call 'continuity' today. Started out as an actress, but I wasn't any good. I knew some people, so I got the job working the script. Worked at the studio for twenty-five years, which is why they let me in here." She pointed around to indicate the Booth Actors' Home. "Harry and Les were a couple of the good ones, who didn't care if you were on the crew. They'd talk to anybody. You know, a lot of the stars wouldn't even look at you if you weren't another actor or a studio big shot."

She started stacking the chips, and I joined in. "Marion, Harry told me something that . . . well, it really disturbed me, and I was wondering if you knew . . ."

Marion looked up, directly into my eyes, with a jerk of her head. "He told you about Vivian?" she asked.

I decided not to lead her. "What about Vivian?"

"That Les set the fire that killed her." Matter-of-fact. But her eyes had a little something behind them . . . Fear?

"Yes," I said. "He told me that."

Marion looked away. "Did he tell you why?"

"He told me what he thinks, but it sounds a little far-fetched to me."

She continued to look away. "What did he say?"

"That Les thought Vivian was having an affair with Harry, and he killed her out of jealousy."

Vivian's lips disappeared into her mouth, and she shook her head. "No. That wasn't it." She seemed to compose herself, and then turned her head toward me again. She looked me straight in the eye. "Les killed her because she wouldn't give him a divorce."

"He wanted a divorce because he thought she was sleeping with Harry?"

She shook her head again. "No. He wanted a divorce because he was in love with me."

16

Marion's story reverberated through my head as I drove the Sonata — with no radiator trouble — back to Moe's. She said she'd been hopelessly in love with Les Townes for a year before anything happened between them, and when it did, it consumed them. To the point that Les had revealed the truth to Vivian Reynolds, and asked for a divorce, which she refused.

Marion said Les had become livid, and for a week before Vivian's death, during the filming of *Step This Way,* he had been almost useless in front of the camera. "If anyone but Harry had been directing, they would have reported him to the studio," she said. Then came the day they were to shoot the dancing scene, and when Harry Lillis called for the cast, Les Townes had been nowhere in sight. She said he'd never discussed his plans with her, and that she was shocked when Vivian died in the fire.

But Marion said that when she confronted him, Les had admitted to the crime, and contrary to what he'd expected, that turned Marion away from him. Marion couldn't bear to turn in the man she loved, but she asked off *Step This Way,* and said that until the Comedy Tonight screening of *Cracked Ice,* she hadn't seen Les Townes again.

She had followed his career, though. And after *Step This Way,* she knew they'd made four more films to complete their contract, but never made a great comedy or a box office hit again. As soon as the contract was complete, the two parted ways, and only occasionally met at charity events or Hollywood parties.

It was a lot to think about in a Hyundai.

Tuesday nights at Comedy Tonight are not what you'd call huge events most of the time. People don't tend to venture out on a weeknight to see a movie that they might or might not have already memorized, and could very easily watch in the comfort of their own homes, on a large-screen, high-definition, plasma TV with a sound system that was probably clearer and louder than the one I had in the theatre. In fact, sometimes I wondered why I didn't just go door-to-door with an armful of DVDs and offer to show them to people in their houses. I'd probably make just as much money.

But I digress.

Here I was, back in the projection booth, wondering what in the name of William Claude Dukenfield (W. C. Fields) I should do with my newfound information. Hearsay from a previous millennium was probably not the strongest evidence in the world, and I had no idea if I should call the FBI, Townes, the LAPD, or Turner Classic Movies. It was a conundrum.

The two kids running the theatre (it was Anthony's night off) had looked at me strangely when I came in, probably because of the dazed expression on my face. Sophie no doubt attributed it to my unfortunate membership in the male gender, while Jonathan was more likely to look into my stunned face and wonder if a very warped mirror had been placed before him, as I wore his usual expression, give or take twenty years. Okay, give. They'd both given me a wide berth, and I was glad to be spending time upstairs, changing reels and not communicating with other humans.

When I looked down into the auditorium, I could see Leo Munson sitting by himself in one row, and a collection of various lonely types scattered about. People came to the movies on dates, to sit next to each other and not have to talk. The ones who talked at the movies were usually already married, and either arguing or explaining the film to each other, most of the time incorrectly. You could see a lot about relationships from the window of the projection booth.

I sat back down, a little too hard, forgetting the tenderness in my nether region. The pain pills Sharon had given me made me sleepy, so I'd stopped taking them. The pain wasn't that bad, anyway, as long as I didn't drop myself indiscriminately on a hard metal folding chair. I made a mental note not to do that again.

Marion Borello had said pretty much the same thing as Lillis, but her perspective was different — she'd been in love with Les Townes. Harry had been in love with Vivian Reynolds. Hadn't there been an easier way to resolve it than burning down the house?

It didn't make sense that Lillis wouldn't tell anyone about Townes's confession. He'd loved Vivian Reynolds, too; was his professional partnership with Townes so important to him that he'd overlook her murder? Was Lillis that cold-blooded?

Or was he so tenderhearted that he couldn't look into his best friend's eyes and turn him in to the police? I'd seen Lillis both ferocious and merciless in his assessments and also sentimental and soft when dealing with people he liked. Which one was the real Harry?

Maybe staying alone in the projection room wasn't such a great idea, after all.

It didn't much matter, because I wasn't alone for long. Just after a reel change, the door to the booth opened, and Jonathan walked in. He'd been in the booth once or twice before, but he continued to stare at all the equipment like a truly devout Catholic in the same room with the Shroud of Turin.

"Mr. Freed?" As they had with Anthony, my attempts to get Jonathan to call me Elliot had failed miserably. I was his first boss, and everybody knew you called your boss "Mr." He was probably disappointed I didn't call him "Goodwin," but I'm used to disappointing people, so I didn't let it bother me.

"What's up, Jonathan?"

"Um . . . do you need anything, Mr. Freed?"

"Not really. Why do you ask?"

He still wasn't making eye contact. "Well, the crowd isn't very large tonight, and I don't really have anything to do . . ." Jonathan never finishes his sentences; he just sort of lets them run their course.

"Do you want to go home early?"

Jonathan appeared shocked — for him. He still didn't look at me, but his mouth dropped open. "No!" he said, and I gestured for him to lower his voice. "Why would I want to do that?"

I found myself on the defensive. "Well, the way you were asking, I thought that's what you meant."

"No. I just wanted to see if you felt like trading Monty Python lines."

The kid scares me sometimes. I know he's a fellow comedy fanatic, but he doesn't seem to understand that I'm not sixteen anymore.

"Not just now. I'm thinking, okay?" I figured that would do it, but Jonathan just nodded, and continued to look around the hot, cramped room. "Something else I can do for you?"

"How about Kids in the Hall?" he tried.

I shook my head. "Not tonight. Thanks, Jon."

"It's Jonathan."

"Mine's Elliot, but you insist on calling me Mr. Freed," I pointed out.

"You're my boss." Go argue with him.

I'd have to be blunt. "I'd sort of like to be

alone for a while, Jonathan. You don't mind, do you?" I gestured toward the door with my head.

"No, it's okay," he said, and headed to the booth door. He reached to open it, then turned back, nodding his head. "Oh. Sophie said to tell you that a package came addressed to you."

So what? We got candy shipments, catalogues, all sorts of packages every day. Sophie knew that. "Was there a reason she thought I should know?" I asked Jonathan.

"Um, I think she said it was ticking."

Even with the buckshot holes in my butt, I made it to the door in record time.

17

The box was as nondescript as you'd expect a box containing a bomb to be: wrapped in brown paper, addressed with a computer label, no return address. Sophie said it had been brought by a messenger she didn't recognize, not by UPS or our normal mail carrier.

And she was right: it was ticking.

Loudly.

I called 911 and got the Midland Heights Police Department. When I told the dispatcher the "nature of my emergency," she seemed to hit the Mute button on her phone, and I got the uncomfortable feeling that she might very well have been laughing at me. But when she came back to the call, she was all business, asking the address and promising to have someone at the theatre "very soon."

I hung up the phone and stared at Sophie, who no longer looked like a radical feminist,

176

but rather like a scared, skinny teenager, and at Jonathan, who looked like . . . Jonathan.

"Get out of the theatre," I told them.

Neither of them moved.

"What do you mean, get out?" Sophie said.

"I don't have time to argue with you, Sophie. I don't know if that package is a bomb or a very loud wristwatch, but I'm going to err on the side of caution and think bomb. So get outside and stay outside until I tell you it's okay to come back in. You too, Jon."

"Jonathan."

"Out!" I shouted, and they reached for their jackets, hanging on hooks behind the snack bar. Sophie looked sheepish, and Jonathan looked confused. I heard the siren in the distance as they reached the door.

Sophie stopped and turned. "What about the audience?" she asked.

I'd forgotten they were there. "I'll handle them," I told her. "Go. And stay gone. Go across the street and get some coffee or something."

"I don't drink coffee," she said. "It's a societal attempt to get women . . ."

Get out! I screamed, and she went.

I took the package to my office and laid it

177

gently . . . *very* gently . . . on the desk. Then I rushed to the auditorium doors. There were perhaps twenty people in the audience. Should I assume that a bomb would destroy the entire building, and they would be in danger, or should I conclude that there *is* such a thing as bad publicity, and that yelling *"Bomb!"* in an extremely uncrowded theatre would be reckless, and small-business suicide?

It was very difficult to decide, I'm ashamed to say. But I did come down on the side of safety for the audience members. I started for the stairs to the balcony, figuring I'd turn off the projector and bring up the house lights first.

But I never made it to the stairs, since the theatre doors opened and two Midland Heights police officers walked in. I could see the red and blue flashing lights through the glass in the front doors.

The one cop I recognized, Officer Patel, came directly toward me. "Where's the package?" he asked.

"My office. I was just . . ."

"What about the audience?" Patel said, looking into the auditorium. "Why are they still there?"

"I was just about to go upstairs and turn off the projector when you came in," I said.

Patel stared for a moment. "What took you so long? The call must have come in five minutes ago."

Sure, stick in the knife while I'm down. "You want to talk about it and let the moments tick by, or do you want to get that package out of my office?" I asked. Vince Lombardi was right about that "good offense" thing.

Patel and his partner were headed for the office, and I was halfway to the auditorium when the front doors opened again, and Barry Dutton walked in, wearing civilian clothing and a bemused expression. "Why is there still an audience in this theatre?" he asked before making it all the way inside.

"I was just . . ." I decided to give up and walked to the auditorium doors. "Your attention, please!" I shouted. The group inside, barely a minyan at bar mitzvah services, turned toward me. "We're having some problems with the heating system. Will everyone please wait outside until we can correct the problem?"

This was Midland Heights, and nobody ever does anything in this town without complaining about how it inconveniences them first. "We'll miss the movie," one man said.

"I'm going to turn it off in a minute.

Please head for the front exits."

Leo Munson, the little traitor, yelled back, "Wait a second. You're having problems with the heat, so you want us to go *outside?* How does that make sense?"

"There's a very small chance it could be dangerous," I said. "So please, head for the exits, and we'll let you know when you can come back in."

"Can we get our money back for the movie?" one woman asked. An hour and forty-five minutes into a two-hour movie, and she wants her money back.

"We're going to let everyone back inside in just a few minutes," I said. "Please just wait patiently, and hold on to your ticket stubs."

"Why?" the first guy asked, grinning. "You afraid we'll get lost in the enormous crowd?" Everybody's a comedian.

Dutton came up behind me, and very easily said, "This is Chief Barry Dutton of the Midland Heights Police Department. Please exit the theatre." He turned and walked toward the office. The audience, as one, rose and headed for the exits.

I went upstairs and turned up the house lights, as promised. I turned off the projector, with maybe twelve minutes of film left to unspool.

Once I made it back downstairs, I found Dutton, Patel, and his partner, who was introduced as Officer Crawford, huddled around my desk, staring at the ticking package. At least ten minutes had gone by since Jonathan had alerted me to the problem, and there was no way of telling how long before that Sophie had told him to let me know. And here they were, staring at it.

"Should I get out a deck of cards?" I asked. Dutton turned and gave me a look that indicated I might have overstepped some boundaries.

"Why aren't you outside?" he asked. Make that *demanded.*

"It's my theatre," I said. "If it's going to blow up, I want to see it happen."

Dutton grimaced. "That's one of the stupidest things I've ever heard."

"I didn't have time to think of something smarter," I said.

He turned his attention back to the package. "Normally, our first priority would be to get this thing out of here and into a secure environment," Dutton said.

"A secure environment?" I asked. "You think it's ticking because it hasn't gotten enough love at home?" This is how I am when I'm petrified. I can't help it.

"Did you move the package since you got

it?" Patel asked me.

I nodded. "Yeah, Sophie received it at the snack bar, because I was upstairs. Then when I sent her and Jonathan outside, I brought it in here."

"How careful were you when you moved it?" Crawford asked.

It was hard not to stare at him. "Not very," I said. "I figured it might blow me to bits at any second, so I juggled it all the way there." Other people get chills up the spine; I break out in sarcasm. But together, we can find a cure — won't you help?

Dutton broke the uncomfortable silence. "With all that shaking, I wonder if it's really all that unstable," he said. "I think it's safe to take off the wrapping. Let's try that first." He and the two officers reached into their pockets and pulled out latex gloves, which they put on. Dutton began very slowly working at the cellophane tape holding the brown paper onto the box.

It seemed to take weeks, but eventually, Dutton managed to remove the paper from the box without tearing it significantly. I produced a large zipper plastic bag from a shelf over my head and handed it to him, and he put the paper into it to keep as evidence.

Inside the paper was a plain shoebox. New

Balance. Size 14EEE. Aside from the company's logo and markings, the box wasn't written on; it had no ominous words in an undecipherable language, and no skull and crossbones to indicate that it shouldn't be opened.

But the ticking was louder.

Dutton looked at his two officers. "Did anybody bother to call the county and ask for the bomb squad?" he asked. The officers did their best to look straight at the box, and not at their chief. "Figures," Dutton said.

"Do you want us to call now, Chief?" Crawford asked. Patel stared even harder at the shoebox, as if he could see inside if he just concentrated hard enough. Too many Superman comic books will do that for you.

Dutton shook his head. "Not now. I don't feel any resistance on the cover. I don't think anything's wired to it." He gingerly moved his fingers toward the top of the box.

"You don't *think* anything's wired to it?" I asked. "Isn't that the kind of thing you want to be absolutely *sure* of before you act on it?"

Dutton exhaled. "I seem to remember telling you to go outside, Elliot," he said.

"No, you asked me why I was still here. That's different."

"Please go outside, Elliot," Dutton said.

"That's different. No."

He didn't argue beyond that. "Then don't question my methods. You had your chance to get out."

"I don't like the way that sounds," I told him.

Dutton didn't answer. He put his fingers back on the box, worked the flap out of the tab in the front (which must have taken half a minute on its own), and very, very slowly raised the top of the box, checking all the while for wires that might have been connected. There were none.

When he lifted the top, Dutton could see into the box. He and the two uniformed officers leaned over it, and blocked my view. I held my breath.

They let theirs out.

"What?" I asked. "What is it?"

Dutton leaned away from the box, and let me see inside. Sitting in the shoebox was an old-fashioned alarm clock, one with two bells on the top, set to the right time, which was currently 10:06. A Goofy cutout pointed at the numbers just to make it look more ridiculous.

Taped to the clock was a printed note (Times New Roman) that read, "If this were a bomb, you'd be dead now."

At that moment, a click came from the box, and the alarm bells began to ring. I came very close to needing a change of underwear.

Dutton reached over, hand still gloved, and turned the alarm off. He turned toward me with an expression of fatigue and annoyance.

"I've begged you to stop bothering people, haven't I, Elliot?" he asked.

18

We let the audience — or what was left of the audience, which amounted to Leo and seven others — back inside, and then Dutton berated me for a couple of hours and asked about my most recent activities in bothering people. We agreed that the clock in the shoebox was most likely sent by one or both of the Towneses. They were the only ones I'd annoyed enough to warrant this much attention, except for maybe Gregory, Sharon's current husband, but he knew Sharon would kill him if he even tried to hurt me again. Besides, he wasn't this witty.

Since the NYPD was already going to harass Wilson Townes about shooting me in the butt, it didn't seem like that much more trouble for them to question him about terroristic threats, transporting a clock across state lines, and copyright infringement. It was one thing to threaten my life and invite the wrath of the states of New York and New

Jersey, but you didn't want the Walt Disney Company mad at you.

"There's no chance that Anthony would do this, is there?" Dutton asked. We sat in the projection booth while I rewound the films and Dutton, screwdriver in hand, started to take up the piece of plywood from the floor again. He had ordered a fingerprint kit from his headquarters for the alarm clock and the box in which it had been delivered, and the kit had materialized a few minutes before.

"Send me a fake bomb because he thinks I took his movie away?" I considered. "No, that's not Anthony's style. He'd do something gorier. Send me a fake severed finger, or something. A fake bomb in a Goofy clock is a comedian's threat. Anthony's more of a Wes Craven kind of guy."

Dutton had gotten the plywood up, and pulled the cans of film out from under the control console. Again wearing latex gloves, he placed the cans very carefully on the floor and began dusting them for fingerprints, something I'd never actually seen done before, and still don't entirely understand.

I couldn't watch for long, because the reel I was rewinding had finished, so I took it off the projector and got ready to rewind the next and last reel, in order to set it up for tomorrow's showing. Being a theatre owner means never having to say you're stuck for something to do.

"You have a vacuum cleaner, don't you?" Dutton asked me. He pointed to the dust he was accidentally spreading all over the projection booth floor. "I don't want Anthony to know what's been going on when he comes in tomorrow."

"He won't," I said. "But I'll vacuum it up, anyway."

Dutton finished with the first film can and started on the second. "Can I dust the reels themselves?" he wondered aloud.

"I'd advise against it," I answered. "I don't know what that stuff would do to the film, and it's Anthony's only copy. Besides, if someone were stupid enough to handle the reels without gloves, he'd probably be stupid enough to handle the cans without gloves, too."

Dutton nodded, and went back to his work. "So, why do you think Les Townes would send you a fake bomb?"

"He doesn't like me asking questions about Vivian Reynolds, and he wants me to stop," I said. It wasn't like I hadn't been asking myself the same thing.

"*I* don't want you to ask questions about

188

Vivian Reynolds, and it never occurred to me to dress up a Goofy clock and suggest I could blow you up with it." Dutton carefully blew a little dust off the film can, noticed a fingerprint, and began to lift it with some kind of tape.

"You just don't have a creative mind, Chief," I told him. "Don't feel bad about it; most people don't."

"What about Townes's son?" Dutton ignored my remark. "Do you think he could have taken it upon himself to warn you off?"

"Wilson Townes is a big, big man, Chief," I told him. "Maybe bigger than you, but I got a strong impression that he doesn't do anything his father doesn't tell him to do."

"At least there aren't a lot of suspects," Dutton said as he saved a slide with the fingerprint on it. "The last time somebody threatened you, we didn't know where to look first."

"Good times, good times," I said.

Dutton finally stood up, brushed some dust off his clothes, and put the slide, along with some of the other equipment, into a kit he'd placed on the console. "I think I got all I'm going to get," he said.

"I'm going to vacuum, then," I told him. "I don't want that dust getting inside the

189

console, or I'll never run this projector again."

I went down the stairs to the closet where we keep the vacuum cleaner, noticing to my pleasure that my war wound suffered at the Battle of Queens was not hindering my movement as much as before; I was starting to feel better. I reached the landing, and walked across the lobby to the closet.

But on my way, some movement caught my eye from the direction of my office. The door was open, and I was almost certain I'd closed it when the uniform cops had taken the "bomb" out and Dutton and I had gone upstairs. There wasn't anyone else in the theatre at this time of night.

Was there?

I changed course, but slowed down as I headed for the office. It occurred to me to go back upstairs and get Dutton, but my butt wasn't feeling *that* much better, and besides, this could be nothing at all. An optical illusion. A trick of the mind.

Instead, it was Jonathan, standing next to my desk.

"What the heck are you doing here at this time of night, Jonathan?"

He stiffened, stood straight up, and turned. I think it was pretty clear I'd startled him. I've seen more subtle moves in Keystone Kops films.

"I was just looking for something to do, Mr. Freed." Wow. That's probably the lamest excuse possible under the circumstances.

"Didn't I send you home an hour ago?" After he and Sophie had cleaned up, and while Dutton was still debriefing me about the package, I distinctly remembered telling the two of them to leave. Sophie had almost left a vapor trail, she'd gone so quickly.

"Yeah, but I wasn't happy with the way the auditorium looked, so I cleaned up a little more in there." Uh-huh. Yeah, that massive crowd we'd had tonight must have done some kind of damage.

"It's after midnight, Jonathan. Go home. Do I need to call your mom to give you a ride?" He only lived three blocks away, but it was late.

"No, I'm okay walking. I'll see you tomorrow, Mr. Freed." Jonathan walked out the office door at sixty miles an hour and headed for the front doors, so stiff he looked like he was concealing an ironing board in the back of his shirt. Picture the Frankenstein monster on methamphetamine.

I assessed the office after he'd left. Was there something he was trying to find? Something he'd want to take home? I didn't know Jonathan very well yet, but I knew he had an eye for some of the memorabilia I keep around the theatre. Still, he could have just asked me if there was something he especially wanted; I probably would have let him have it.

It didn't occur to me until I noticed where he'd been standing, right over the desk, a few feet away from the iMac I keep there. I ran my eyes across the desk, wondering what might have attracted Jonathan's attention.

The only thing that looked like it had been moved was my Rolodex. Yes, I know, I can keep all those files on my computer — and at home, I do — but I appreciate the old cards and the feeling of flipping through that thing randomly. Besides, a computer program has never really been able to absorb my "system" of filing names. That whole alphabetizing thing is so twentieth century.

Walking to the desk, I looked more closely, and sure enough, the dust that had settled all over the rest of the desktop (nobody ever accused me of being especially neat) had a Rolodex-sized break in it, a few inches to the left of where the Rolodex was now. I leaned over to see if I could discern what Jonathan had been looking at.

The Rolodex was turned to one of the

newest cards, one I'd added less than a week before, white and crisp among the yellowed, worn, dusty ones.

The card with Les Townes's address and phone number on it.

19

Thursday

"You think Jonathan Goodwin is conspiring with Les Townes to threaten you?" Sharon could barely hide her amusement, although to be fair, she wasn't trying very hard. "You seriously believe that sixteen-year-old kid is trying to help an eighty-year-old man cover up a murder that took place in 1958?"

The restaurant, trying its very best to be quaint, was stopping short of rustic. Called The Settlers Inn, it was meant to be a colonial dining experience, when in fact the only thing the least bit colonial about it was the presence of goose on the menu. And you had to call a day in advance to get that. We hadn't.

"I'm not saying it's a perfect theory," I countered. "But Chief Dutton took it seriously enough to consider it."

"Did he call Jonathan in for questioning?" My ex-wife's large green eyes were drinking in my discomfort like wine. Assuming eyes drink wine.

"No."

"Did he call Jonathan's mother?"

"No."

"Did he ask the New York cops to talk to Townes about it?"

I waited a beat. "So. How was *your* day?"

Sharon giggled. "Just lovely," she said when she'd reigned in her amusement. "I treated a man with shingles and a woman with a persistent cough, among many others."

"You should be flattered I'm even breathing near you, considering the germ factory you must be by the end of the day," I told her.

"I'm very clean," Sharon said.

The waiter, an unfortunate young man with a fake ponytail and a three-cornered hat, came over to explain the specials, most of which came with succotash, and some with a wild rice medley. I couldn't remember one hit song that wild rice had ever recorded, but it certainly sounded better than succotash, so I went with a chicken dish of some sort that included the rice. Sharon, adventurous soul that she is, went for a fish dish that sounded downright rustic and came with succotash.

And to think, I had chosen this restaurant myself. I should have known better.

"Where were we?" I asked when the waiter retreated back behind redcoat lines to give our orders to the Hessian at the grill.

"We were discussing my level of cleanliness," Sharon answered.

"Perhaps it's time to move on to another topic, then."

"Yes, let's talk about someone sending you a bomb, and how you think that Jonathan Goodwin is involved." Sharon's hundred-watt smile never so much as flickered.

"You're a fine first date," I told her.

"I'm a better second date."

"I remember."

She gave me a pointed look to remind me that we were starting fresh. "I can't believe you suspect Jonathan. You're so paranoid. That boy is like a little lamb; you just want to hug him."

"He's five foot ten and stares at the floor all the time," I countered. "There are people I can think of I'd rather hug."

"You keep on being mean, and you're not going to get lucky tonight," my ex-wife said.

I widened my eyes. "You mean I actually have a chance on the first date?"

"No. But why shouldn't I give you the illusion of hope?"

The waiter came over with some brown bread and "freshly churned" butter that was ostensibly from a cow here on the "farm." Forget that the pats all had "Land O Lakes" stamped on them. I have been well trained, so I waited until he walked away before I tore off a hearty portion and began slathering it. I hadn't eaten much today.

"Look," I told Sharon through a mouthful of bread (I'm not as good on a first date as she is). "I don't *want* to suspect Jonathan. But I walked in, he was there when he shouldn't have been, he was acting guilty, and the Rolodex was open to Les Townes's card. Now, you tell me how I should interpret that without being, as you would say, paranoid."

"Maybe he just wanted to talk to Townes. He's a movie nut like you." Sharon used the serrated knife I hadn't noticed to cut herself a "human-sized" slice of bread. Women can be so civilized it hurts.

"And it's just a coincidence that he's there past midnight right after I got a threatening package that we assume came from Townes?"

"Precisely. Coincidences do happen, you know."

"Yeah, in Dickens novels. In real life, they're just way too . . . coincidental." I was

197

losing, and we weren't even having an argument. "But let's forget this whole thing. I came here to have a night with you."

"An evening. A night, you don't get on the first date," Sharon said.

"I believe you might have mentioned that. So. Tell me what kind of medicine you practice." If she wanted a first date, I could give her a first date.

Sharon's face brightened; she liked playing this game. "Well, I'm a family practitioner. That way, I get to treat everyone from kids to grandparents, and I find that really rewarding."

"That's really interesting," I said, voice dripping false fascination. "Do you treat pets as well?"

Her eyes fell to half-mast. "You don't play this as well as you used to," she said.

I put on my most innocent expression. "Used to? I thought we'd never met before."

"Let's go back to talking about how Les Townes is trying to kill you. It was more fun."

I had a devastating quip to use as a retort — no really, I did — but my cell phone, in my inside jacket pocket, began to vibrate. "Uh-oh," I said, reaching for it. "This could be Sophie. I knew I shouldn't have left them . . ."

But the number was one I didn't recognize, although the area code indicated it was
from North Jersey. I looked at Sharon, and
she nodded: go ahead. I pushed the talk
button and said, "Hello?"

Harry Lillis's voice came through my cell
phone, which only a week ago would have
been enough to leave me speechless for an
hour. Now, it was just a little scary. "I took
your advice," he said.

"Harry?" Sharon looked surprised when I
said the name, and we made eye contact.
"What advice?"

"About doing the show here at the
Home," he answered. "I decided to be in
the one they're having next week. Les is
coming up to rehearse tomorrow."

What did he just say? "Les?" I asked.
Sharon looked even more concerned.

"Sure," Lillis answered. "We're a team. I
invited him to come up and start working
on something for the show. I imagine we'll
be seeing a lot of each other over the next
week. And it's all because of you, Elliot."

Well, I was speechless again, but for a different reason.

"I'm afraid I haven't shown you a very good
time," I said.

We were standing on the stoop in front of

my town house, in front of the door painted (according to the bylaws of the condo association) so green it actually can bring on nausea (I'm not the owner; I rent). Sharon wasn't standing close enough, but there would be time for that on future evenings.

"Don't be so tough on yourself," she said. "We had a nice dinner and we talked like adults. That's not a bad evening for those of us on the dating scene."

I smiled; she could still do that to me. "I spent the whole night worrying about Harry Lillis," I reminded her. "You must have thought I was insane."

"No more than usual. Look. You tried to explain to him that you thought it was a bad idea to reunite the team, and he didn't want to hear it." (That was true; I'd spent at least ten minutes trying to dissuade Lillis, who was unimpressed.) "And just because Les Townes is a little miffed at you doesn't mean he'll take it out on Harry."

"A little *miffed?* He told his son to shoot me and tried to blow me up."

"No one tried to blow you up," she said, voice loaded with eye rolling. "The note pointed out that if they wanted to, they *could* blow you up. That's different. And besides, you don't even know for sure that it was

200

Townes."

"Yeah, what was I worried about?"

Sharon shivered beguilingly. "It's getting chilly."

"Do you want to come in?" I asked, with almost no ulterior motives.

She gave me a knowing look. "Not tonight. I'm going home." But she leaned over and kissed me very nicely, which took some of the sting out of rejection.

"Now *that* I remember," I said when we were finished.

"You would."

"No fair. You can't take it back," I told her. "That was a really good first-date kiss, and it was your idea."

"And if you ask me on a second date, we'll see where it goes from there." Sharon turned and started for her car.

"I'm asking," I said.

She turned back and smiled. I can still do that to her.

20

Friday
Never Give a Sucker an Even Break **(1941)**
AND *Box Office Bozo* (THIS WEEK)

Sophie, having recently arrived in her (beautifully) restored Prius, was busy at work organizing candy into configurations that would best dramatize the struggle of women through the centuries, which I believe meant moving the Junior Mints to the bottom shelf and the Mary Janes to the top. There is no gesture too subtle for the true believer.

She'd given up parting her long hair down the middle and letting in hang down in Goth disinterest, and instead had cut it to her jawline, adding bangs to her style. She looked like Ringo Starr in 1964, but with a smaller nose.

Having just gotten in myself, I had little to do that was urgent; we wouldn't be opening for two hours. So I ambled over to the snack bar, friendly employer approaching trusted employee, and leaned on the glass case. Sophie gave me a dirty look, and I realized I had smudged the top, and she'd have to clean it again. I straightened abruptly.

"How's the car?" I asked her.

"Fine." She couldn't be grateful for my having it repaired, because that would indicate a state of indebtedness to a man. I had noticed this didn't stop her from cashing her paychecks, but I wasn't going to be petty about it.

"May I ask you a question?" I said.

"That *is* a question." I moved out of the way so Sophie could Windex the mark I'd left on the counter. She would have Windexed me if I hadn't.

"That's true." No sense getting her more annoyed. "Is it all right if I ask you another question?" Then I quickly added, "After that one, of course."

Sophie didn't look at me. "Yeah."

"Forgive me if this is too unenlightened, but when I saw you right after we had the damage to the theatre, you were acting very differently than when you came back to work a couple of weeks ago." I thought that was pretty diplomatic.

"That's not a question."

So *don't* nominate me for the Nobel Peace Prize. "Well, did something happen during the time away that . . . Are you acting differently than you used to?" I asked. I refrained from pointing out that this *was,* in fact, a question. No need to pat oneself on the back, you know.

"No."

"Don't elaborate, Sophie, you wouldn't want to give away too much." I started to walk away.

She called after me. "Elliot?"

I turned to face her again. "Sophie?" I said. Hey, I can do petty as well as the next fella.

"We're low on Buncha Crunch."

I told her I'd order more and went back to my office. Well, maybe I'd order more, and maybe I wouldn't. We patriarchal types can be unpredictable. (Who was I kidding? Buncha Crunch was one of our better sellers when we had family films — parents bought it for their children, and then ate half the box. And wondered later why they couldn't lose weight, as they "hadn't eaten anything at the movies.")

The phone was already ringing when I reached the office door, and Sergeant William Dunkowitz of the New York City Police Department (he said all that stuff — it prob-

204

ably killed him not to add his middle initial) was on the line.

"Mr. Freed, I wanted to call with a few more questions about the alleged incident at Mr. Townes's home in Queens," he said.

"*Alleged* incident? Should I get my doctor to send you some of the *alleged* shotgun pellets she took out of my butt?"

He didn't react at all. "We questioned Mr. Townes and his son, and they were adamant in their explanations that the incident was a misunderstanding."

"A misunderstanding? Did I fail to understand that he was trying to shoot me when Wilson aimed a shotgun at me and pulled the trigger? What kind of misunderstanding are we talking about, Sergeant?"

"Mr. Townes, senior, said that was a joke that got out of hand," Dunkowitz said. His tone indicated he was keeping a straight face while saying it, but I don't have a video phone, so I can't say for sure.

"Well, I'm a big fan of Mr. Townes, senior, but I'm not laughing," I told him.

"I'm just letting you know what was said, Mr. Freed," Dunkowitz said.

The guy was just doing his job. "What is it you'd like to know from me, Sergeant?" I asked.

"Your chief of police called me with

information about a second incident, when someone sent you a package that might have been explosive?"

Now that I'd had a little time to get past the sound of the ticking, the "bomb" episode was just a little embarrassing. I must have reddened, but again, the lack of a video component saved any further humiliation. "It wasn't explosive, Sergeant. It was a Goofy alarm clock with a note on it that indicated it could have been a bomb if the sender had desired it to be."

"What was odd about the alarm clock?" Dunkowitz sounded perplexed.

I thought maybe he hadn't understood me. "It had this note . . ." I began.

"I understand about the note. You said the alarm clock itself was 'goofy.' What did you mean by that?"

"I meant it had a picture of Goofy on it." There was no response. "You know, the dog that hangs out with Mickey Mouse?"

"Yes, I've heard of Goofy, Mr. Freed." There's a sentence you don't hear often. But I didn't have time to savor the moment. "Now, your police chief seems to think that you believe the clock package to be related to the alleged incident in Queens. Can you tell me why you think that might be the case?"

I dunno; it seemed obvious to *me*. "I don't get ticking packages all that often, Sergeant," I said. "When I get one soon after being shot at, I tend to assume that the two incidents, alleged or not, have some relation to each other. Is that unreasonable?"

"It wouldn't be a district attorney's favorite piece of evidence," Dunkowitz suggested.

"The shoebox was for size 14EEE," I offered. "What size does Wilson Townes wear? I don't know anyone short of Yogi Bear who has feet that big."

Dunkowitz let some air out. "My first question in suspected bombing interrogations is not usually, 'What size shoes do you wear?' I didn't ask," he said.

"Nonetheless. Did you ask the Towneses about the package?"

"I mentioned it."

"Don't tell me," I said. "They said it was just a joke."

"No. They denied any knowledge of it at all."

Dunkowitz promised he'd keep in touch — for what that was worth — and I hung up the phone. It wasn't three seconds later that Anthony walked in, followed by a determined-looking Vic Testalone.

This was turning out to be one of those

days when it wasn't fun to be a theatre owner.

Where Anthony had been somewhat surly in our past conversations about *Killin' Time* and its whereabouts, this time he was more mournful than anything else. He was a parent whose child had been kidnapped, and he was now bargaining with the fiends who had perpetrated the crime, still stunned by the pure evil being exhibited.

He walked into the office with his head down, and Vic, behind him, watched in fascination.

Anthony raised his eyes just enough to look into mine, and asked in an injured voice, "Why didn't you tell me?"

For a horrible moment, I thought Anthony had discovered the film in the storage compartment under the projector console. But then I realized what he was asking. Clearly, Vic had made some inquiries about Anthony's state of mind, and his willingness to talk to the people at Monitor Films. He had, to coin a phrase, hung me out to dry. I looked at Vic with fire in my eyes.

"Glad to know I can trust you, Vic," I said.

"You asked me for a couple of weeks. It's been a couple of weeks. Where did I let you down?" Vic tried his best to look genuinely puzzled, but the smugness was bleeding through. There must be other distributors who stocked old comedies.

Anthony was still staring into my eyes. "Is that why you stole my film, Mr. Freed? To keep me from making a deal with a distributor and give me no choice but to stay in school?"

"I'm going to say this for the last time, Anthony, so listen carefully: *I did not steal your movie.* You can assume, you can accuse, and you can even try to get me arrested if you think you're right, but I'm hurt and disappointed that you think so little of me. I didn't take your movie. I don't know who did take your movie. I wish I did. I would give it back to you." That part was technically true, but I'd had to be very careful in my phrasing.

For the first time, Anthony appeared to be listening to me. His eyes widened at the idea that he'd done me wrong, and he started to stammer. "But . . . but . . . but . . ."

"But nothing," Vic said. "It's been a couple of weeks. You asked me for that time. Now I want the movie back, Elliot."

"I thought we were friends, Vic." It was a cliché, but the first thing that came to mind.

"We are," he answered. "But this is business. You're keeping me from a lot of money."

Clearly, he and I had differing concepts of friendship.

"Anthony," I said, "I want to talk to you. Come with me to the auditorium. Vic, don't even think of following us." And before either of them could protest, I took Anthony by the arm and led him out of the office. Vic blinked a couple of times, but did nothing else.

Anthony said nothing until we were behind the closed auditorium doors. "Mr. Testalone said you had talked to him about Monitor Films the night of the screening," he said. "He said you didn't want me to have the meeting. Why are you trying to stop me from starting my career?"

"You really have an inflated idea of my involvement in your life, Anthony," I told him. "I'm just the guy you work for. I care about you, because you're a nice guy, but I'm not your dad. It's your father's job to worry about your staying in school. You should talk to him; he makes sense."

Anthony snorted. "Well, if you didn't steal the film, I'll bet he did. He just keeps telling me over and over that I don't have any sense, and I'm chasing a ridiculous dream."

I sat down; row U, seat 101. "I don't think the dream is ridiculous, and I'll bet he doesn't really, either," I said. "He's just scared that you're going to do something that will ultimately make you unhappy."

He raised his eyebrows. "How could getting the film distributed make me unhappy?"

"Okay. Suppose you drop out of school and your movie gets distributed to some art house theatres; that's what Monitor is good at. Suppose it doesn't do well — they don't have a huge advertising budget, and your movie isn't going to be at the top of their priority list. What if it's not a hit? What if they don't make back their investment? Do you think you'll be able to raise financing for another movie?"

"I don't know. Maybe not," Anthony said. The truth was starting to hit him between the eyes, and as in most cases, it wasn't being gentle.

"So if you've dropped out of school at that point, what are your options?" I asked in what I hoped was a friendly voice.

"I guess not great," he admitted.

"And that might make you unhappy, no?"

Anthony hung his head a little. The poor kid had cold, hard reality dropping down on his head, but it was necessary. "I guess that's what everybody's been trying to tell me," he mumbled.

"Who besides me and your dad?" I asked.

211

"Oh, a couple of people. Carla, a little, but she won't really say anything she thinks will get me mad. Danton. Even your ex-wife was trying to talk me out of dropping school the night of the screening."

That was a surprise. "Sharon?" I asked.

"Yeah. She cornered me when you were in the office talking to Mr. Testalone. Told me an education was the foundation for any career, even in movies. Or something like that. I was surprised she cared that much." Anthony looked a little overwhelmed, like he was trying to walk through a downpour with a paper napkin held over his head for shelter.

"That's Sharon," I told him. "If she thinks she can help, she'll do pretty much any . . ."

"What?"

Dutton had suggested I talk to Sharon. He'd gone out of his way to say he didn't think she'd taken the film, which might have been his way of saying he *did* think she'd taken the film. He'd played with my head before. Sharon knew where I kept the key to the projection booth. She was in the theatre the night the film disappeared, and she would, given the circumstances, think she was doing good.

Could my ex-wife have stolen Anthony's

movie? *Would* she have stolen Anthony's movie?

You don't really know that much about a woman you've been out with only once, after all.

I walked Anthony out of the auditorium and toward my office. He still seemed a bit dazed, but I believed I'd talked a little sense into him, and felt better for it.

When we arrived at the office door, we found Vic Testalone sitting in my dilapidated chair, feet up on my dilapidated desk, cigar in his mouth, unlit match in his hand.

"Put that down or face the consequences," I said, and Vic, startled, put the match down without striking it. He looked at me like I was his mother, and had found him with the *Playboy* magazines he kept under his bed.

"Jesus, will you make a noise before you show up in the doorway?" he exclaimed. One doesn't often get a chance to hear a man with a cigar in his mouth exclaim. It's overrated.

"Pardon me for walking into my own office," I said. "Now get out of my chair and take your cigar out of here."

Vic stood, flattening his lips in an expression of dismay. "You didn't talk my friend here out of selling his film, did you?" he asked.

"I'm not trying to talk him out of that," I said. "If he can sell his film, I hope he does extremely well. But I do think — and it's only my opinion — that he should stay in school either way." I inched my way around Vic (the man really did resemble a beach ball with a cigar in its mouth) and managed to ease myself into the chair without wincing.

"Thank you, Mr. Civics Teacher," Vic said. "I'd rather he was working on his next movie, maybe make a deal for that." He turned toward Anthony, slowly. "When you make your millions, you can donate a building to the college." He saw the look on Anthony's face and stopped walking. "You're not listening to him, are you?"

"I . . . I don't know," Anthony said. "It doesn't matter, anyway. The film is still missing, and I can't afford . . ."

"If I have to, I'll pay for a new print out of my own pocket," Vic said. "Call it an advance. Did you shoot it in high-def?"

Anthony shook his head. "I didn't use video," he said. "I like the warmth of film."

Vic's beach ball deflated. "You used *film?* This whole thing isn't on a hard drive someplace waiting to be turned into a movie because you wanted *warmth?*"

Anthony stood up a little taller. "Kurosawa never used video," he said.

"He would if it had been *invented!* Okay, so maybe I *won't* buy a new print." Vic picked up his catalogue case and started to usher Anthony out of the office. But he wasn't entirely engrossed in his "humanitarian" activity. He turned back to me. "You all set for the next four weeks?" he asked.

"I'll call you."

"Okay." He started out with Anthony again, and then remembered something. "Elliot," Vic said, "Harry Lillis left a message on your machine." I must have looked surprised, because he nodded. "Something about Les Townes trying to kill him." He chuckled, shook his head, and ambled toward the door. "Those guys," Vic marveled. "They never quit."

I reached for the phone.

21

"He *didn't* try to kill me," Harry Lillis said.

"You said he threatened to kill you," I answered. "What does that mean?"

I had listened to the message on my answering machine by now, and knew that Vic had been just a little off in relating the message.

"Which word didn't you understand?" Lillis asked.

"No wisecracks, Harry. This is serious."

Lillis sighed. What was the point of talking if you couldn't make wisecracks? "Okay," he allowed. "Les came up to rehearse for this grand pageant they're throwing here, and we started doing our old barbershop routine from *You're Making It Up.* Never did it in a movie, but it seemed appropriate. It's this scene where Les is a barber, and I'm a guy who comes in for a shave and a haircut, but . . ."

"Harry," I said. "He threatened your life.

Remember?"

"I remember," Lillis groused. "You know, there was a time that interrupting the world's most beloved raconteur would have gotten your kneecaps broken. I had friends whose businesses weren't always legit."

"Luckily, that time has passed," I said. "When did Les threaten you?"

"I told you, last night. We're doing the barbershop sketch, and we get to the part where he's going to start shaving me. So Les picks up the razor and gives me a funny look. I say, 'What's the matter?' and he says, 'Is this a real razor?' I say, 'Hell yes, it's a real razor. Where would I get a fake one living in a nursing home?'

"And then Les looks at me like he's Colonel Sanders and I'm Foghorn Leghorn, and he says, 'You know, I could cut your throat with this thing if I wanted to.' " Lillis's voice was as calm and steady as if he were giving me a grocery list. "I thought he was kidding, so I said, 'Real nice, cutting the throat of an old man in a wheelchair.' And Les keeps staring that Boris Karloff stare and says, 'You keep telling your lies to that movie theatre guy, and you'll see how funny it is.' "

I was breathing a little heavily. "He mentioned me?" I asked.

"Yeah," Lillis answered. "But just for a minute, could this be about my life being in danger, if you don't mind?"

"Sorry," I said. But I thought it was still a *little* about me.

"He tells me you came out there and so much as accused him of killing Viv, and that the only way you could have found out about that was if I told you," Lillis continued. "Said the cops had already been to his house, and if they came back with questions, the next one who'd end up dead would be me."

"Jesus, Harry!" Not exactly original, but it fit the moment.

"Yeah. Look, I'm seventy-nine years old, and I don't expect to live to be a hundred, but I'll be damned if I'm gonna become the next victim of the Comedic Killer." I knew he couldn't resist, so I didn't comment. That was Lillis, and there was no changing him.

"I won't say another word, Harry, I promise," I told him. "I'll forget about it this minute."

"No," Lillis replied, his voice full of conviction now. "You keep pressing. I'm pissed off now, and I have a plan."

My throat was suddenly dry. "A plan?" I croaked. "What kind of a plan?"

"A *secret* plan," he said. "And since I now know you to be a blabbermouth, it's gonna stay that way."

"Harry . . ."

"I know what I'm doing, Elliot," he said. "You keep poking around. Ask about the insurance records. Call Les again and taunt him with what you know."

"That's fine for you, Harry, but I've already gotten one fake bomb that could have been real, and I'm not seventy-nine years old. I'd like to be around a few more decades." I looked down and noticed that I'd absentmindedly straightened out seven paper clips, which were now sitting on my desk looking annoyed.

"Don't worry about it," Lillis said. "The man's all bluff."

"*All bluff?* He killed his wife and threatened to kill you, and he's all bluff?"

"Les killed Viv by accident," he said without a lick of inflection. "He was trying to scare her and squeezed too hard. He burned the place down to cover it all up. The man couldn't look you in the face and kill you."

"His son could," I tried. Maybe I could scare Lillis into calling off his cockamamie plan.

"Don't worry about that boy," he dismissed me.

"Boy? The guy's gotta be fifty, and he's the size of a baseball team I was on once."

"That's not bad, Elliot. Where'd you get that line?" Lillis was leading me.

I'd been caught. "From you," I admitted. "It's from *Peace and Quiet*."

"I know. I wrote it. Good work, Elliot," Lillis said, and hung up.

That had not been a satisfactory conversation. I considered calling Lillis back, but that seemed pointless. His twisted comedian's mind had wrapped itself around this "secret plan," and I was apparently part of it. The question, then, was: What was *my* next move?

I could do nothing. That seemed the most rational position to take. Doing nothing meant that Les Townes wouldn't be any more irritated — and therefore no more homicidal — than he was now. Lillis wouldn't be in danger, and neither (I'm embarrassed to note) would I.

The problem was, Lillis seemed hell-bent on implementing his plan, and if I didn't play my part, it might collapse around him, leaving him vulnerable to an angry Townes. Besides, Townes had told Harry that if the police came to his house more than once, Harry would be held responsible. Surely the cops had come to follow up on the fake bomb. That would be twice, and Lillis could already be in serious jeopardy. Assuming Townes and/or his son hadn't been arrested.

Another option was to call the police. But *which* police? Townes lived in New York City. Lillis was in Englewood. I was in Midland Heights. Vivian Reynolds had died in Bel Air, California. Unless the FBI decided to get involved (which seemed unlikely), I'd have to decide which jurisdiction to call.

And then, tell them what? That there had been a threat against Lillis, which he'd probably deny? That I'd gotten a fake bomb? Dutton and the NYPD already knew about that. And I'd be amazed if Townes didn't look them right in the face and say he had no idea what they — and by extension, I — could be talking about.

The third, and least attractive possibility, was to call Townes and do what Harry Lillis had asked me to do. It seemed the stupidest plan by far, easily the most dangerous, and also the only one I could do right now.

So I picked up the phone and rolled my 'dex to Townes's number.

I admit I was nervous as the phone was ringing; the last time I'd spoken to Townes, it hadn't gone especially well. But I couldn't leave Harry Lillis twisting in the wind. Maybe I could find a middle ground.

The voice that answered could have been Townes or his son. "Mr. Townes?" I asked.

"Yeah." That didn't help. They were *both* Mr. Townes.

"Mr. Les Townes?" And they say Aaron Sorkin writes snappy dialogue.

"Dad!" Well, now I knew which Mr. Townes it was. "For you!"

At least twenty seconds went by, and I remembered how slowly Townes seemed to be moving when I was at his home. Finally, his voice came through my receiver. "Who's this?" he asked.

"Mr. Townes, it's . . . Elliot Freed." I waited for the explosion and got none.

Instead, Townes sighed a little. "What is it now, Mr. Freed?"

"I felt bad about the way we left things the last time we spoke," I said. Diplomatic, no?

"I'm not surprised," Townes answered. "I've had the police here twice since then. It seems unlikely we're going to be pals." Okay, so maybe diplomatic, no.

"I'm not going to press charges," I offered. "The police won't be back."

"That's great," said Townes with a flat affect. "I'll sleep so much better tonight. What is it you want, Mr. Freed?"

"I just don't understand, Mr. Townes. Why did you have your son shoot at me when all I did was ask a question? Why send me a ticking package?"

"Yeah, the cops asked about that the *second* time they came by," Townes said. "How do you know it was me who sent you a ticking package? You strike me as the kind of guy who could annoy whole armies of people without trying very hard."

"I'm really not like that," I responded. Rarely has a man sounded weaker.

"No, I'm sure you're a real swell guy and your mother loves you," Townes responded. "Is there anything else I can do for you?"

"Do you remember Marion Borello?" I asked him.

It seemed to take him by surprise. "Marion . . ."

Of course. "You knew her as Marion Hunter. She married Harold Borello years later."

"Marion Hunter. Yeah. Couldn't act, so they put her in the script department. She was at the showing of *Cracked Ice.* What about her?"

This man was, as much as Harry Lillis, a giant of my youth, and a hero. Maybe he didn't have Lillis's biting wit, but he was funny, and he actually had given Harry some of the "ad-libs" Lillis had used on-screen. I was afraid to ask the next question, because I wanted my idol to like me. Even if he was a killer and an arsonist.

"Um . . . did you know her well in those days?"

"Know her well? What do you mean?" My idol wasn't making it easy.

"I mean, did you guys date, or anything?"

Townes's voice sounded tired and aggravated. "Date? What are you, *Hollywood Confidential*? It was fifty years ago, and I was married, for crissakes. What's your point, Freed?"

"I don't know," was all I could think of.

"Then maybe you should let me get back to *American Idol*," he said. "It's Motown night."

"Just one thing . . . Is there a reason you've been in touch with the sixteen-year-old who works in my theatre?"

Townes hung up.

He was right about one thing: it was unlikely we'd end up as pals.

22

Sunday

We were cleaning up after the Sunday night showing of *Box Office Bozo,* an unfortunately named comedy about a clown whose accidental stunt almost kills him — and makes him a star. It was actually better than average, which is saying something for a contemporary comedy. Sophie had made sense of the snack bar and was cleaning the glass on the poster frames in the lobby. Anthony could be heard rewinding the film upstairs. Jonathan was "helping" Sophie, which seemed to consist of watching her and asking her questions that made her scowl.

I felt bad about not telling Anthony where his film was hiding. The kid might not be spending every moment of every day agonizing over his lost baby, but I was willing to believe the majority of his time was spent in that pursuit. I could ease his mind if I wanted to . . . Well, that wasn't entirely true. I *did* want to; I just needed permission from Chief Dutton. After that, maybe the chief would let me go to bed without being tucked in and everything.

Standing in the lobby of Comedy Tonight, I considered simply going upstairs to the projection booth and lifting the plywood panel to show Anthony his film. I could go from being the chief suspect to being his hero in seconds. It would take what had so far been a pretty miserable month and put a positive spin on it.

But I had sort of promised Dutton that I wouldn't give up his secret, and you really don't want to double-cross the chief of police in the municipality where you do business. Bad form, you know. Especially when said chief is bigger than two of you, and probably works out more often than the twice a year that you do. Practicality must prevail once in a while.

I made a mental note, though, to call Dutton the next morning and ask when we could let our hostage go.

My staff, ragtag bunch that they were, didn't really need any assistance from the boss (that's me) at the moment. I marveled at their dedication to their work. Okay, so one of them thought I had stolen his film, one thought I was oppressing her just by being male, and I suspected the third of conspiring with a homicidal comedian to send me a threatening package, but they were nice kids. I liked them.

"Will you just go away?" Sophie yelled, and pulled me out of my reverie. I turned to see her aiming her wrath at Jonathan, who stood rooted to the spot, as unable to move as I had been the first time I met Harry Lillis. "You're just annoying!"

I started to walk toward them, but instead, Sophie threw down the paper towels she was using on the frames and stomped in my direction. She caught me midway, shouted, "Why don't you hire more *women?*" and kept walking. She got her jacket and left.

Jonathan didn't move a muscle the whole time, until Sophie was out the front doors and gone. Then he picked up the paper towels and the Windex, and slowly started back toward me. "What was that about?" I asked him.

"What?" he asked.

I let him walk by. He also got his jacket and left.

Waiting for Anthony to come downstairs, hopefully not glower at me, and go home, I decided to head into the office and clean up some paperwork. But once I reached my office, it seemed I'd get a little less done than I'd planned.

Wilson Townes, all nine-foot-whatever of him, was standing next to my desk, leaving little room in the office for anyone else. In fact, he wasn't leaving a lot of room for the desk.

I scanned the room for the shotgun, and was glad not to find it. "Something I can do for you, other than stop breathing?" I asked.

"You're going to leave my father alone," he said.

I tried to squeeze by him, but there was no "by him," so I retreated and stood in the doorway. "That works for me," I said.

"You're a smartass, but I mean it." Wilson loomed over me, which didn't take much effort on his part. "You're not going to call him, you're not going to come by; I don't want you writing him a letter. You got that?"

"Absolutely," I told him. "I won't be in contact with Les Townes. Is there anything else?"

Clearly, Wilson had rehearsed this scene with another reply from me in mind, because he just kept going. "Because if you do try to contact him, I'm going to come back. And I'm going to kill you. Understand?"

"Let me see if I've got it straight." I made a show of thinking hard. "I don't get in

228

touch with your father again, and I get to live. Is that about right?" Now he was just starting to irritate me.

Wilson picked up a snow globe I had on my desk. Now, I'm not much for snow globes, generally speaking, but this one had some sentimental value. I'd made it all the way to the top of Pikes Peak in Colorado (granted, there's a train — I mean, I didn't *climb* Pikes Peak; I'm not Pike), and bought myself that globe to celebrate my not dying from the lack of oxygen at the summit.

In Wilson's hand, the snow globe looked like a Corn Pop would look in my own. He closed his hand, then made a face that, if you've ever watched ESPN during an off day when they have Strong Man competitions, you'd recognize as the face of someone with enormous muscles really exerting himself.

The globe exploded.

Water splashed over my desk, which was bad enough, but it splashed on my pants, as well. Now people who saw me riding my bike home would think it had just been too long since I'd been near a bathroom. But the glass from the globe also shattered, and a large shard was sticking out of Wilson's palm, which bled impressively.

"Do you want a Band-Aid brand bandage?" I asked him, making sure to adhere to trademark laws.

Wilson growled, and picked the glass out of his hand. "*Now* do you get it?" he asked me.

"I *always* got it. You didn't have to do that little demonstration, although next time, I'd recommend the tear-the-phone-book-in-half trick. The worst you'll get there is a paper cut. But here's the thing: now you've got to go to Pikes Peak and get me a new snow globe." He growled, and I added, "What size shoes do you wear?"

Wilson licked the blood from his hand, sneered at me in the way that all the incredibly large men do when encountering average people, and headed for the office door. I got out of his way, and he stomped his way to the front doors and left.

I watched after him, and stood stunned for a moment. Then, just loud enough that I could hear myself, I said, "Of course you realize this means war."

23

Tuesday

"War?" Sharon asked.

For our second "date," we had decided Sharon would come to my town house, and I'd make her dinner. This was a significant commitment for each of us: as I mentioned, Sharon doesn't like to enter the town house, and I don't like cooking, because I'm as skilled a chef as I am a shrewd business-man.

But since she was separated from Gregory, yet still living in the same house with him, going to her place for dinner would have been, at best, unbearably awkward. At worst, it would have ended up on the police blotter the next morning. We had decided to avoid that scenario.

So here she was, the woman of my dreams (anxiety, dirty, and otherwise), the woman of my past, possibly the woman of my future, sitting in my furniture-impaired home, at the dinner table (which I'd bought three days ago and assembled today), eating fettuccine alfredo, assuming that the label on the jar was accurate.

Sharon was lovely as ever, her huge eyes looking fondly at me and making me feel like I was sitting in a hot spring. Cold in many spots, warm where it counts. She ignored the spartan surroundings, and my obvious inadequacies as a chef, and smiled.

"War?" she repeated.

"Okay, maybe not *war*," I countered. "But the coming-to-my-theatre-and-threatening-me thing was a step too far. I can't just sit by and take that." I offered her another glass of the very good red wine (Sharon had brought it), and she accepted. I poured.

"Even though you said you would? Even though it's the most logical way to avoid bodily injury beyond what I had to pick out of your butt?" My ex-wife is the only woman I know — the only human I know — who can say the word "butt" elegantly. I'm not quite sure how she does it.

"He came to my place of business and wouldn't take 'yes' for an answer," I said. "There have to be limits."

"I can hear a 'besides' on its way," Sharon said.

I nodded. "Besides. He broke my snow globe."

She pouted with her lower lip. "Aw. The one from Pikes Peak?"

"Yeah, and you know how hard I worked to get that one."

Sharon nodded sympathetically. "Yes. That train was a terrible chore for you."

"Mock me if you will."

"I will," she said. "But you were telling me about the war." She actually slurped fettuccine into her mouth without getting sauce on her lip. I sat in awe for a moment.

"Perhaps 'war' was too inflammatory a word," I admitted. "But I am going to look deeper into the Vivian Reynolds thing."

We declared dinner to be over, and I took our plates to the dishwasher, which, as usual, was completely empty. I wasn't even entirely sure I had dishwasher soap in the cabinet. But appearances are important, so I put the dishes in the appliance and closed it before Sharon could see how lonely they were in there.

"Shall we repair to the theatre?" I gestured toward the living room.

"Why, is it broken?" Sharon asked. She tries. It's sad sometimes.

The only real furniture in my home — aside from the newly purchased dining table

233

and chairs — were the floor-to-ceiling video shelves I'd had installed two months ago. They'd been expensive, but there was no other way to house the thousands of movies that had dropped into my lap.

We'd agreed that Sharon would choose the evening's entertainment. I didn't want to go to the movies, since I spend virtually all my nights at a cinema, and besides, I was petty enough not to give the competition my business. She stood in the center of the room, staring with some amazement at the vast array of titles.

"It looks like a very specialized Blockbuster," she said.

"And the scary part is, there are still titles I want that I don't have," I said.

"That is scary." Sharon frowned, thoughtfully trying to narrow her choices down to a few hundred. I have spent a good number of afternoons scanning these titles, and I know how intimidating it can be.

She took her time. Sharon always takes her time making any decision, because she wants it to be right. It's what makes her a really good doctor. It also makes her an excruciating movie-chooser. But one learns to overlook these things, particularly when one hasn't had sex in a very long time.

It wasn't just that. Yes, I still found my ex-wife incredibly attractive. Yes, I was a man who had the same urges as the vast majority of men. Yes, it had been a really long time. And yes, Sharon still looked very, very good, standing there in a pair of jeans that were just tight enough and a thin sweater that, for my money, could have been tighter.

I'm sorry: What was the question, again?

We had a long and complicated history, Sharon and me. But no matter what had happened, each of us was certain we'd be involved in each other's lives until one of us, at least, had no life left. The issue tonight, the question hanging from the ceiling and not being discussed, was whether this was the beginning of a new phase, in which we moved forward into a new relationship (or was that backward?). We could stay as we were, of course, since it was working just fine for the time being, but maybe we were correcting a mistake we'd made that took us away from the path we were destined to walk together.

Sharon and I had made a very strong — and deliberate — effort to have a civil divorce. That was the idea of the weekly lunches together. It was the goal, when we had both gone through the anger phase of our separation, to avoid the sniping, pettiness, and greed that characterize most divorces. A lawyer friend of mine once told me she'd worked for a family attorney for one summer during law school, and "the things people do to each other when they're getting a divorce are unbelievable. Everyone starts out thinking they'll be reasonable, and by the time it's over, they're physically threatening each other over a fork."

Well, we'd managed. It had taken some effort to get past the anger (especially on my part), but we'd done it. And now, we were tentatively, cautiously, okay, nervously edging back toward a more romantic relationship. And that could be the most dangerous step we could take right now. Maybe it would be best to leave things as they were.

On the other hand, those jeans looked really good.

"Come on," I said after a couple of eternities. "Hamlet took less time to make a decision."

"Don't rush me." Sharon was lingering in the romantic comedy section.

"I'm not. It's just that I'd like to put on a movie before I start getting mail from AARP."

She stuck out her tongue at me. But with great dignity.

I sat down on the foam rubber futon that was pretending to be a sofa. I should have considered that move more carefully, because if Sharon ever did manage to choose a movie for us to watch, I'd need a spotter to get me back to my feet. The futon is a little low to the floor. Ants have been known to look down on it.

"Here," she said, and handed me *Adam's Rib*. A good choice, and appropriate to the company. Now if I could just get to a standing position . . .

Sharon regarded my efforts to slither across the floor and asked, "Do you need some help?"

"That's a rather existential question," I attempted.

She held out a hand, and feeling idiotic, I took it. She helped me up.

"This is just a thought, but maybe you should have invested in furniture that could hold *you* up before the furniture that holds up the DVDs," Sharon said as I approached the video system.

"I had a responsibility to safeguard the collection," I said.

Sharon sat down heavily on the "sofa." "Ouch," she said. "You have a responsibility to safeguard my behind."

I put the disc into the player and pushed Close, then walked back to the futon. "I'll try to keep your behind at the top of my priority list." I sat down, sank, and mentally vowed never to move again.

Naturally, with a video collection that vast and important, I'd had to replace the twenty-two-inch television I'd been using with a flat-screen, high-definition beauty that had an audio system far superior to the one in my theatre, which I charged people money to hear. So *Adam's Rib* had never looked nor sounded better.

I wasn't paying much attention, though. Just to my right, a warm, loving, sensitive, intelligent woman in jeans that were just tight enough was close enough to touch.

So I did.

To be specific, I put my left hand on her right forearm, and left it there. Sharon looked at me and smiled, and everything inside my body melted into a gelatinous, lava-related substance. I was, in a word, lost.

She leaned over and put her head on my shoulder. "Watch the movie," she said.

"I can't help it. You look better than Katharine Hepburn."

Sharon's head came up and she stared into my face to see if I meant it. She gasped. "That's the nicest thing you've ever said to me," she said. She leaned over to kiss me, and we spent a few perfect minutes doing just that.

"Do you really want to see this movie tonight?" I asked her finally.

"I've seen it before," she answered.

"You've seen lots of things before," I told her. "I hope that doesn't mean you won't see them again."

"Don't spoil it." And we kissed some more. Finally, Sharon broke the clinch, and managed — without help, I noticed — to stand up. "Come on," she said.

Having planned ahead, I put my hand on the side table (needed for drinks when watching movies and baseball) and got up on my own. "But the movie," I protested, grinning.

"I'll tell you how it turns out."

We had made it to the stairs when the phone rang. Sharon looked at me, and I shook my head. We started up the stairs, and then I heard Barry Dutton's voice on the answering machine.

"Elliot. I called the theatre and they said you were at home. This is Chief Dutton. Get back to me as soon —"

I had no choice; I ran to the phone and picked it up. "What's the matter, Chief?" I asked. "Did something happen at the theatre?"

"No," he said, but his tone didn't calm me down. "Something happened up at the

239

Booth Actors' Home in Englewood. There's been a fire."

"Chief . . ."

"Elliot, Harry Lillis is dead."

24

There are moments when everything goes well; don't be frightened, it won't last.
— JULES RENARD

Sharon looked at me with concern; I must have been as white as Wonder Bread. I put my hand over the mouthpiece — for no reason; I didn't have to keep Dutton from hearing me — and said to her, "Harry's dead. A fire." She gasped, and sat down on the stairs.

"What happened, Chief?"

Dutton's voice was deep and serious. "The Englewood PD put it on the radio about a half hour ago. I called over there, and it seems that a gazebo on the grounds behind the main building went up in flames, and there was a body in the center of it, burned beyond recognition. They counted up inside the home after the fire department got it under control, and Harry was the only resident who wasn't accounted for."

"How sure are they it's him?" I asked Dutton. "Just because Harry isn't jumping up and down and yelling, 'Lookit me,' doesn't mean he's the body in the fire, Chief. He could be out for the evening or something. Remember, he's in a wheelchair."

I could practically hear Dutton nod. "I know, but he'd have had to sign out, and he didn't. The body matches his general description, and once they get everything under control and remove it to the ME's office, there should be confirmation. I'm sorry, Elliot. They're pretty sure it's Harry Lillis. There were traces of clothing that matched what people saw him wearing at dinner, and like I said, he's the only one missing. But they haven't finished investigating the scene yet. We don't know what they're going to find."

"How did the fire start, Chief?" I didn't want to think about Lillis being dead. Distracting myself with the details was considerably easier and more therapeutic.

"I don't know yet, but I'll ask the Englewood department to keep me informed. Tell them there's a similar case I want to keep track of, or something."

"Can I talk to them?" I asked.

"In what capacity, as a guy who met Lillis

a few weeks ago?"

Sharon had gathered herself, walked down the stairs toward me, and put her hand on my arm. I responded by wrapping the arm around her waist. "He didn't have any children. Could I say I'm his son, or grandson, or something?"

"Let me get this straight," Dutton said. "You want the chief of police to advise you to lie to another police department? Of course, Elliot! And be sure to mention my name, won't you?"

I switched gears as quickly as I could — there'd be time to consider approaching the Englewood cops soon enough.

I needed to sit down, and my kitchen phone doesn't provide a natural place for that. "Thanks for letting me know, Chief," I said, and I meant it.

"I'm sorry I had to be the one," Dutton said, and we both hung up.

I let out a long breath and guided Sharon back to the stairs. She understood that I wasn't suggesting anything more than sitting on the stairs — the only real means of support in my downstairs living space even if you count the futon. I didn't look her in the face until we sat down, she just to my right.

She was crying.

I put my arms around her and held her close to me. I felt her tears dampen my shirt, and just pulled her closer. There was nothing sexual about the way we embraced; nothing at all suggestive in my fingers on her skin.

"It's so crazy," she said. "I barely met the man. I've seen him in a few movies, only since I met you. But now . . ." Sharon drew a hard breath, and didn't say anything else for a while, but her head, down on my chest, continued to move just a little as she sobbed.

"I know, baby," I said. "I know."

Sharon went home about an hour later, and I went to bed, but I couldn't sleep.

If the Englewood firefighters were so sure it was Harry's body in the gazebo, had they seen his wheelchair nearby? Did they have some DNA samples they could match with the remains? Were they sure Lillis wasn't simply sitting somewhere playing the guitar? Had anyone looked?

My problems were twofold: first, I wasn't a cop, and I didn't have any friends in Englewood, so I couldn't insinuate myself into the investigation and ask all the questions I had. I'd be relegated to the news coverage and whatever information I could squeeze out of Chief Dutton, which wouldn't be much. I was a civilian. And I hated that.

Second, and more disturbing: a fire.

Exactly the way Vivian Reynolds died.

Fifty years later, a replay of the initial crime? Or simply a coincidence?

And that's where my natural cowardice took hold: after having been warned off by Wilson Townes, did I really want to get myself involved in the exact activity I'd been warned about? Did I want to get Les Townes, suspected double murderer, and his son, who had probably doubled for King Kong in long shots, mad at me? Or more to the point, *madder* at me?

It didn't make for a frame of mind that was really conducive to sleeping, so I didn't sleep.

The next morning, having "awakened" at six, a good four hours earlier than usual (which didn't really matter much under the circumstances), I hit the Internet again, and started taking notes and printing out any-thing — any slight hint — that made Vivian Reynolds's death look like something other than a tragic accident.

There wasn't much beyond what I'd already found. Vivian Reynolds had been a minor celebrity, and while there were count-less websites devoted to similarly minor celebrities, most of what was available consisted of "tribute" sites, with pictures, appreciations, filmographies, and other means of justifying the site owner's slavish devotion to the bit player, second (in some cases, third or fourth) banana, or one-hit wonder.

It was astonishing, even to a classic movie maniac like me, that you could find sites devoted to Dwight Frye, Margaret Dumont, J. Carroll Naish, and Zasu Pitts. For Vivian Reynolds, the material concentrated, not surprisingly, on her work with Lillis and Townes. She was rarely mentioned as an actress separate from the team.

Aside from the site I'd already accessed, www.whokilledviv.com, there was nothing specifically focusing on Reynolds's death. But there were mentions on some sites, most simply that she'd died in a fire on November 10, 1958.

Bits and pieces did point to some oddities in her death, though. On www.fabulous50s .com, Reynolds's demise was mentioned, but the "suspicious circumstances" attached had suggested the fire was not accidental. An article from the *Los Angeles Times* two days after the fire expressed some skepticism over the fact that the arson squad of the LAPD had not been assigned to the case. But it didn't elaborate on what details of the fire made it seem at all suspicious.

It wasn't until I got to www.studio coverups.com that I found anything at all helpful. This wiki site, devoted to virtually every conspiracy theory ever proffered in the movie business (apparently James Dean's brake line was cut, possibly by Sal Mineo but more likely by space aliens), had only a few paragraphs on Vivian, but the fanatics who posted had managed to find a colossal plot behind her death.

Even in my current mental state, I found it hard to buy some of the claims the site (hosted by an unnamed poster) put forth — that Vivian was having an affair with Natalie Wood, for example — but others were eerily plausible, especially given the events of last night.

According to whomever was posting (backed up, it should be noted, by filed blueprints of the house in which Reynolds died), a steel plate in the wall between the kitchen, where the fire started, and the upstairs bedroom, where Vivian was found, should have contained the fire before it reached her.

In addition, there was reference made to the "official autopsy report" (which was not reproduced here) that suggested the victim "should have noticed the smoke and been alerted before the fire reached her location," but for some reason had stayed in the bedroom. "Had she been drugged?" the site asked. "Was she dead *before* the fire was set?" No answers were offered, but it was fairly clear where the poster came down on the subject.

The most damning evidence, however, was in the form of an in-house studio memo, which *was* reproduced online. Granted, it was shown as a PDF file that assumedly represented a carbon copy of the original, but it looked authentic (which I suppose is the point if you're trying to prove a conspiracy, true or not).

The memo, from the studio's head of publicity Milton Kresge to H. R. Mowbrey — the studio owner himself — was dated the day after the fire, Veterans Day, 1958. It put forth the case for a studio cover-up (hence the name of the website) to keep Les Townes, and by extension the studio and the movie being filmed, clear of any suspicion in Vivian Reynolds's death.

"It is necessary to establish that Mr. Townes was on the set at the time of the fire," the memo read. "Toward that end, the production staff should provide the sign-out sheet without Townes's name included. Since it is not (some of this sentence was smeared and therefore unintelligible), an alternate sheet might be provided."

The memo, three pages long, went on to suggest that "any hint of wrongdoing in this case could be avoided" by "cooperating completely with the police investigation, and by — (more smeared copy) — the investigating officers."

It was clear, through my talk with Sergeant Newman, that there had been no serious investigation of the fire as anything other than an accidental electrical mishap that had turned tragic. But this memo, if it were accurate, would indicate something much darker — that the studio executives in charge of *Step This Way* had decided to deliberately impede the police investigation, and it could be inferred, if you stretched a little, that there might have been some studio bribery of the police. Dynamite.

But what could I do with the information? I wasn't sure that it was accurate, and I didn't know how to verify anything I saw online. It's easy enough to find websites confirming beyond a shadow of a doubt that Elvis was seen at a Wal-Mart in Iowa a couple of weeks ago, or that eating a Big Mac every day was actually beneficial to one's cholesterol numbers. I hadn't worried too hard about the accuracy of things I'd found on the Internet before, mostly because it hadn't mattered all that much before.

This mattered.

I didn't want to call Dutton or Meg Vidal with questions about this — not just yet — so I convinced myself that I needed crime investigation advice less than Internet advice this morning. I resolved to call Ned Overberg, a computer expert I know from college, as soon as possible, but since it was seven thirty a.m., it would probably be counterproductive to do so now.

Instead, I skipped breakfast (I hadn't eaten in the morning since I'd bought the Rialto and turned it into Comedy Tonight, mostly because I was rarely awake much before lunch) and took the bike to the theatre. I figured I could do some repairs on some of the auditorium's shakier seats until the rest of the world was at work. This being an early riser might result in more work being done, but was that really a good thing?

Astonished, I found Dad standing at the door of the theatre when I rode up.

"How could you know I'd be here this

early?" I asked him when I caught my breath.

"I saw the news about Harry Lillis last night," he said. "I told your mother you wouldn't sleep. Figured you'd be here early."

I took the front wheel off the bike and chained it to the water pipe in the alley next to the theatre. "You frighten me sometimes," I told my father.

"Then my work here is done."

"Far from it. Come help me fix seats."

We went inside and got some tools from the storage closet (is there a closet in which storage is not the whole idea?), then headed for the auditorium. Dad didn't mention Lillis again until we were trying — with little success, initially — to secure a row R seat back to the cement floor. My father isn't the man he used to be, and I never was.

"When was the last time you talked to him?" he asked, not bothering to clarify who "him" might be; I knew what he meant.

"A couple of days ago," I said. "He said Les Townes had threatened his life, and I told him to be careful, but he didn't want to hear about it from me."

Anyone else would have a violent reaction to the news that Lillis's life was threatened by his ex-partner days before he died. Not my father. Arthur Freed has the power of

251

an internal calm. I got my metabolism from my mother.

"Did you believe him?" he asked me.

"Yes. After all that went on with Townes, I was pretty sure Les had a pretty hot temper."

"Hold that steady," Dad said, pointing to the bolt I was keeping still and he was tightening. "A temper doesn't automatically make the guy a murderer."

"How about threats?" I asked.

"Circumstantial. Yes, it means he's thought about being violent, but the man is in his late seventies, at least."

"You're almost seventy," I told my father. Because he might not know how old he was.

"Thanks for reminding me. Do you think I could drag a six-foot-tall man out to a gazebo and keep him unconscious long enough to set him on fire?"

"Maybe Townes lured Lillis out there and then knocked him out. You could hit someone with a wrench, or something."

Dad stood up, holding the heavy steel wrench in his hand. "Like this one?" he asked.

"It was just a thought."

"Elliot. You're grasping at straws. You want to believe Les Townes is a killer because then you can come riding to the rescue and solve the crime, and let Harry Lillis rest in peace. The sad truth is, he'll rest how he's resting, either way." Dad shook the seat a little to see if it was solid; it was. "What's next?" he asked.

"Next?" I thought about that. "I think next is to let the police do their job."

"I meant with the chairs, but okay, let the cops investigate. Without your help?"

"Help?" I asked. "Ask Chief Dutton how much help I am. After he's done laughing, he'll be able to draw you a pie chart that proves I actually cost the taxpayers of Midland Heights money with how much help I am."

"So what are you going to do?"

"I'm going to help Anthony get his film back. *That* I can do."

25

Friday
The Ghost Breakers (1940) AND *Boo!Ya*
(THIS WEEK)

"Elliot, if I knew anything else, I . . . might or might not tell you."

Chief Barry Dutton sat back in the swivel chair we have for Anthony in the projection booth. It took a good deal of convincing to get Barry Dutton to come to Comedy Tonight in order to retrieve *Killin' Time.* I hadn't seen the point, really; I thought I was just as capable of loosening four screws and removing a piece of plywood as the next man. Dutton (who apparently *was* the next man) saw it differently, saying he wanted to see Anthony's face, as well as Sophie's and Jonathan's, when the film was returned. "Helps eliminate suspects," he said. I thought he didn't have enough crime to keep him busy, but kept that notion to myself.

He'd even made me wait an extra day for the "revelation," possibly in an effort to prove he did indeed have other crimes to solve. But first, I was pumping him for information on Harry Lillis's death. He didn't have much, but he did tell me that the medical examiner was working on an autopsy report, which would probably take a couple of weeks to be made public. Over my protests, he added that a couple of weeks was "actually faster than usual" in such cases, especially since Bergen County, where Lillis died, is the largest in New Jersey (by population; if you want sheer square mileage, you go to Burlington County), meaning that a good number of people died there on the average day. More than one of them did so in mysterious ways that required a county medical examiner's attention.

"Have they determined for sure that it was Lillis?" I asked, again. I was clinging to the irrational hope that someone else — one of the other residents, perhaps — had wandered out to the gazebo at the Booth Actors' Home and gotten caught in the fire. But Dutton just pursed his lips, trying to restrain himself. So I'd become a broken record (that's a reference for the vinyl

crowd). Fine. But nothing had been definitive yet.

"They're sure," Dutton said. "For goodness' sake, Elliot, it's been two days. Harry
Lillis isn't in his room and hasn't been seen
on the grounds. Everyone else who lives and
works there is accounted for. Who do you
think died in that fire? Frankenstein's monster?"

"There aren't many police chiefs who say
'for goodness' sake,' you know." I had to get
a dig in.

"There aren't that many who can back it
up," Dutton noted. Touché.

"Were there any visitors at the Home that
night? Maybe someone else . . ."

"Maybe, maybe, maybe." Dutton shook
his head. "I didn't get the complete report;
I don't think it's even written yet. Elliot.
Lillis is dead. You'll have to accept it eventually."

"Why can't I talk to the Englewood cops?"
I asked him. "They're not telling you everything."

His eyes widened, and he looked amused.
"So they're going to tell *you?*"

"I want to talk to them." When in doubt,
act like a four-year-old.

"Be my guest," Dutton said, hands laced
behind his head, relaxing. "How do you

think you'll talk your way in? You're not going to pretend you work for a fake newspaper again, are you?"

I hung my head, but looked at him. "You knew about that?"

"I'm the chief of police. I see all, and know all."

"I thought that was a guy in the justice department. Look, Chief, I'm going up there to talk to the Englewood detectives working on the case. Now, I'll keep your name out of it . . ."

"Big of you," Dutton said.

". . . but I *am* going up there. And I don't care what kind of deception I have to use, or what lies I have to tell. Harry Lillis was an important figure in my life, and I'm not going to just let him die without anyone looking into it deeply enough. These guys probably think that it was only an accidental fire, just like the cops in L.A. fifty years ago thought Vivian Reynolds died in an accidental fire. It's the easy solution, and you'll have to forgive me, but cops generally like easy solutions. They're not going to dig unless someone makes them, so I am going up there."

Dutton hadn't liked the comment about cops and easy solutions, and he raised a finger to scold me, but he didn't get a chance. The phone rang, and, still staring at him, I picked it up.

"Comedy Tonight."

"Is this Elliot Freed?"

I admitted it was.

"This is Detective Lieutenant Benjamin Honig of the Englewood Police Department. Mr. Freed, we are looking into the death of Harry Lillis, and I'm afraid I'll have to ask you to come in for an interview."

I stared at the phone for a moment. "I'm not sure I can make it," I said. Hell, all of a sudden the cops were looking for me? Did I need a lawyer?

"It's very important," Honig said. "But I can tell you that you're not in any trouble, Mr. Freed. We're hoping you can help us. Some aspects of the incident are not entirely consistent."

"Can you send a car?" I asked.

After gloating for a few minutes to Dutton, I summoned the staff to the projection booth so we could begin our little scripted pageant. I found Anthony at the base of the stairs to the balcony, apparently in the midst of an argument with his father, who looked smaller than usual as his son berated him. It was one of those moments when I didn't mind not having children.

"It's my life, not yours," Anthony was saying to Michael Pagliarulo. "If this is because you pay my tuition . . ."

"It's not about money. You *know* it's not about money," his father told him. "If it was about money, I'd *want* you to quit school, so I wouldn't have to pay for it."

"Meeting upstairs," I said, hoping the next few minutes would defuse the tension between the two of them.

Anthony looked confused to see Dutton in the projection booth, as did Sophie and Jonathan when they arrived, but Anthony's look was a warier one. Could he have known why the chief was there? Could this really have all been a scam of some sort on Anthony's part?

Sophie, all teenage impatience, lowered one eyebrow and looked through her bangs, which were hanging in her eyes. Anything involving men had to be bad, and she was stuck in a room with five of them. Well, four and a half men: Jonathan was wearing a SpongeBob T-shirt and the same leather flip-flops he seemed to wear in all weather. Sophie barely looked at him.

Dutton took charge, being the largest, most weapon-carrying person in the crowded room. "I'm glad you were all available on such short notice," he said.

"We all work here," Sophie told him. She was an equal-opportunity obvious-noter. "Except Anthony's dad." Michael Pagliarulo nodded in her direction, seemingly afraid to get on Sophie's bad side, and I didn't blame him.

"Yes," Dutton had to agree. He did his best to regain what little dignity could be had in a room built for one person that was currently holding six. "As you know, the night of the screening of . . ." He actually referred to a reporter's notebook he pulled from his back pocket.

"Killin' Time," Anthony said, his voice so dry I swear dust flew from his mouth.

"Yes," Dutton said again. After being abused by my staff for months, there was a certain guilty pleasure, I admit, in watching them do it to someone else. "On that night, the only copy of *Killin' Time* vanished from this booth right after the show."

Sophie gave him a look that would probably have vaporized a weaker man. "Do you think one of *us* stole Anthony's movie?" she hissed.

"That's just the point," Dutton answered. He picked up the screwdriver from the control table and knelt down to begin opening the panel on the floor, which we had loosened earlier (Dutton wanted to better heighten the drama of the moment). It took just a few seconds to get the screws loose. "I don't think *anybody* stole Anthony's movie."

The booth door opened, and Sharon stuck her head in. "Elliot?" she called. "You in here?"

"Yeah, come on in," I offered. "We're reenacting the stateroom scene from *A Night at the Opera*."

Sharon squeezed her way into the booth and took in the scene. I'd told her Dutton was coming to the theatre, but hadn't told her why.

"What are you talking about?" Michael Pagliarulo asked Dutton. "If nobody stole the movie, where is it? Wouldn't it still be here?"

"Exactly." Dutton was savoring his moment. "Wouldn't it?" He pulled up the plywood panel and set it aside.

I watched their faces. Nobody looked especially guilty, although Sophie did stifle a yawn.

"Are you saying the reels are in there?" Anthony asked, spoiling Dutton's surprise.

The chief was gracious about it; he didn't shoot Anthony for spilling the beans. "Yes, that's what I mean," he said. And he reached inside the storage compartment.

Then Dutton's expression changed from one of slight disappointment but great anticipation to one of utter confusion and more than slight disappointment. He reached inside the compartment again. Deeper. Until his arm was pretty much out of sight.

Anthony got down on the floor next to him. "What's wrong, Chief?" he asked. "Can't you lift them?"

Dutton stared directly at me when he said, "No. The problem is the reels aren't here anymore."

Anthony and Sophie turned their heads to stare at me, too. I could feel their eyes burning into my cheeks, and it wasn't a pleasant, warming feeling. Anthony's father looked at the chief, wondering why such a man would play this mean trick on his son.

"Wow," Jonathan said, squinting into the storage compartment. "There's all kinds of wrenches down there."

But I was staring at Sharon, who looked strangely amused.

26

Saturday

Detective Lieutenant Benjamin Honig was a tall, broadly built man with curly hair going prematurely white. He had a prominent nose and stared down it at me, but I wasn't intimidated. I was sitting in front of his municipal desk, in a metal chair with a leather cushion on it, drinking coffee that wasn't all that bad, but I had to make believe it was, because it had been brewed in a police station.

I took a sip and made a face. "Ugh." I can play along.

Honig nodded. "I know," he said. "It's really amazing. You can go out and buy the best coffeemaker on the market, and if you install it in a police station, the coffee comes out tasting like mud." He slurped down much of his freshly poured cup, and sat behind his desk. "Now then," he said, lumping two words with opposite definitions against each other. "Harry Lillis."

It's possible that at the drop of Lillis's name, I was supposed to go to my knees and confess, because Honig just looked at me for a long moment. I didn't confess, because I was relatively sure I hadn't killed Lillis, so Honig eventually moved on.

"Harry Lillis," he repeated, but didn't wait as long for my tear-soaked breakdown this time. "The body was discovered in an unrecognizable state in a gazebo seventy-five yards from the rear entrance of the Lillian Booth Actors' Home. Firefighters on the scene reported it was there when they arrived, lying on the wooden floor of the gazebo, which was engulfed in flames." He was reading from a report he held on a clipboard. Underneath the report, also attached to the clipboard, was today's *New York Times* crossword puzzle, folded neatly to fit on the board.

"Thank you," I said. "Can I leave now?"

"We haven't even gotten to you yet," Honig said, apparently having missed my masterfully ironic tone. He went back to the report. "Body was badly burned, no fingerprints left, no hair, no clothing, except for a few pieces of burned cloth that appear to match the shirt Lillis was seen wearing earlier that evening."

264

"Dental records?" I asked. What the hell; I was drinking the man's coffee, and actually got up to refill the cup.

"Lillis had a full set of dentures, which were found next to the body. Took us a while to find them in all the ash, but they were there."

I stopped in mid-refill. "Next to the body? Not in his mouth?"

"Apparently they fell out as the body burned. They were a few inches away, on the floor, a little melted." Honig wasn't wearing glasses to read, unlike Dutton, who favors half-glasses. Maybe he was wearing bifocal contact lenses.

"We sure they were his?" I asked.

Honig gave me a look that read, "What's this *we* stuff, kemosabe?" He said, "Dentures are made with the patient's name on a small piece of paper that is molded directly into the plastic. They were Lillis's teeth, all right."

That took the wind out of my sails.

"I'm sorry for your loss." Homicide detectives must say that in their sleep.

"He was a legend. And he was getting to be a friend." I bent my head, and my right thumb and forefinger went to the bridge of my nose. Harry was dead. I looked up at Honig. "Lieutenant, why am I here?"

He glanced back down at the report. "Four nights before Lillis died, he called you from the Booth Actors' Home. Is that correct?"

I nodded.

"He told you that his ex-partner had threatened to kill him."

I blinked. "How did you know . . . ?"

"Chief Dutton in Midland Heights told me about that. We also have reports from the NYPD of two complaints you made, and then withdrew, against the ex-partner, Mr. Townes, and his son. Said they shot at you and sent you a cartoon character clock in a box."

"Well, when you say it like that, it doesn't sound scary," I said.

"Did Lillis tell you Townes wanted to kill him?"

I thought about exactly what Harry had said. It seemed like months ago, but it had only been a little more than a week. "He said that Townes had implied he *could* kill Harry if Harry made any more comments about Townes possibly killing his wife."

Honig's jaw dropped a couple of feet. "Townes killed Vivian Reynolds?" Oh lord, another classic comedy freak. Somehow, they all find me, eventually.

"That's what Harry said. I don't know if

it's true."

"How?"

I grimaced. "Harry said he strangled her and then . . ."

"And then what?" Honig's eyebrows had merged.

"And then set their house on fire to cover his tracks."

Honig sat back in his chair and blinked a few times, digesting the information. "Lillis set the fire in Bel Air?" He *was* a fan. "Did he use kerosene?" he asked.

That made *me* blink. "To set the fire?" Honig nodded. "How the hell would I know? Why? Was there kerosene found in the gazebo?"

"We're not sure yet," Honig answered. "Could be kerosene, could be chemical fertilizer from the garden shed. That stuff is pretty flammable."

"Was it in the gazebo?"

"It was on the body," Honig said. "A *lot*."

Wait a second; I'm slow on the uptake. "So we're talking about a murder here, for sure?" I asked.

"Unless Lillis decided to immolate himself, I'd say yes," Honig answered. "And for that matter, even if he didn't."

"What does that mean?"

Honig's lips flattened out; he looked like

he'd tasted something awful. "It means —
and I don't want this repeated anywhere —
that the head was set at a strange angle, and
might have had a broken neck. As if . . ."

"As if someone strangled him, and then
set the body on fire to cover his tracks." I
sat back and forgot the coffee.

"So I need to know from you, Mr. Freed,
exactly how much you know about the Vivian Reynolds case, and how it relates to Les
Townes."

I spent the better part of an hour detailing
for Honig the research I'd done on Vivian
Reynolds's death, and how none of it could
be substantiated. I told him about my visit
to Les Townes's home, about his son Wilson, about the attack with the shotgun and
the ticking package delivered to Comedy
Tonight. I told him about Wilson's visit to
threaten me and about his breaking my
snow globe. I talked for so long, I think I
might have told him about the time my
mother made me go trick-or-treating
dressed as a stalk of celery. I went through
a good deal of police station coffee. Honig
made a new pot. I took two bathroom
breaks.

He took notes. He wasn't a great listener;
he didn't let me forget I was being questioned in a crime investigation. But he was

a *good* listener. He didn't miss anything, he asked for clarification when he needed it, and he asked questions that made sense. By the time I was finished, I felt like my brain had been emptied. Tomorrow, I'd relearn that "walking upright" thing I'd mastered a while back.

Finally, Honig stood up, indicating the interview was over. He reached a hand across his desk and I took it. "Thank you for coming in," he said.

"I didn't have much of a choice, Lieutenant," I answered. "You sent a car." I got up to leave, and did my best Peter-Falk-as-Columbo impression: "There's just one thing, if I may ask."

"I have no reason to tell you anything about an ongoing investigation," Honig said.

I ignored that. "If you knew that Townes had threatened Harry's life, and you knew that Harry had been murdered, and didn't just die in an accidental fire, why didn't you immediately go to Queens for Les and his son?"

Honig's eyes narrowed. "What makes you think we didn't?"

"And?"

"And, they were gone. The house was empty of everything but furniture. They'd taken their clothes and left. There was noth-

269

ing there, and nobody has seen them for
over a week."

27

I asked Honig if Officer Broeker, the uniform who had driven me up from Midland Heights, could take me to the Booth Actors' Home before the return trip. He grumbled about it, but agreed after a minute or so. I figured that I'd already made the trip to Englewood, and was less than two miles from the Actors' Home. It would be foolish to go home and then borrow a car to drive back up.

My chauffeur in blue came in with me, and followed silently wherever I went. When I inquired at the front desk about seeing Lillis's room, the woman behind the counter looked worried, and called for Walter Lee, who arrived in less than a minute.

Luckily, Walt recognized me, and visibly relaxed. "We've been a little jumpy recently," he said. When I asked again if I could see Lillis's room, he glanced briefly at Officer Broeker.

"He's not here to investigate," I said. "He's my ride for the day." Broeker's expression went from stony to . . . stonier.

Walt walked me back to the room where Lillis had lived. There were traces of police crime scene tape on the doorjamb, but most of it had been removed. He unlocked the door and let it swing open, but seemed reluctant to walk inside. Maybe Walt was squeamish. For that matter, maybe *I* was squeamish, because I hesitated for a second, and then went in. Walt said the room would have been cleared out by now to make room for a new resident — he was fond of mentioning the lengthy waiting list — but the police had insisted on not touching anything in there until the medical examiner's report on Lillis's autopsy was released, and that hadn't happened yet.

The room was untouched — no, make that unchanged. The cops had been through it, had opened drawers and moved furniture, but had been respectful, not tossing the place like they would if it had been a suspect's residence. It was still neat, but there had clearly been some activity recently.

The bed was made, waiting for Lillis to come back.

I looked for the wheelchair, but it wasn't

here. "Did they find his wheelchair?" I asked Walt.

"His wheelchair?" he responded.

I must have added three permanent wrinkles to my forehead. "Harry had injured his hip in a fall," I said. "Didn't you know that? He could barely stand up the last time I saw him, and was complaining that the physical therapy on his hip wasn't helping."

"Physical therapy?" Walt seemed incapable of starting a response without repeating something I'd just said. "Mr. Lillis wasn't receiving physical therapy."

"Why not?"

"He didn't need it," Walter Lee answered, for once using his own words. "All the tests our doctors ran indicated he hadn't injured himself. We assumed he'd done a pratfall to entertain the people watching, because he didn't even land hard. Mr. Lillis insisted it was worse and requested a wheelchair, which we gave him gladly, but he never really needed it."

My head started to hurt. It was as if all the strange information I'd been getting all day was collecting in my sinuses. "I don't understand," I told Walt. "I saw Harry just a few days before he died, and he needed me to wheel him outside. Everyone here saw me doing that."

Walt nodded. "Yes, we did, but I can assure you that not two hours before you visited that day, Mr. Freed, Harry Lillis walked himself to the dining room and back with no sign of pain at all."

"You're sure?"

"I saw him myself."

I felt like I had to prove him wrong. "So where is the wheelchair now?" I asked. Ha! Answer that, Mr. Smarty Pants!

"I believe it was discovered near the gazebo that night, wasn't it, Officer?" Walt looked at Officer Broeker, who nodded so slightly it was hard to see the movement.

"So whoever killed him must have wheeled him out there," I said aloud. "Why did you ask about it like you didn't know he was using it anymore?"

Walt widened his eyes a little in a facial gesture meant to convey bafflement. "I knew he still had it, but I assumed it was a security blanket sort of thing, since I knew he had been walking under his own steam rather well for quite some time," he said.

I walked to the desk, and gestured at it: "Is it okay if I touch this?" I asked. Walt glanced at the cop, who hesitated, then gave the eensy-weensy nod again. I opened the top drawer of Lillis's desk.

There wasn't anything special in any of

the drawers, just some stationery, a few photographs, some cassette tapes (apparently Harry wasn't much for the digital revolution), and a few bottles of prescription medication.

"What are these for?" I asked Walt, showing him the bottles.

He examined them. "Blood pressure," he said, looking at the first, then "acid reflux" for the second.

Walt put a third bottle into his pocket. I thought about asking what it was for, but he deflected me by asking if I was ready to leave.

I gave the room another careful look, but there wasn't much to see. There were books on two shelves over the desk and the bed, mostly about show business, biographies, and criticism. One section, however, seemed to be devoted to Shakespeare. A comedian never lived who didn't have a serious side.

"Was anything removed from this room?" I asked.

"Nothing except . . ." Walt started to answer, but the cop in the corner moved suddenly, shaking his head "no," and catching his eye. "No. Nothing."

I started to ask about that exchange, but saw the look in the officer's eyes, and decided to take the question up with someone more forgiving. Like Barry Dutton.

"Is that all you wanted, Mr. Freed?" Walt asked.

I took a last look. "Yeah, I guess so," I said. We turned to leave the room, and just then, I noticed something in one corner, at the foot of the bed.

Lillis's acoustic guitar was propped against the bed frame, and somehow, it looked so lonely and sad sitting there, I was reminded of my new friend's loss all over again. I bit my lips, and walked to the guitar. I picked it up.

Walter Lee must have sensed my feelings, because he waited a moment, and then asked, "Would you like to take that with you, Mr. Freed?"

Harry Lillis's guitar? For me? The offer was overwhelming. "Really?" I asked, sounding like a nine-year-old being given a valuable baseball card.

Walt nodded. "Mr. Lillis didn't specify that it be given to anyone in particular," he said. "He had no next of kin. You know, his brother died a number of years ago, and Mr. Lillis never had any children."

I felt the polished wood in my hands, and was more overwhelmed than I should have been. "Thank you, Walt," I said. "I'd like to take it."

We walked out of the room, and Walt locked the door again. The three of us walked down the corridor, past the dining room, and toward the main entrance. Just before we made it to the door, I asked Walt if I could see the gazebo where Lillis died.

"I'm afraid there's not much left to see," he told me. "The structure was pretty well destroyed in the fire. All that's left is a black spot on the ground."

"I'm not expecting much," I said. "Would it be all right?"

Walt blinked, then nodded. He showed the officer and me the way, and led us out the back door of the main building and toward the spot where the gazebo had been.

The area still smelled from the fire, a smell that reminded me of barbecues when I was a boy — my father is a lousy griller. If you took a ream of paper, soaked it in water, waited for it to dry completely, and then burned it, you could get the same general scent. It wasn't pretty.

Walt had been right: there wasn't much to look at, just a burned spot, very large and remarkably symmetrical, round. Almost as if it had been designed.

It was still fenced off, but the fence was close enough and low enough that the spot could be seen clearly. Small pieces of wood, once painted white, were visible in the brown grass and the mud.

To one side, leaning on a walker near the police tape, taking no note of us, was Marion Borello. I think the walker was more for support when she was standing still than for when she was walking.

I kept my distance out of respect for her feelings.

"Where was the wheelchair?" I asked.

Broeker pointed to a spot near the top of the circle, nearest the natural path to the gazebo when it had been standing. He said nothing.

"You were here that night?" I asked him. He nodded, a cigar store Native American with a crick in his neck.

"A lot of officers were here," Walt said. "EMS came, too, but by the time the flames were under control, there was nothing that could be done for poor Mr. Lillis."

I knew it was pointless to spend much time in the area; the cops had seen everything there was to see, and I didn't want this mental picture to linger for me. Harry's death had hit me harder than I was willing to admit, more than it should have for someone who, technically, I had met only a couple of weeks before. But Harry Lillis had been a hero of mine all my life, and to lose him this way, so soon after meeting him, hurt more than it would have a month ago.

Marion seemed to decide something, then walked toward us, not very slowly, with the walker.

When she reached us, I said, "I'm so sorry, Marion."

She didn't even look at me. She just kept walking. I watched for a long time as she made her way back toward the building.

"Let's go," I said. My voice was hoarse. I clutched the guitar respectfully by the neck and started toward the parking lot. On the way, I thanked Walt for taking the time, and for letting me have the guitar, an impressively generous gesture.

"You were the first guest Mr. Lillis had had in quite some time," he said. "I know Mr. Testalone spoke with him, but you were the first one to come specifically to see Harry Lillis. I know that meant a lot to him, because he spoke of you often after that."

"I'll bet he insulted me," I said.

Walter Lee grinned. "Maybe a little."

"I can't believe nobody else wanted the guitar," I said as we reached the police cruiser.

"Nobody asked for anything," Walt answered. "I haven't heard from anyone."

"There must have been a next of kin on

your records when Harry first applied here," I said. "There has to be a name as a beneficiary on his life insurance."

Walt looked uncomfortable. "Yes," was all he said.

I narrowed my eyes as Officer Broeker opened the car door for me to place the guitar in the back. "There was someone. You checked," I said.

Walt's mouth flattened out. "Yes," he said. "I did check. And it was odd."

"No beneficiary?"

He shook his head. "No, there was one. Mr. Lillis's life insurance listed one beneficiary. Wilson Townes."

28

The drive back to Midland Heights was as quiet a ride as I can recall taking. Officer Broeker, chatterbox that he was, spoke only when absolutely necessary, and sometimes not even then. I had a lot of time to think, and that wasn't my best option at this moment.

I realized that my coming to Englewood was supposed to be helpful for the police, and not necessarily for me, but I couldn't help ruminating on the idea that I'd come home with more questions than I had when I'd gotten out of bed this morning. A lot more questions.

Wilson Townes was the beneficiary of Harry Lillis's life insurance policy. How did that make any sense? Lillis had hardly seemed to remember that Townes *had* a son when I'd mentioned him, and certainly hadn't exhibited any affection, outward or otherwise, when Wilson's name had come up. Sure, Lillis had no children of his own, but Wilson Townes was barely an afterthought. Why leave him the death benefit (my favorite oxymoron) from Lillis's policy?

But that was just the beginning of the questions I'd compiled after meeting with Honig. Why had Lillis been using a wheelchair if he didn't need one? I had no reason to disbelieve Walter Lee, who said he'd clearly seen Harry Lillis up and walking around at the Booth Actors' Home, even though Lillis had insisted on using the chair when I'd visited. Was Lillis putting on a performance for my benefit? Why would he want me to think he was seriously injured if he wasn't? Did that tie in with the insurance policy? Would there have been some kind of claim that I'd have been expected to testify about?

And what was the look that passed between Walt and Broeker when it was obvious something had been removed from Lillis's room? I asked Broeker about it, and he responded in no uncertain terms that, "I was told to drive you. I'm driving you." And he didn't say anything else.

All this confusion was making my brain hurt, and since Broeker was unwilling to stop at an ice cream store to ease my pain (some people are so rigid!), I decided to take a walk after he dropped me off at Comedy Tonight. I'd left a key for Sophie in her family's mailbox, as I'd prearranged (over Sophie's objections that I was "using a woman like a slave") before Broeker had picked me up at the theatre. Since I figured the three kids could run a matinee well enough for an extra half hour, I headed to Big Herbs, a vegetarian restaurant on Edison Avenue, for a quick bite. Well hell, I couldn't get ice cream. I go from one extreme to the other when under stress.

I was hoping Belinda McElvoy would be behind the counter today, and I was lucky. Belinda, an African-American woman with striking good looks and an overwhelming serenity, could make you feel good about the seventh day of rain in a row. It was only cloudy today, so I figured I was already one step ahead.

"What's good today, Belinda?" I asked as I took a stool. Big Herbs is a slightly renovated diner, at one point called Big Bob's Bar-B-Q Pit, which had probably been closed by the Board of Health over cholesterol issues. Midland Heights being the kind of town it is, public demand was voiced for a vegetarian restaurant, and so Big Herbs was born.

Of course, most people are hypocrites, so

Big Herbs was usually pretty empty, like today. Saturday afternoon at lunchtime, and there were three other people in the place besides Belinda and me.

She looked at me. "You don't think I actually eat this stuff, do you?" she asked, and I laughed. Belinda was a woman whose tastes ran to pulled pork and french fries. She would have been better off working at Big Bob's. And she stays perfectly trim. There are days the very sight of her could move me to violence.

"In that case, give me a Caesar salad," I said. "Heavy on the croutons."

"You a growing boy?"

"In all the wrong directions," I told her.

Belinda went to place the order at the window behind the counter, then came back with a bottle of water that she knew I'd want, a napkin, and a counter setup. She took a long look at my face and asked, "Now, what's the problem with you? Elliot, you look like somebody ran over your puppy dog with a steamroller."

"I lost a friend," I told her, and she frowned.

"Sorry," Belinda said. "I shouldn't have said that."

"It's not your fault."

"Was it a good friend?" she asked.

"Not really. Well, maybe. Yes. I don't know."

Belinda walked away for a moment to deliver something containing a good deal of kale to one of the tables, then came back to pretend to clean the counter when she was actually talking to me. "Is that what's got you so down?" she asked, as if the conversation hadn't been interrupted at all.

"I guess. Thing is, my friend died under . . . odd circumstances. And I'm trying to figure it out. And it won't figure." I don't know when, but Belinda managed to bring my salad while I was being incoherent. She knew I liked the dressing on the side, and had delivered it that way, so I poured a little on and started in. Charlie Brown once noted that, "Some psychiatrists say that people who eat peanut butter sandwiches are lonely. I guess they're right. And when you're really lonely, the peanut butter sticks to the roof of your mouth." Of course, Charlie never had a Caesar salad for lunch. Or perhaps people who eat Caesar salads for lunch aren't lonely; they're bedeviled by a murder.

Okay, maybe not *all* of them.

"Tell me about it," Belinda said. Others have a friendly bartender or a source at the telephone company to help in their detection. I have Belinda, the waitress at the vegetarian cafe. Of course, Belinda's not only a very intelligent woman, but she's also studying for her PhD in psychology. No, really.

"My friend was an old man. He wasn't going to be around forever. But somebody went out of their way to kill him, and it doesn't add up. What was to be gained by killing him?"

"Money?" Belinda asked. "On *CSI,* they always say people kill other people over money or sex. How old was your friend?"

"Around eighty."

"Probably not sex, then."

"Could be revenge," I said. "There was this other guy who thought my friend was fooling around with his wife, and the wife ended up dead the same way as my friend. But that was fifty years ago. Why wait that long for revenge?"

"You really need to tell me the whole story from the beginning, Elliot," she chided.

So I did. I told her all about Lillis and Townes, the fire in 1958, Townes's suspicion that Harry was having an affair with Vivian, the wheelchair, the insurance policy.

Everything.

During which Belinda managed to serve up two veggie burgers, an omelet (it's vegetarian at Big Herbs, not vegan), and some whole-grain pasta with zucchini, all while listening to my twisted tale. I managed to eat about half the salad (it was huge) and drank the whole bottle of water.

When I was finished, Belinda gave me a long look and sighed. "Sounds like quite a mess," she said.

"You got that right. But what do I do about it?"

Belinda looked puzzled. "Why do you have to do anything about it? That's why the police were invented, isn't it?"

"You ever lose a friend, Belinda?" I asked.

"Yes," she said quietly.

"How can I *not* do something?"

She thought for a long time. "Well, the cops aren't going to share information with you, and you don't have any witnesses you can talk to on this side of the country. Seems to me that if you think there's a connection, you have to look into the Hollywood murder. You going to fly out to L.A.?"

"Seems unlikely," I said. "What with this theatre to run and everything."

"Not going to be easy from here. You know what you need, Elliot?"

"What?"

"A big juicy hamburger."

I laughed. "Seriously," I said. "What do I need?"

"What you need," she said, "is to think about something else. That's when you'll get your best idea."

Damn it. She was right. "How is it that you and I never moved past the 'banter' stage?" I asked her.

Belinda considered me for a moment, and grinned on the right side of her lovely face. "Honey," she said. "You couldn't handle me."

29

My first order of business on returning to the theatre was to check on the staff, who couldn't possibly have cared less that I hadn't been there for a few hours. Sophie, at her station behind the snack bar, reported there were forty-seven members in the matinee audience for *The Ghost Breakers,* which unfortunately was about what I'd expected. Sophie said one African-American woman had come out about a half hour into the film, demanding her money back because the way Bob Hope treats his valet Willie Best in the film was "racist." Which it unquestionably was, but 1940 will remain 1940 on film for all eternity, and there's not much one can do about it. I'd already limited myself to comedy films, and half the time to those made at least a quarter century ago. To further limit myself to comedy films from at least a quarter century ago that contained no material offensive to a Midland Heights audience would be to ensure constant showings of *Guess Who's Coming to Dinner* for the rest of my life, which wouldn't be long, since I would soon commit suicide. The movie's heart is in the right place, but, oh boy, is it dull!

Luckily, after listening to a few minutes of Sophie's feminist invective, the woman was more incensed about Bob's dealings with Paulette Goddard in the film, and rushed back in to see how it would turn out, and probably to break up with the guy who'd brought her to the film. It is our pleasure to serve our audience.

Anthony was upstairs, still reeling (you should pardon the expression) from his film's latest disappearance, and no doubt concocting more reasons that it was all my fault. Or his father's. One of the two of us was clearly responsible for all the evil in the world, because his father loved and cared and worried about him and paid for college, and I gave him a paycheck every couple of weeks and ran his film for him to show all his friends and family. Yup, we were a pair of blackguards, Michael Pagliarulo and I.

Jonathan stood at the auditorium entrance, looking tall and baffled in a Firesign Theatre T-shirt and his ubiquitous flip-flops.

I breathed a sigh of relief that at least he'd cut his toenails, and wondered if a) he had conspired with a man I now believed to be a murderer to threaten me, and b) if he'd wear those damned flip-flops in a couple of months when the temperature would be in the twenties.

I called Barry Dutton at his office, then Sergeant Newman in Los Angeles, then Detective Honig in Englewood, then Meg in Camden, peppering them all with questions about Wilson, and Harry's will, and the Bel Air fire in 1958. Everyone gave me roughly the same answers: *Why should the police share any information at all with a movie theatre owner?* Actually, Newman was less discouraging, giving me names of ex-studio employees who might still be alive, and a B-list of cops who hadn't been on the force at the time but might know something, though he did still ask the question.

Strikingly, I had no answer to give, even the fourth time. You'd think out of sheer repetition I'd have come up with something.

When I'd asked Dutton what might have been removed from Harry Lillis's room at the Booth Actors' Home, he'd sounded downright hostile when he said, "You may not realize this, Elliot, but the Englewood Police Department doesn't rush right to the phone and call me whenever they get a clue in a case." If he kept up that attitude, I'd start to think he didn't *want* me looking into Harry Lillis's murder.

The Internet provided little more of use; I'd pretty much tapped out any sources of information about Vivian Reynolds's death. Despite encouragement from a vegetarian restaurant waitress, I was running into a brick wall.

Fortunately for me, I had plenty of other frustrating things to consider. I decided not to think about Sharon's curious expression when Anthony's film turned up missing again. But I'd try and find the copy of *Killin' Time,* so that Anthony would stop scowling at me. It had gotten so bad, I made Jonathan taste my food for me when Anthony was in the theatre. It wasn't doing me much good, since Jonathan seemed unfamiliar with the "tasting" concept, and would generally eat whatever I'd intended for myself and leave me with nothing.

Sharon aside, the only other person I could think to contact was Anthony's roommate Danton. He was in when I called, and although he offered to come to the theatre, I didn't want to risk Anthony seeing him at Comedy Tonight. I said I'd meet him at the apartment, which I'd visited once before.

I left the office and went to the snack bar to tell Sophie I'd be gone for an hour or so. Her hooded eyelids said more than her voice when she responded, "Fine," so I asked her if my absence would be a problem.

"Wasn't a problem all morning." She sighed. "Why would it be now?"

"What, exactly, happened to give you this attitude, young lady?" I asked.

"Elliot," Sophie said, "you've never talked to me like my father does before."

That took me aback, and I might have blushed a bit. "Well, I . . ."

"I've always liked that about you," she added.

I made it to Guilden Street in New Brunswick in about twenty minutes on my bike. Danton opened the door of the second-floor apartment and let me in. The place looked exactly like it had when I'd seen it a few months before: slovenly, cramped, unsanitary, and littered with pizza boxes. About standard for an apartment with four undergraduates infesting it.

We sat in the "living room," a space occupied by a couch with holes in its cushions and permanent Cheez Doodles stains on its arms; milk crates holding up books, CDs,

DVDs, and more DVDs; a Salvation Army armchair that smelled of beer; a large cardboard Amazon box being used as an ottoman; and a sixty-inch flat-screen LCD HDTV television with surround sound. You have to have priorities.

"I'm not sure I can help you much, Mr. Freed," Danton said when I explained my mission (but left out the part about him being my current prime suspect by default, since I didn't want to consider my ex-wife/current, um, girlfriend?). "I saw all the same stuff you saw that night. I don't know what happened to Anthony's movie."

"Well, you know what the cops say: maybe you saw something and didn't realize you saw it." I couldn't explain that sentiment, but I wanted to get the police into the discussion. Maybe I could sweat a confession out of the kid.

"I don't know what that means," he said.

Danton was a lanky guy in a white T-shirt and shorts that had last been washed when gasoline was 89 cents a gallon (pardon me: 88.9 cents per gallon — do they think they're *fooling* anybody with that one?). He had the easy smile of a young man who has always gotten every girl he wanted to fall in love with him. I ignored all that and asked exactly where he'd been after the screening.

"Well, they were doing all the toasts and stuff," he answered, making a show of thinking. "I was on the steps to the balcony at that point, because I remember looking down at Anthony and Carla."

"What about after the group broke up?" I prodded.

"I hung out with Phil and Dolores in the lobby for a while, and then I took off," he said.

Dolores was another of their roommates. It was a very relaxed apartment. "Who's Phil?" I asked. "Dolores's boyfriend?"

Danton grinned a little and shook his head. "Nah. Phil's our new roommate. Lyle graduated last year. Phil and Dolores are just friends." His grin betrayed his definition of "friends."

"Did you leave with them?" I asked. Dolores's love life was none of my business.

"Nah. They took off before I did. I was trying to talk to this one babe, but she didn't want to know me."

"One of the other film students?" I asked.

"Nah. Older lady, but easy on the eyes. Didn't matter, though. She wasn't interested." He sounded a little surprised, because *all* women should have been interested, in Danton's opinion.

"Older?" Danton nodded, so I went on.

"Long, dark blond hair, big eyes, dressed in a skirt with a slit up the side?"

Danton grinned wider. "That's her. You try for her, too?"

"She's my ex-wife," I said.

Danton's expression took on a more respectful attitude. "Cool," he said.

"So you were talking to her for a while." I tried to get him back on track before I felt the need to hit him over the head with a wet sack of manure.

"Yeah. But she shot me down, so I left. Nobody else there who was that interesting."

"You leave with anybody?"

Suddenly it struck Danton that I was trying to establish an alibi — or not — for him. "You think *I* took Anthony's movie?" he asked.

"I don't think anything," I said. "I'm trying to eliminate things so I can focus on what's left."

"Well, you can eliminate me," he said. "I had no reason to steal it."

"You weren't even a little jealous that Anthony got his film made? Maybe you had a script that was better, but you couldn't get the financing, especially not the way he got it?"

Danton looked like he was going to make

a fart noise: both his lips turned out and flattened in an expression of dismissal. "I'm a history major, Mr. Freed. I don't have any scripts at all."

"You don't." There went an hour's worth of kangaroo court in my head.

"Nope. I'm tickled for Anthony. Let him go make his movies. Maybe he'll get rich and I can hit him up for a loan. No reason I wouldn't want him to have his movie. What kind of a guy do you think I am?"

I stood up. "Sorry if I offended you," I told him. "I wasn't trying to make you a suspect." I believe my nose grew just a bit after I said that. "I'm just trying to . . ."

"Eliminate things," Danton said.

"Exactly. Consider yourself eliminated. At least, from my list."

I walked to the door. Danton didn't say anything else until I turned and faced him again. "Just one question," I said.

He didn't look happy. "Yeah?"

"Is Danton your first name or your last name?" I asked.

The kid grinned one last time in a Cheshire cat fashion. "Yes," he said.

30

My conversation with Danton had made me uneasy for a number of reasons. For one, I never like being in the room with someone who is sure he's cooler than I am, especially when I'm sure of it, too. For another, I believed him, which meant I couldn't blame him for Anthony's missing movie, and I wanted to. The fact that he had even considered hitting on my ex-wife, a woman easily fifteen years older than he was, made my stomach uncomfortable. And there was something about Danton's manner that had me feeling suspicious of him on a subliminal level: even if he hadn't taken *Killin' Time,* I felt he'd done something else equally reprehensible, although I couldn't imagine what that might be.

But more than anything else, it worried me because suddenly, Sharon was my best — and to be fair, only — remaining suspect in the Case of the Missing Movie.

Even if her motives were altruistic (and I could certainly imagine her trying to save Anthony from himself), I didn't want to think that my ex-wife had committed burglary for a good cause. Mostly, I didn't want to be there when she was accused. I've seen Sharon when she's not pleased, and it isn't something I wanted to experience again if I don't have to.

All of which made the prospect of our upcoming date (set for the following Monday night, a mere two days away) somewhat daunting.

Clearly, my only recourse was to find evidence supporting the theory that Carla, Anthony's girlfriend, had taken the film. I resolved to begin doing so shortly.

I got back to the theatre after my interview with Danton just in the middle of the second feature, a comedy about a ghost who finds a career as a sports announcer that wasn't as funny as the average Tampa Bay Rays game. Jonathan was nowhere to be seen on my arrival, which I took to mean he was inside the auditorium. Sophie sat behind the snack bar, her back to me, on her stool. I couldn't tell if she was reading, sleeping or — for all I knew — sticking pins in an Elliot-Freed-as-all-men voodoo doll, but her head was down when I walked over.

"Everything going okay?" I asked in the most benign, yes-I'm-male-but-I'm-not-the-enemy tone I could muster.

Her head jerked up, alarmed. Geez, maybe she *had* been napping! "Sorry," I said. "I didn't mean to startle you."

Sophie turned around and looked at me as her hand went, palm up, to her cheek. Was that a tear I saw being wiped away? "You didn't startle me," she said, but the quiver in her voice betrayed her words. "I was . . . doing inventory."

"No, you weren't. Now tell me what's bothering you."

"Nothing!" She ran, literally, to the ladies' room, where she knew I wouldn't follow. I guessed I'd be selling candy for a while until she came out.

Jonathan emerged from the auditorium just as I was sitting down on Sophie's stool, and realizing that there was still some residual ache in my butt from the buckshot. I made a mental note to buy a softer seat for the snack bar, and wondered how Sophie, with her almost total lack of padding in that area, had withstood it all this time.

"Did someone yell?" Jonathan asked. "I thought I heard something out here."

"Sophie was being dramatic," I told him.

"She'll be back soon."

Jonathan looked around, making sure I wasn't actually holding Sophie hostage somewhere, and then looked at me. He seemed to be staring at the area just under my chin, not making eye contact. When someone does that, it has a tendency to make me self-conscious, as does most everything else.

"What are you staring at?" I asked. Jonathan didn't answer. I took a deep breath, and figured, what the hell. "You talk to Sophie a lot," I said to him.

Before I had a chance to finish the thought, Jonathan widened his eyes and looked me in the face. "No, I don't," he said.

"I'm just wondering if you'd have any idea why she's upset," I said. "Maybe she told you something."

"Not me," he answered. "I didn't do anything."

"Nobody thinks you did. I'm just wondering if she said something to you that she wouldn't say to me."

Jonathan seemed to find that concept confusing. "What wouldn't she say to you?" he asked.

This line of questioning wasn't getting me anywhere, so I decided to ask what I should have days ago. "Jonathan," I said, "have you been in touch with Les Townes?"

You'd think I'd just asked him for the definitive word on Einstein's theory of relativity and its relation to the work of Steven Spielberg. Jonathan's eyes seemed to recede into his head, and his mouth puckered, like I'd mentioned lemons out of context. "Les Townes?" he asked. "Of Lillis and Townes?"

No, Les Townes of Black Sabbath. "Yes," I said. "Of Lillis and Townes."

"You mean have I ever spoken to him?" Jonathan made a face like he was trying to hear me from very far away: eyes squinted, head leaned forward.

"I know you spoke to him when he was here that night," I said, thinking I sounded like a kindergarten teacher with an unusually naive student. "I'm asking if you've spoken to him or heard from him privately since then."

"Why?"

That struck me as odd. "Why am I asking? Because Mr. Townes is missing and the police are wondering if anybody's heard from him."

Jonathan shook his head. "Why would I have been in touch with him? Did he say something to you about me?" Jonathan appeared to be asking if Townes wanted to be

302

his friend.

"No, I was just wondering if you'd talked to him. Or his son."

"He has a son?" Jonathan asked.

This conversation really wasn't going anywhere. "Yes, Jon. He has a son."

"Jonathan."

"No. Wilson." No point to it anymore.

"My name isn't Wilson." Jonathan must have thought I was a complete idiot.

It was time to stop beating around the bush. "Jonathan, the night I came downstairs and found you in my office. Were you . . . ?"

The door to the ladies' room opened and out came Sophie. Her face was not wet and her eye makeup, what little there was, had not streaked. She marched to the snack bar and glared at me.

"What are you doing behind there?" she asked.

"Somebody had to be here," was the best I could do.

"I'll bet nobody came out for a snack," Sophie said. "You just don't trust a woman to handle the situation."

"*What* situation?"

"May I get back to my workstation, please?" Sophie asked. *Workstation?*

I got out of the way and turned to face

303

Jonathan. I didn't care if Sophie heard the question now.

But Jonathan was gone.

Sophie went back behind the snack bar, and as she sat down, I thought she winced a little. Well, good. Maybe I wouldn't get her that new stool, after all.

31

No one will ever win the battle of the sexes. There's too much fraternizing with the enemy.

— HENRY KISSINGER

Monday

It is never easy for me to knock on the door at Sharon's house. Since she and Gregory moved in together (about twenty minutes after she moved out of my house), I've felt like I did on the set of *Split Personality:* that someone had taken something that was mine and turned it into something I could barely recognize, while I stood by and watched.

Of course I know (before Sophie can get on my case about the previous sentence) that Sharon never belonged to me, and that she is still the same woman she was when we were married. But there's something unnerving about seeing a person with whom you were that intimate move on to someone else. I have enough of an ego for it to hurt, deeply. So entering their home had always been awkward.

Tonight, though, took the prize for weirdest yet, because I was knocking on Sharon's door for our third date since starting this experiment. We were going out to a play being performed at the George Street Playhouse in New Brunswick (Sharon's idea), but instead of her picking me up at the town house, from which we could have walked to the theatre, Sharon had suggested first having dinner at her house. Gregory was in Las Vegas, at a convention of people who put other people to sleep for money. I hoped there'd be a hypnotist working the hotel lounge, just for the irony.

But somehow, the two thousand miles between us didn't seem quite far enough.

Sharon opened the door and, as usual, immediately riveted my attention. She doesn't favor low-cut tops, but the one she was wearing was tighter than usual, and she had on those jeans again.

She knows exactly what effect they have on me.

"Come on in," she said, gesturing. The house, as befitting a two-physician income, was large and well furnished. Sharon doesn't show off, but she has really good taste. As evidence, I offer the fact that she divorced me. As more evidence, I offer the fact that she was divorcing Gregory. She doesn't always get it right the first time, but, eventually, she manages.

I offered the red rose I'd been holding behind my back, and she took it, smiling. I didn't tell her I'd bought it at the Shop Rite, but the UPC code on the wrapping may have betrayed my lack of class. She pretended not to notice. "It's beautiful," Sharon said. "Thank you."

And she leaned over and gave me a kiss that would kill a normal man.

"Wow," I said when we came up for air. "If I'd known the flower would get that kind of reception, I'd have bought the whole dozen."

My ex-wife smiled the smile she thinks is mysterious, but is really just adorable. "The night is young," she said.

"That doesn't make any sense, but I'm really turned on," I told her.

"Good. I made dinner," she said. "Are you hungry?"

"That's one of the things I am, yes."

I followed her into the dining room, where Sharon had set the table and put out covered dishes. We sat, feeling way too formal, and she served out chicken Kiev and rice pilaf, as well as asparagus and a white wine that I'm sure has a name, but don't ask me to repeat it. She is a wonderful cook, but I could barely eat a bite for the first few minutes. The atmosphere was just a little too intense.

Finally, hunger took over, as well as my fear that I seemed less than enthralled with the evening Sharon had planned. "This really beats the dinner I made for you," I told her. "I'm embarrassed."

"Don't be. You're very good at things that aren't cooking."

It wasn't like Sharon to be this forward, but I certainly wasn't complaining. I think we'd both felt disappointed — and ashamed of our petty disappointment — when the call about Harry Lillis's death had interrupted us the previous week. We were picking up where we'd left off, and it was making the atmosphere in the room a little strange.

It didn't help that I was flirting madly with another man's wife in that man's house. The fact that the man in question had done the same with my wife in my house provided little solace. I can't say whether revenge is a dish best served cold, because Sharon was serving a hot dinner. In a number of ways.

Eventually, we settled into our normal pattern, although the underlying tension was still there. We started to discuss Lillis, the implications that Townes or his son had killed him, and Sophie's odd behavior of late.

Neither of us said a word about *Killin' Time.* I was, frankly, afraid to break the mood — women respond so unpredictably when you accuse them of robbery. I can't vouch for Sharon's motivations.

"The problem is, I really don't *want* Les Townes to be the killer," I said. "I grew up watching the guy in movies and wishing I could be more like him. I can't just tear down that part of my character and start fresh now."

Sharon's eyes were sympathetic. "I'm afraid you may have to get used to the idea," she said. "It seems everything Harry said about Les was true."

"I know." I sighed. "I'll admit, all the evidence is circumstantial, but Lillis was killed in almost exactly the same way that Vivian Reynolds died in 1958. I'm not sure how reliable my Internet evidence on that one is, but the parallels are eerie."

"How much more can you find out about Vivian without going to L.A.?" Sharon asked.

"I'm not sure I could find out much more even if I did go," I told her. "All of the studio insiders are dead now, and so are most of the cops. There's nobody to ask."

"Did you check on the insurance?"

"Yes." I hadn't told her this before. "I called the insurance company saying I was researching a book on famous insurance claims in Southern California."

"You didn't. And they bought this?"

"Hook, line, sinker, pier, and coastline," I said. "They were thrilled to be included in such a long-overdue project."

Sharon giggled. I could have eaten her alive.

"Anyway, the diligent girl working in the records department spent about an hour digging into the archives and called me back. The house had fire insurance, of course, but it was for the right amount — nothing inflated, just what the house was worth — and Townes didn't appear to be in any serious financial straits. Vivian's life insurance named Wilson the beneficiary, but in trust to Townes."

"Does the plot thicken?" Sharon asked. We had finished eating, so I helped her carry the plates into the kitchen and put them into the dishwasher.

"I don't know. It's natural she'd leave her

money to her son. The policy had been changed when he was born, but Townes had signed it, too, and changed his own to mirror Vivian's."

"So the money went to Wilson, who was where when the fire started?" Sharon was all attention now.

"He was at his grandmother's. Les Townes's mother."

"So what does this all mean?" Sharon closed the dishwasher, and I was standing right behind her. I didn't move back to give her room.

"It all looks awfully normal, from an insurance point of view," I said. "Now, we'd better get going, or we're going to be late for that play."

Sharon grinned mischievously. "Well, here's the thing about the play . . ." she said.

"Yeah?" I moved a little closer. It was that kind of a grin.

"I never actually bought the tickets," she said.

I put my hands on her hips and pulled her just slightly toward me. Sharon moved close enough to kiss. "You didn't?" I asked.

"No. I didn't want to see it. It sounded dumb."

"Then why did you invite me to the play?" I said. "Is this how the whole dating thing is going to go?"

"I knew you don't like coming here, so I had to pretend we were going out," she said. "It's practical."

"No, practical would have been if we'd gone to my house. That's practical."

"I don't like going to your house," she said. "I wanted this to happen here."

"You wanted *what* to happen here?" I asked. It was going to come from her, not me, if I had any say in the matter.

"This," Sharon said, and gave me another coronary-threatening kiss. This time, I didn't try to come up for air very soon.

When we finally did start to breathe again, I said, "Here's good."

Then we didn't talk again for quite some time.

32

Tuesday

I woke up in a strange bed in a strange room in a strange house, something I hadn't done for a very long time. That odd feeling of disorientation is overwhelming for a brief period, but it usually dissipates quickly.

Not this time.

It didn't help that Sharon wasn't there when I woke up. I could hear the water running in the shower, so I knew she was still in the house. But her absence from the bed made for extra weirdness, and that was something I didn't really need.

A lot of men wake up after spending a night in bed with a woman and wonder what they might have been thinking the night before. I knew exactly what I'd been thinking, and didn't mind having thought it. But I was asking myself a lot of questions in the bright morning light.

What did that mean? Were we back together

again on a permanent basis? Was last night a result of our history? Did Sharon sleep with me simply because I was the most comfortable choice? What happens now?

There was one other question that hung over the room, and having cooled down considerably from the night before, I could ask it now: *Did Sharon steal Anthony's movie?* Suppose she had — for altruistic reasons, surely — then what would I do? What *should* I do?

Men also make a lot of ill-considered choices after a night like I'd just spent. And I was no exception: I decided that being alone in Sharon's bedroom (which these days thankfully bore no traces of Gregory, not even a tie clip — he'd occupied the guest bedroom since returning to the house in this weird arrangement they'd worked out), I had a rare opportunity to eliminate the possibility that my ex-wife had committed robbery, so it was my right — no, my *duty* — to prove her innocent.

You can talk yourself into all sorts of things after you've had a night you've been dreaming about for a long, long time.

I got out of bed, after doing a quick visual scan of the room for hiding places that could hold large cases of film reels. Discounting the closet as too obvious, I started by dropping to the floor and looking under the bed. But there was nothing to be seen except shoes and a baseball bat. Sharon considers a baseball bat the first line of defense against nighttime burglars. She believes in strict gun control, but insists the Second Amendment guarantees each citizen the right to wield a Louisville Slugger.

Maybe the closet wasn't too obvious after all. I crossed the room and opened the door, and took a few moments to drink it all in.

I've never lived in a home that had a walk-in closet. The best I've ever been able to do is an arm-in closet, which allows an arm to be extended all the way in if a shirt is far in the back. But this was almost a whole room.

It had a full-length mirror, and shelves on three sides, as well as a closet pole on each wall, holding Sharon's suits, skirts, and blouses. It was all so tidy, she could find anything she needed with a quick glance. My closets in the town house, on the other hand, were more receptacles for piles of clothing, out of which I would pull what was needed at any given moment. I'm clean, but I'm not neat.

The thing about such a well-organized closet, with everything immediately visible, was that it drove home the point: there were

no cans of film here. But there were plenty
of shoes. Women seem to need a truly hor-
rifying number of shoes, despite the vast
majority of them having only two feet.
Males don't understand this, but we put up
with it because, well, they're women. As
long as they're nice to us, we figure they
can indulge that shoe jones anytime they
want.

Hang on, though: the floor of the closet
was built up on a riser, meaning there was
storage space beneath the shelves on one
side. Storage space with a door that was
closed, hiding the items being stored.

Just enough space for film canisters.

This bore investigation. I walked to the
spot where the raised section began, and
got down on the floor to reach for the
handle. I stole a quick glance toward the
closet door, saw no one there, and opened
the storage space.

It was in shadow, and difficult to see
inside, so I lowered myself closer to the
floor, face almost inside the storage area. If
I'd had a flashlight, I'd be able to see in,
but maybe . . .

I reached inside and felt around. Something grazed the back of my hand, so I
grabbed for it and pulled it out.

It was a fuzzy blue slipper, the left one,

with a two-inch heel on it. I vividly remembered a very interesting evening that had begun a few years ago with that slipper and its brother on Sharon's feet. Yes, I remembered that fondly. But it wasn't a can of film. I put the slipper back where I'd found it and closed the door.

About four feet farther into the closet was another section with a door. I crawled toward it, scraping my knees on the carpet, and resumed my position, face inches from the floor, and felt for the door handle.

"Okay, I give up. What the heck are you doing?"

I'm crazy about hearing Sharon's voice, but it wasn't what I was hoping for at that moment. I spun, as well as a man can spin on his bare knees, and faced her. She had her hair in the traditional female towel-turban, but that was all she was wearing.

"You're naked," she said.

"So are you."

"I was coming in here to get my clothes. What's your excuse?" She walked into the closet and I stood up, somewhat painfully. My knees weren't made for friction, no matter how plush the carpet.

"Ah, I was . . . See . . ." S. J. Perelman would have been proud of the razor-sharp wit, no?

"Elliot," my nude ex-wife said, "I don't understand why you're naked in my closet. And the weird part is, it's more the 'in my closet' part than the 'naked' part that's confusing."

There was no point in concocting a story. "I was looking for Anthony's film," I said.

"And you thought the most logical place to find it would have been in my underwear drawer?"

"Well, I didn't *know* it was your underwear drawer, did I?" There's a sentence you don't get to say often.

"Wait a minute — you were looking for Anthony's movie in my closet? You think *I* stole it?" The expression on her face was exactly the one she'd had at our divorce settlement — disappointed, sad, and angry all at once.

"I don't think you stole it, but other people might," I answered, feeling only slightly hypocritical. "I was trying to prove that you hadn't."

Sharon walked past me to what I now knew was her underwear drawer, and started pulling out various garments. This morning wasn't shaping up the way I'd hoped. "That's so gallant of you, Elliot, accusing me of the crime and then trying to exonerate me all by yourself. Would it be prying to

318

ask why in the name of Wolfgang Amadeus Mozart I would steal Anthony's film?"

"Um . . . because you wanted him to stay in school," I mumbled. I was starting to wish my underwear were in here as well.

Sharon was almost completely dressed now. "I think maybe you'd better go," she said. "Put some clothes on." And she walked out of the closet.

Nope, not the way I'd hoped for at all.

33

If waking up alone in a strange house was
weird, trust me, it had nothing on getting
dressed alone in a strange house and beating it out the door as quickly as is humanly
possible. Sharon was nowhere to be seen,
and I wanted to be gone before she re-
appeared. I had too many thoughts running
through my head — all bad — at the same
time, and the loudest one was screaming,
"Speed!" So I found my clothes, put them
on, and tried as meticulously as possible to
eliminate all traces that I'd ever been there
at all. I even started the dishwasher before I
left.

The twenty minutes it took me to get to
Comedy Tonight was enough to allow some
of the other competing voices in my mind
to sort themselves out and speak freely.

"You're an idiot," one said. "You were
finally back with the one woman you've ever
really loved, and you threw it away over a

suspicion you never seriously believed, anyway."

"You didn't see that smile on her face in the projection booth," I defended myself.

"Of course I did," it countered. "I'm a voice in your head." Touché.

"What about Anthony's movie?" another one piped up. "If Sharon didn't take it, who did?"

"Carla?" the first voice ventured. "She's the one who *really* doesn't want to see Anthony leave New Jersey for Hollywood."

I was much too tired for a bout of schizophrenia this morning. "Can we leave that to Dutton, finally?" I tried. "We've done everything we can do." The voices didn't answer back, but I got the impression they were giving me a disapproving look.

A third chimed in, "You're nowhere on the Vivian Reynolds and Harry Lillis murders, you know," but I ignored it. I hate negative head-voices.

It went on like that the whole way. The debate going on between my ears could have filled an hour of time on a cable news talk show, if I could have increased the volume to dangerous levels. You can't purposely change the volume in your head. Seriously, try it. Can't be done.

By the time I reached the theatre, I was

thoroughly discouraged about pretty much everything from international relations to the price of dog food, and I don't even have a dog. When I get going on being discouraged, I'm a pro.

I dragged myself into Comedy Tonight a good eight hours before I needed to be there, dropped myself into my office chair, ignored the lingering sting in my butt, and wondered what the hell I should do with the rest of my short stay on this planet. I had certainly destroyed any chance I had of spending my life with Sharon, even if she did get over this latest outrage. I figured she would eventually, but then I'd just come up with another and another down the line until finally she saw the colossal error in her ways and broke off all contact with me entirely.

The three oversized children with whom I spent my working hours would eventually grow up and leave the nest, to be replaced by others (Rutgers University and Midland Heights High School will have an endless supply of cheap labor for the foreseeable future) who would also ingratiate themselves to me and then take off to start their actual lives, while leaving mine in a perpetual neutral gear.

The shining achievement of my professional life had been writing a novel that was pretty good but took enough out of me emotionally to be my only effort in that area. And it had been turned into a truly lousy film that had made everyone forget there was a book to begin with. Now I played dusty old movies to an indifferent audience — a small one, at that — and took a solid financial loss every night I stayed open.

The sad fact was, I'd never been happier than the night I'd introduced Harry Lillis and Les Townes in front of a packed house at Comedy Tonight. But that memory was now, let's be fair, just a little tainted, as it seemed to have triggered a set of events that ended with Townes murdering Lillis and then disappearing into the night. Talk about your downers.

I had begun to make friends with one of my honest-to-goodness heroes in this life, and had ended up helping to hasten his death. That wasn't going to be a real strong line on my interpersonal resume.

I couldn't even find Anthony's movie, and hadn't told him where it was when I actually knew. Nice guy I was.

What had begun as a minor case of self-pity was growing into a full-blown inner tantrum. Sadness was being overrun by anger. Was I going to just let the circumstances of my life roll over me? Was I that defeated, at the relatively tender age of thirty-seven?

Yeah, pretty much.

But I didn't have to take it lying down. I could fight back at the karma that had brought me to this rotten Tuesday morning. I could choose one of the things that was tormenting me and attack it frontally, just to prove I could do it. It was just a question of summoning the determination, persevering when the inevitable hardships arose, and not even considering the possibility of failure.

I decided, after three cups of heavily caffeinated coffee from the Dunkin' Donuts down the street (in New Jersey, there's a Dunkin' Donuts down *every* street), to avenge my friend Harry Lillis. Not the comedian; not the legend. My friend. Because somebody had done something unspeakably bad to a man I cared about, and it was time to get the word out that you didn't do that on Elliot Freed's watch.

I'd solve Harry Lillis's murder, prove Les Townes had killed him and Vivian Reynolds, and see justice done. And if that's not a bold plan for a Tuesday morning, I've never heard one.

The way to prove my suspicions was to illustrate the parallels between the murder of Harry Lillis and the death of Vivian Reynolds in 1958. It was way too large a coincidence that they had died under almost identical circumstances, and that Townes could not account for his whereabouts either time (to be fair, no one knew if Townes could account for his whereabouts the night Lillis died, because no one knew where Townes was now). So I started calling the few remaining names that Sergeant Newman had given me of ex-studio employees who might still be alive.

It took a great deal of the morning. Who am I kidding — it took the whole morning, and part of the early afternoon, and I spoke to a number of people. Some of the numbers were either disconnected or had been passed to new Verizon customers who had no idea what the hell I was talking about. Other numbers led to people who were still alive, but hadn't had any direct contact with either Lillis or Townes on the day of the fire, or didn't remember. I heard the sentence "It was fifty years ago" at least fifty times. But, eventually, I reached Estelle Mason, who had worked in the commissary at the studio while most of the Lillis/Townes films were being made. She lived in, of all places, Edison, New Jersey, not fifteen minutes from the uncomfortable chair in which I was sitting. But I didn't ask to see her face-to-face; I wanted my answers immediately. Mrs. Mason was kind enough to indulge me.

"I remember that day all too well," she said. "I knew poor Viv; I'd worked with them on *Cracked Ice* and a few of the others." I suppressed the urge to ask about behind-the-scenes details of the Lillis and Townes films and managed to stay on subject. I asked Mrs. Mason why Townes hadn't shown up for shooting that afternoon.

She sounded as if I must truly be demented. "But he did," she said. "I was in the room when Les heard the news of the fire. He looked like someone had drained the blood out of his body, he was so white. All he wanted to know was 'What about Viv? Is Viv okay?' He left that minute to get to the house."

What? Now Townes *was* at the studio after three in the afternoon? "But I saw a studio sign-out sheet that had him leaving long before the fire began," I said.

"I don't know anything about a sign-out sheet," Mrs. Mason said with a firm tone. "I know Les was there waiting for the scene to be lit. We were playing cards in the commissary for hours."

When I got off the phone with Mrs. Mason, I was stunned, but not entirely convinced. The story contradicted everything Marion Borello had told me; it didn't seem possible Mrs. Mason was right. So I called one of the "secondary" names on Newman's list, an arson cop who had not been on the force at the time of the fire (he was twenty years too young), but who, Newman said, had made a "hobby" of old Hollywood fire cases and would know this one as well.

I reached Martin Donnelly at his home in Mentor, Ohio, and he immediately owned up to being a former Los Angeles police lieutenant, now retired. It was amazing how many people left L.A. as soon as they could. Considering the number of people who are attracted to the place with celluloid fantasies (now being rapidly replaced with computer-generated digital fantasies), I guess things evened out.

"I won't waste your time, Mr. Freed," Donnelly said. "I spent six years looking over every report, every piece of evidence, every newspaper account. I've even looked at the Internet stuff. I can tell you one thing: nobody set that fire. It began as an electrical fire in the kitchen wall. What was criminal was the way that house was constructed, but you can't blame anyone at the time for that; it was thirty years old *then*."

"There weren't any traces of kerosene, chemical fertilizer, no igniters on the scene?" I asked.

"Nothing. And they went over that place with a fine-tooth comb, I'm telling you. The Reynolds woman must have fallen asleep upstairs and by the time she woke up, it was too late to get out. No good escape route in that house, and she didn't have a ladder to get down from the second story. No, she was trapped, no question. It's even possible she died of carbon monoxide poisoning, and never woke up at all."

"Was her neck broken?"

"Her neck? Hell, no. The skeleton, after it was removed, was determined to be in perfect condition. No breaks. Why, do you have evidence her neck was broken?" Donnelly sounded amazed.

"I guess not," I said, and thanked him for his time.

For a long time, I sat there and stared. It was starting to look like Vivian Reynolds hadn't been murdered after all.

34

Estelle Mason's firm insistence about Les Townes's presence on the soundstage when Vivian Reynolds died took a good deal of wind out of my sails, and there hadn't been much more than a light breeze to begin with. If Townes had been at the studio, then he couldn't have set the fire, nor could he have been seen taking his possessions out of the house before it began. Les Townes couldn't have killed his wife.

And I couldn't hang this one on Wilson Townes, either, as he'd been less than a year old at the time, and probably incapable of standing up, let alone strangling his mother and setting the house on fire before he managed to get out, put on adult clothing, and start hauling mementos out of the house. If his present-day physique were any indication, even at that age, Wilson might have been big enough, but not mature enough to do all that. I was only marginally sure he was mature enough now.

Besides, Donnelly's information, which sounded awfully official and comprehensive, made it seem pretty clear that no one had murdered Vivian Reynolds — she'd just been a sad, unfortunate victim of bad luck. The smokescreen (no pun intended) by the studio, if there had really been one, was probably just a hysterical response, an attempt to keep two bankable stars bankable.

Sophie walked by the office door, shoulders slumped, head down. If she'd been followed by an enormous cloud of dust, she could have been Pigpen from an old Peanuts cartoon. I decided against trying to wrest the source of her angst out of her, assuming it had something to do with her oppression by the Male Establishment, of which I was the most convenient symbol. I had enough women angry at me today.

That meant I couldn't call Sharon; there'd be no point. And I couldn't call Dad, because he'd ask me about Sharon and I'm incapable of lying to him successfully. So I called Chief Barry Dutton, because at least I could be cynical with him. Besides, I figured he'd probably be out of his office.

As with most other things that day, I was wrong. Dutton answered his phone, and I started with, "By the way, nice job on the missing film. Yup, you sure cleared that one up."

"I'm sorry; are you trying to get sixty-two speeding tickets attached to your record?" Dutton asked.

"I don't own a car."

"What's your point?"

"Chief, what are we going to do about Anthony's movie? We knew where it was, and then . . ."

"And then the person who hid it there decided to move it on us. Or more specifically, on *you*. The security in your theatre is atrocious, isn't it?" Dutton was getting back what I'd taken from his dignity.

"I can't imagine how someone got up there without a key, twice," I said. "And I'm sorry I made a wiseass remark."

"You can't help it; it's deeply ingrained in your personality," Dutton answered. "But you need to think about when you left the key unattended, or put back into play the possibility that Anthony is doing this to himself."

"That doesn't make any sense," I told him, dismissing the notion. "Anthony wouldn't do that in a million years. He's too protective of that film, and besides, what evidence is there that he even has any insurance on the movie? My guess is that he's being blackmailed, but that leads us right back to the idea that somebody has been in and out of my projection booth on a regular basis, and I don't know how that could happen, either. There are only two keys, and Anthony never lets go of his."

"Could one of his roommates have gotten hold of it?"

"I spoke to Danton, and he doesn't have a motive," I said. "I've never met the others. But they'd have to work pretty hard to swipe Anthony's key to the projection booth, steal the movie, put the key back so that he wouldn't miss it, and then do all that *again* a second time."

"Couldn't they just get the key copied while he was sleeping?"

"I guess it's possible," I said, "but that would mean that Anthony sleeps at night. I usually don't send him home until after midnight, and I'm pretty sure he just stays up watching movies or playing video games until dawn. I think he only ever actually sleeps in class."

"I see your point. Well, that leads us to your key," Dutton said. "Do you always have it on your person?"

"Nah. It ruins the line of my jeans."

"So did that pillow you had stuffed down the back of your pants the other day, and that didn't seem to worry you. Where do you keep the projection booth key?" Dutton asked.

I figured there was no harm in telling the town's top cop. "I have it on a hook in my office," I said. "It's not marked, and I lock the office when I'm not using it."

"Always?"

"What do you mean, 'always'?" I asked.

"If you get up to go to the bathroom or something, do you always lock the office door?"

I had to admit I didn't, but added, "It's unmarked, and you really have to know where to look to find it."

"Who would know?" Dutton said. "Consider everybody."

"Me," I answered, more to myself than to him. "Anthony, but he already has a key. I guess Sophie, although she has no interest in knowing anything about the theatre that doesn't take place at the snack bar." I hesitated.

"What?" Dutton asked, hearing my reluctance.

"I don't want to say it, but Sharon knows where I keep the key," I said.

"Don't be an idiot. Your ex-wife didn't steal the film," Dutton said. "She has no motive, and she's too smart."

"You couldn't have told me that yesterday?"

"What about Jonathan?" asked Dutton. "Does he know where you keep the key?"

"He really hasn't been around the theatre that long, but he might," I told him. "Jonathan thinks the projection booth is where the Great Oz lives. But remember, he wasn't working here back then."

"Right," Dutton agreed. "Besides, he doesn't an obvious motive. Unless — could he be blackmailing Anthony?"

"Jonathan blackmailing Anthony?" It was too bizarre a concept. "Jonathan isn't awake enough to blackmail somebody."

"You thought he was in cahoots with Les Townes to threaten you. He was awake enough for that."

"At best, I think he could be tricked into it," I said. "And by the way, 'cahoots'? What kind of cop are you?"

"You should know by now."

"I withdraw the question. What about Carla?"

"Carla Singelese?" Dutton asked. "We questioned her, and she couldn't really come up with an alibi for when the film was taken, but then, we don't actually know when the film was taken, do we?"

"So what do you think I should do?" I

asked him.

"Start locking your door when you leave the office," Dutton said. "Hang on, I have a call on another line. I'll be right back." And there was a click on the line.

I looked around my office, and specifically at the key on the wall (try not looking at something you've discussed at length when it's in the room), as Anthony skulked by, rethought his disposition, walked back into my doorway, and nodded at me. I gestured him in, as I was on hold.

"What's up?" I asked.

"Didn't you wear those clothes yesterday?" he asked.

I ignored that. "What did you want, Anthony?"

"I forgive you," he said.

"You forgive me."

"Yes."

"For what?"

"For stealing my film," Anthony said.

I did a Moe Howard burn and said, "I *didn't* . . ." There was a click on the line, and Dutton's voice came back on. Anthony turned and left the office, having said his piece.

"That was the Englewood Police," Dutton told me. "Detective Honig."

"What's up with good old Benjamin?" I asked.

"They're sending you something," Dutton said. "He wanted me to know before you got it." His voice sounded odd, a little confused.

"What?" I asked him. "What are they sending me?"

"I'm not sure. Honig said they found it in Harry Lillis's room, and it was clear Lillis wanted you to have it."

It took me a moment to realize he wasn't referring to Lillis's guitar, which I already had at the town house. This was something the cops *had* found in Lillis's room! And he wanted me to have it? What the hell did that mean?

"What the hell does that mean?" I asked Dutton.

"I have no idea," he said. "But you'll have it later tonight. They're sending someone down."

That was odd, but neither Dutton nor I could explain it, so all there was to do was wait until the Englewood cop showed up with my inheritance. I said good-bye and had barely hung up the phone when Sophie appeared in the doorway.

"What's going on?" I asked.

"We're low on Goobers," she said. "Were

336

you wearing those clothes yesterday?"

That was it; I stood up and reached for my jacket and the bicycle's front wheel. "No," I said. "I'll be back in an hour."

"Where are you going?"

"Home," I told Sophie. "To change."

She didn't even look amused when I squeezed by her on my way to the front door. I made sure to lock the office door on the way out.

It occurred to me just as I got out into the cool early autumn air that I'd gotten progressively more confused every day since the screening of *Killin' Time*. Everything that had happened since then had, instead of clarifying matters, made them murkier. I was at a point where I was starting to *expect* things to be more baffling as they developed.

Now the Englewood Police Department was sending me a mystery memento from Harry Lillis. I had been elated to own the great comedian's guitar, but that was different: this was something he'd apparently left instructions should be given to me. Given my current mood, I was sure it would just mystify me to the verge of exasperation.

I turned the corner and walked into the alley next to Comedy Tonight. Shaking my head at the glass-half-empty thoughts in my head, I tried to look at whatever bright side

337

was available: Maybe the package Honig was sending would actually help. Maybe it was a lost Lillis and Townes artifact, like the missing seven minutes of *Bargain Basement* that had been cut by the Hayes Office and were rumored to have been shown on British television in the 1970s. Yeah, I was sure it would be something like that. Maybe things were taking an upturn.

And then I noticed that my bicycle seemed to be standing at an odd angle, chained as always to the water pipe next to the brick wall of the theatre. In the twilight, it seemed to be turned almost backward. I picked up the pace and moved closer.

The bike was bent, twisted at its frame, into a grotesque pretzel of aluminum alloy. It seemed as if every tube, every handlebar, every rod, was pulled into an impossible position. And in some places, the metal was perforated with small holes in a pattern that also seemed to have penetrated the brick in the wall behind the bicycle.

Someone had shot at the bike with a shotgun. Like the one Wilson Townes had shot at me with.

35

"You know, pretty much all the crime in Midland Heights happens right here at your theatre," said Chief Barry Dutton. "I'm thinking of opening up a branch headquarters in your lobby to cut down on our response time."

We stood in the alley, with the lights from Dutton's car illuminating what was left of my bicycle. The twisted mass of metal didn't look any better with repeated viewings. I felt like someone was using my stomach for an accordion. Tears were not entirely out of the question.

"It had to be Wilson Townes," I said with great hoarseness. "You should issue an arrest warrant for Wilson Townes."

Dutton looked back at me, surprised by the depth of my hurt. "With all the arrest warrants issued for Les and Wilson Townes, I don't think one more is going to make a huge difference." He studied the look on my face, and nodded. "But I'll put out one for questioning," he added.

"He just came by and shot it and twisted it and . . ." I babbled. "It was just sitting here by itself." I had to stop talking.

Dutton decided to distract me. "That fingerprint came back, the one that I took off the film can in the projection booth. It was yours."

But I wasn't being taken in. "You just don't understand," I said to Dutton. "That bike . . ."

"Let's go inside," Dutton said. "The officers will take care of it." He motioned to Patel and his partner, who were standing on the sidewalk looking slightly amused. I wanted to throttle them. They walked over as Dutton gently led me back toward the front door. "Give me the key, Elliot," he said.

The key? "It's hanging up in my office, Chief," I told him. "We discussed it."

"The key to the bicycle lock," he said. Oh. Yeah. I handed it to him, and Dutton gave the key to Patel. I didn't want to watch. Dutton and I walked inside. We walked through the lobby and sat on the stairs to the balcony.

I leaned forward and put my head in my hands. "This is too much," I said. "You can shoot at me if you want to. You can send me a fake bomb. Hell, you can send me a *real* bomb. But you don't go after my only mode of transportation. I've had that bike for fourteen years."

Dutton actually reached over and put his hand on my shoulder. "I'm sorry for your loss," he said, and I don't think he was being ironic.

I looked up at him, partially because I wanted him to see that I wasn't crying. "What can we do?" I asked. "There has to be something we can do."

"The NYPD and the Englewood Police — not to mention the New Jersey State Police — all have warrants out for the Towneses. We'll add our own. Sooner or later someone's going to spot them. If Wilson was in your alley today, he can't be too far from here." Dutton didn't make eye contact, because he knew I wouldn't think that was enough. "We'll find them."

"No, you won't." Dutton stared at me, but I went on. "No offense, Chief. But they've been looking for Les and Wilson since Harry Lillis died — days ago. I don't think the bicycle thing is going to fire up the state troopers that much."

Dutton stood up, and I had to crane my neck to look at his face. The man is tall.

"Elliot. I know it seems bad now, but we're searching for an eighty-year-old man and his fifty-one-year-old son. We know what kind of car they were driving, and the license plate number. Even if they've switched cars, they're not going to be hard to spot. Les Townes is a famous man. People will notice."

I shook my head. "Nobody remembers Les Townes," I said. "People like him and Lillis are anonymous in these days of Paris Hilton and Brad Pitt. They live in crowded neighborhoods in Queens and at nursing homes in northern New Jersey, and even their biggest fans like me don't know it. I could have met Lillis years ago, could have asked Les Townes to appear at the opening of Comedy Tonight last year, but I never even thought to look for them. If someone like me, who has memorized every frame of film they ever shot, doesn't know enough to drive forty-five minutes to see them in person, why would anyone else recognize them in the street?"

"I promise you, we'll get them," Dutton said. "I'll see to it. I will personally arrest Les and Wilson Townes for what they did to your bicycle."

I stood up. I still couldn't go eye-to-eye with Dutton, but I could get closer. "Don't patronize me, Chief. I'm upset because this has come home to me, but the bigger issue is that Harry Lillis is dead, and those two are probably the ones responsible. Yeah, I'm mad about the bike, but let's not trivialize what's happened. I just want you to promise me one thing."

"What's that?" Dutton looked worried.

"I want you to swear to me that you'll share what you've heard from the other cops, and that I can be a part of bringing those two to justice. Tell me I can do that."

"Elliot, I can't even swear to you that *I'll* be involved," Dutton said. "If some cop in Albany spots the car, or even if Honig in Englewood gets a lead, they're not necessarily going to share it with me. The only way I have any jurisdiction at all is if the Towneses are caught right here in Midland Heights."

I don't know where the words came from, but I said them. "Suppose I can arrange that," I said.

Dutton clearly thought the bicycle trauma was hitting me too hard now. "How are you going to do that?" he asked.

I never got the chance to answer — which was lucky, since I had no idea what I was talking about — because Officer Broeker of the Englewood Police Department came striding purposefully into Comedy Tonight. He noticed Dutton immediately (it couldn't be helped; the man is essentially the Washington Monument in pants) and strode purposefully again, directly toward us in the straightest line imaginable. Broeker had to be an ex-Marine.

Under one arm was a small cardboard mailer, the kind that online services use for audio CDs and DVDs. Broeker stood straight as a totem pole between Dutton and me, and faced me directly. I was relatively sure he hadn't blinked since entering the theatre.

"Have you been drinking, Broeker?" I asked. "You seemed a little wobbly on the way in." Dutton gave me a disapproving look.

"Negative," Broeker said. "I don't drink."

"My mistake."

He reached under his arm and pulled out the mailer. "Detective Lieutenant Honig requested that I give this to you," Broeker said. "It was obvious that Mr. Lillis intended you to have it." He held out the mailer in a hand that miraculously was ungloved, and I took it.

"What is it?" I asked.

Broeker was silent, which apparently was his best thing.

The mailer was sealed, Honig being a stickler for protocol, so I broke open the seal and reached inside. Dutton craned his neck over my shoulder to see. Broeker stared straight ahead, no doubt waiting for General Patton to give him the attack order.

Inside the mailer was a small videotape cassette.

"What the heck is this all about?" I said, not to anyone in particular.

"It's a videotape," Dutton said. "Maybe it's famous outtakes or something from Lillis and Townes movies."

I looked at Broeker, who didn't move a muscle, and I shook my head. "I don't think so," I told Dutton. "This is a digital tape, one that would probably have come from a camcorder. This is a home recording, and a relatively recent one." I turned to Broeker. "And you've already seen it, haven't you?"

"Affirmative," Broeker said. How his eyes could stay open all that time without drying out was a mystery. "What you have there is a copy. Detective Lieutenant Honig retained the original."

"What's on the tape, Broeker?" I asked.

Broeker blinked.

"I don't think you're going to enjoy it very much," he said.

36

Harry Lillis looked me directly in the eye and said, "You see, Elliot? I told you I had a plan, and this is it."

Lillis stared out at me from the screen of a monitor we keep in the projection booth that hooked up to a camcorder Anthony provided from his car. As a film student, Anthony has access to every piece of technology short of nuclear launch codes. Probably.

Anthony, Dutton, Broeker, and I were gathered around the console, watching the fifteen-inch monitor. I didn't hear anyone in the room so much as breathe.

"I'm going to go through the rehearsal for the show, and get Les to repeat his threat to kill me," Lillis continued, placing the camera on something high (I was relatively sure it was the bureau in his room) from which it could take in the view from the top of the window to the top of the bed. The light on the dresser, next to the window and in the camera's view, was on, but there was no light near the camera, so the lower half of the room was in shadow. "See? I told you I can stand, but walking is still a problem." He sat back down in the wheelchair in a white dress shirt and dark slacks, exhaled broadly, and looked up at the camera.

"Once he says he's going to kill me again, it'll be on tape, and we can have him arrested," Lillis said to the camera. "I'll see if I can get him to confess to killing Viv, too. But right now, I'm going to use this remote control to turn the camera off until Les gets here. See you soon, Elliot."

"You see," Broeker said to me. "The frequent references to you. That's why Detective Lieutenant Honig thought Mr. Lillis wanted you to have the tape."

"Maybe he knew someone else named Elliot," I said, but Broeker shook his head, and I knew it was nonsense, too. I just didn't want to see what was coming.

The image on the screen flickered again, and suddenly, Les Townes was standing next to Lillis and his wheelchair. He took off a nylon jacket he was wearing and threw it onto Lillis's bed. Townes wasn't facing Lillis, and didn't see him put down the remote control next to his left leg on the wheelchair.

"After all these years, Harry, a Saturday night show for a bunch of old people? Why is this so important to you?" Townes asked his partner.

"It's these uppity snobs from *the theatah*," Lillis replied. "Always going on about the thrill of a live performance and how us film hacks don't know anything about *real* acting. I had to show them what we were really all about. You have no idea what it's like to live here, Les. For a burlesque clown like me, there's just nobody to talk to."

Townes sat down on the desk chair. "Okay, you got me here," he said. "What's your plan?"

"The barber bit," Lillis said. "I can do it sitting down, and it won't be any different than the way we used to do it."

"This doesn't make any sense," I told Dutton. "Lillis is explaining what sketch he wants to do, and he told me Townes had threatened him with the razor the last time they rehearsed. Why doesn't Townes know that already?" Dutton shook his head.

On the screen, Townes nodded. "Sounds easy enough. We did that bit so many times, I don't even know why we're rehearsing."

"So let's get started," Lillis replied.

Townes found a leather vest hanging on

348

the doorknob, and put it on over his white shirt.

Lillis rolled his chair to the center of the room — directly in the line of the camera, I noticed — as Townes came over. Lillis pointed at a little table he'd set up behind himself, and to the right (down camera).

"There's the props," Harry said.

Townes gave a careful look at the objects on the table. "That's a real razor," he said. "Since when do we use a real razor?"

"This is the exact conversation Harry said they'd had at the first rehearsal," I told Broeker and Dutton.

"Maybe Mr. Townes has a faulty memory," Anthony said. "Alzheimer's, or something." We turned our attention back to the screen.

"You think I could get a prop razor here in the old folks home?" Lillis asked his partner. "Just don't slit my throat and everybody will be happy."

Behind Lillis's back, Townes made a face at him, puffing up his cheeks and crossing his eyes. I laughed in spite of myself; he'd made that face at Lillis in *Step This Way.*

"So what'll it be today, Mr. Hansracker?" Townes began, in character now and snipping at the air with his scissors.

"Just a trim and a shave," Lillis answered. "I'm getting married tomorrow, and I want

349

to look neat."

"You're getting married? Aren't you old to get married?" Townes then broke character and looked down at Lillis. "Funny what we used to think was old, isn't it?" he said.

Lillis frowned. "Don't stop in the middle. Keep going."

"Excuse me, Mr. DeMille." Townes composed himself, and resumed the scene. "Aren't you old to get married?" he repeated.

"You're only as old as the woman you feel," Lillis said.

"That's not the line. You're stealing from Groucho now." Townes looked annoyed.

"I'm not stealing. I made that up."

"You didn't. That's Groucho." Townes's eyebrows lowered.

"It's me."

"You know I hate when you do this, Harry," his partner warned.

"Do what? I'm spicing up the scene. The old line was tired." Lillis reached for the wheels on his chair to move, but they seemed stuck. "You just . . . you don't . . . goddamn this thing, I can't . . ."

"Don't turn around!" Townes ordered, fists clenching. "Finish the scene! You were so worried about putting on a show for the old people; let's get it right. Now, do the line the way we always did the line!"

"Jesus Christ, Les, you always had a stick up your ass. What's wrong with the new line?"

"Do the old line!"

Harry Lillis gathered himself, then looked up at his "barber" and said, "Old? I'm not old; I just worry."

But Townes couldn't let it go. "Even after all this time, Harry, you have to try to make it harder. I always felt like you were trying to get a rise out of me and not the audience. Why couldn't you just do the act?"

Lillis shook his head sadly. "I'm trying to just do the act now, Les. Do your next line."

"What's the point? You'll just do something to annoy me. You always did. I never understood it."

And Lillis sealed his fate. "Viv understood," he said in a low voice.

Les Townes's face morphed into something you'd be likely to see on a rampaging animal. His eyes widened, his nostrils flared, and his mouth became a tight line of frustration and pain. *"Leave Viv out of it!"* he hissed.

"She told me," Lillis continued, as if his partner hadn't spoken. "She said that you just learned the lines, but I was always listening onstage, even when the cameras

351

were rolling. She said you were like that in other circumstances, too. Just doing what you were supposed to do, while I was always looking for a better angle."

"Stop it!" Townes said, and reached for the handles of the wheelchair.

Lillis tried to turn at the same time, but the brakes were applied to the wheels, and he couldn't move. When Townes tried to move him and jostled the wheelchair hard in his fury, Harry Lillis tumbled forward and fell out of the chair. It wasn't possible to see the floor, but it appeared that Lillis landed headfirst.

"Harry, you son of a bitch!" Townes said, and rushed around the chair. There were mumbles from the floor, but the camera angle made Lillis invisible.

Townes, still looking crazed, disappeared from view, and appeared to be reaching for Lillis as he knelt down. The camera looked at what appeared to be an empty room, but it was possible to hear what sounded like very heated grunting. "Take it easy, Harry," Townes said. "This'll go easier if you take it easy."

And then there were some terrible gurgling sounds for a long period, followed by wheezing.

"This must have been when his neck was

broken," Broeker said.

None of us spoke after that for some time.

The next time there was movement on the screen, we all started just a little bit. Even Broeker, who had seen the tape before. Coming up from the floor, facing the window, Les Townes was breathing heavily. And he was dragging Lillis's lifeless body back into the wheelchair.

"Come on, Harry," he said when the body was slumped in the chair. "Let's go out to the gazebo for a little air."

And he pushed the chair out of the picture. The sound of the door opening and closing was all that was left, while the same still view of the room, now silent, occupied the screen.

Broeker looked over at Anthony. "It stays that way for the rest of the tape," he said. "Another forty-three minutes. After a while, you hear fire alarms."

Anthony nodded, and turned off the camcorder. He started to rewind the tape.

None of us made eye contact with each other for a long moment. The whirring of the rewinding videocassette was the only sound in the room. Finally, Dutton coughed, and we all looked at him.

"I guess that makes it pretty clear what happened," he said.

"Yeah," I said. I looked at Broeker. "Do you need the tape back?" I asked.

He shook his head. "No. That one's yours to do with as you please."

"I doubt it'll make my collection of favorites," I told him.

Broeker's face showed no emotion at all, but he said, "I'm sorry I had to show it to you." Then he spun on his heel and left the projection booth.

"Yeah," I said. "Me, too."

37

Wednesday

"It was horrible," I said. "Just the callous disregard for another human being. I'm still shaken up."

Bobo Kaminsky looked at me over half-glasses that normally hung from his neck on a chain. "So somebody beat up your bicycle," he said. "Geez, Elliot, did they steal your lunch money, too?"

We stood in what Bobo likes to call his "showroom," a dingy storefront that houses every possible type of bike imaginable, from racing models to dirt bikes to things that young parents put their kids into so the toddlers (and infants) can experience urban biking close-up, sucking in exhaust fumes from passing buses in the name of an "outdoor experience." Maybe it's me.

"I just feel so violated," I said.

"Suck it up," Bobo scolded me. "I'm a bike salesman, not Dr. Phil. Now, I can show you something that'll take your mind right off that old hunk of tin." Bobo is under the impression that I have millions stored away from the sale of my novel to Hollywood and am just being obstinate in not sharing the wealth, mostly with him. He doesn't seem to have noticed that I spent a large percentage of the movie money (which wasn't anywhere near millions) buying a white elephant of a movie theatre and bringing joy to a large . . . a group of people every night.

"I'm not spending thousands of dollars on a new bike," I told him. "I want to know if you can fix the old one."

He looked as if I'd asked him to build the Empire State Building out of mashed potatoes. "Are you out of your mind?" he asked delicately. "From what you've told me, your old bike looks like a Jackson Pollock painting done in metal and rubber. What's left to restore?"

"Well, if you're not up to the challenge . . ."

Bobo let the glasses drop from his face and dangle around his massive chest. "Who do you think you're talking to?" he asked. "Does a lame negotiating tactic like that really work with other people?"

"Some."

"I mean the ones with cognitive function," he said.

"No need to get snippy. If you can't do it, you can't do it. I'll see if I can find somebody who can."

He raised an eyebrow. "I didn't say I *can't* do it. I said it was *stupid* to do it when you could buy something much better and brand new for the same money."

"Okay," I said, and headed for the door. "See ya, Bobo."

Bobo sighed. "Where is the Wreck of the Hesperus now?" he asked.

"At police headquarters. I can get it to you this evening," I told him.

"I'll see what I can do, but I make no promises. It'll take two weeks."

"Two weeks! That's my only mode of transportation!" I said.

"I could sell you something right now and you could ride it home tonight," Bobo countered.

"How about a loaner?"

Bobo twisted up one side of his face. "A loaner? What am I, your tristate Lexus dealer?"

"You're getting my business," I said. "You get my business on a regular basis. Let me borrow one of your bikes. Who knows; maybe I'll love it so much I'll want to buy

357

it, just like you're always telling me."

"Yeah, and if you don't, I'm stuck with a bike I can't sell as new. No way, Elliot. Take cabs."

I gave him my best pathetic face, and Bobo remained unmoved. "You're losing my business, Bobo," I told him.

"Fine. Go to one of the big-box stores and see if *they'll* try to fix your bike for you." He was good.

"I just hope I'm still here to pay you after walking home late at night over the Albany Street Bridge for two weeks," I told him.

"You're breaking my heart."

"What with being depressed and all over my sense of violation, and the trauma I've been through . . ."

"Oh, for Pete's sake," he said, or words to that effect. "I'll give you a loaner."

"You're a prince, Bobo."

"Yeah. Prince Sucker."

I signed the papers to get the remains of my bicycle away from the Midland Heights Police Department, and was given assurances that it would be brought to Midland Cyclery by an officer as soon as possible. On the way out, I knocked on Chief Dutton's door, and he yelled, "Come," so I went in.

"Don't you have a show tonight?" he asked.

"I've been finding lately that I'm not really necessary at every showing," I told him. "Sophie and Anthony are running the place tonight. It's Jonathan's night off."

Dutton gestured at the chair in front of his desk. "Sit," he said.

I did. "That was something," I said. We both knew to what I was referring.

Dutton nodded. "Uh-huh," he said.

"You've seen worse?"

"Once or twice," he acknowledged. "But that doesn't make this any easier. It does make for quite a case against Les Townes, though. I'm sorry for you."

That surprised me some. "For me?"

"Yeah. How are you going to watch those movies again with that image in your mind?"

"I haven't really thought about that yet," I lied. "I'm trying to take it one step at a time, but I don't know what the next step is. How are they going to find Les and Wilson?"

"Well, let me ask you this: What do you think was the point of the attack on your bicycle? Why do that, if they're trying to stay under the radar?" Dutton wasn't asking as if he already knew the answer; he sat back and laced his fingers behind his head, thinking.

"To scare me off. To get me to stop asking questions. The same day I started calling people about Vivian Reynolds again, this happens to my bike. I think that's pretty clear."

Dutton closed his eyes. "Except that it doesn't add up," he said. "How would they know you'd made phone calls to studio employees from decades ago? And why worry about you, when two states and I don't know how many police departments are looking for them?"

I hated it when he made sense. "So what are you saying?" I asked. "That they're trying to get caught? They're interested in making a big enough splash that they become visible again? How does that make sense?"

Dutton opened his eyes, and shrugged. "Some criminals don't make sense," he said. "They don't have a set plan; they improvise as they go along."

I stood up. "I'm throwing in the towel," I said. "I'm no detective, and I'm tired of being a target. You let me know when they catch these two, and I'll be happy to go and spit in their faces in jail. Beyond that, I'm happy to let those of you who do this professionally take the lead. As my people say, *abi gesundt.*"

"What does that mean?" Dutton asked.

"I'm not sure. I think 'wear it in good health.' " I started for the door, and then it occurred to me. "Chief, what about Anthony's movie? We've got to find it for him."

"Two seconds ago you were retiring from police work, which would be a relief to everyone in uniform on the East Coast, and now it's 'we'? How does that work?" But Dutton's smile gave him away.

"Nobody's shooting at me or destroying my property over Anthony's movie," I said. "I think I can handle it."

"All right, let me give you a puzzle," Dutton offered. "The movie was there for the showing, and then it wasn't there. It was there when we looked in the storage space, and then it wasn't. Who was in the building on all those occasions? Those have to be your only suspects."

I went through the incidents in my mind. "You're right," I said. "I think I've got that one figured out."

38

It would take a day or two to organize the group I hoped to assemble in the Case of the Missing Bad Movie, so I concentrated on running my theatre for a change. I called Vic Testalone to give him my order for the next four weeks, but as usual, Vic refused to listen to my choices on the phone, and said he'd be at Comedy Tonight the day after tomorrow. Then I went into the lobby and put up one-sheets for the attractions that would begin on Friday, then went back into the office and called the candy distributor, reading from a list in Sophie's handwriting, which was revealingly girlish.

But getting the right group together also meant calling Sharon, and that was something I'd been putting off. We hadn't exactly left each other on a soaring note the morning before, but I didn't want to believe that was the last contact we'd have. I wasn't sure we were meant to cohabitate, but that wasn't the only option left to us, was it?

My stomach had the same tight feeling it had decades before when I'd call a girl from my geometry class to ask for a date. I hoped that my voice wouldn't crack when Sharon answered.

She must have read the caller ID, because it took a few rings while she decided whether she'd pick up the cell phone, and when she did, it was with a curt, "What is it?"

"Is that how far we've fallen?" I asked. " 'What is it?' "

"You slept with me and then accused me of a crime," Sharon said. "Were you expecting, 'Hi, honey'?"

"After all we've been through together, I was hoping for the benefit of the doubt," I said.

"So was I."

"You had it. I didn't accuse you of anything; I was trying my best to prove that you *didn't* do it."

I could hear the scowl. "You'll forgive me if I'm not overwhelmed by your gallantry," Sharon said. "Why are you calling?"

"I was hoping you could come by Comedy Tonight on Friday afternoon," I said.

"Why?"

This was the part I had been dreading

more than the rest, and I spoke too quickly. "Because I'm going to get Anthony's movie back, and I want you to be there."

There was a long pause. "What?"

"I think you heard."

You could light a match on her voice. "Are you inviting *all* the suspects?" Sharon asked.

"Yes."

"Well, how could I pass up an invitation like that?"

She hung up.

"I'll e-mail you with the details," I said to no one in particular.

Well, that had gone well. I stood up and tried to shake it off. I would have lifted some weights, if I'd owned any. And if I'd known anything about lifting weights. And if I ever intended to get into shape in any way other than riding my bicycle.

Somehow, lifting weights seemed to be the wrong response to my situation.

I could have worked off the tension on the new bike Bobo had loaned me. Unwilling to part with one of his top-of-the-line beauties on a temporary basis (and I didn't blame him, but I couldn't tell him that), he'd lent me a bicycle that had probably been sitting in his "showroom" for a couple of years. Still, it was quite a bit newer than mine, and I had to admit, it rode more smoothly.

But that wasn't the point. I'd already lost my Pikes Peak snow globe. There was a limit to my personal suffering, and the bike was beyond what I was willing to endure.

The phone rang, and I stared at it for a moment. Did I really want to talk to Sharon if she was as angry as I imagined? Who else would be calling in the early afternoon? The theatre wasn't scheduled to open for another five hours; even the staff was still in school, not due for some time. I decided to take my medicine, and picked up the receiver.

"Comedy Tonight," I said. "The Funniest Movie Theatre in New Jersey." I made that up on the spot. Impressive, huh?

"You're not gonna stop, are you?" It was a bad attempt to disguise the voice.

"Is that the best you can do, Wilson?" I asked. "You sound like you, trying not to sound like you."

"That's very funny. I guess this call is being traced."

"By whom? You think I have the FBI in my office? You've seen my office. *You* barely fit into it."

"So I'll be quick," he said, as if I hadn't spoken. The man stuck to the script, like his father. "You're going to stop asking questions, or you're going to end up looking like that bicycle outside your theatre."

"That was going too far, Wilson," I told him, my voice signing a boldness check that my stomach couldn't cash. "You crossed a line that you shouldn't have crossed."

"So have you." Did I hear a voice behind him, telling him what to say? It was hard to tell. "And you're gonna pay for it." Wilson hung up.

I immediately called Dutton, and although he wasn't there, a detective took the information and said he'd pass it on to the chief when he came back. He also said he'd get going on obtaining phone records for Comedy Tonight that might determine from where the call had come. But he didn't sound especially interested, particularly when I told him the call involved a mangled bicycle. I could have mentioned the murder, but from the tone of his voice, I didn't think even that would have lit a fire under this detective.

Don't ask me to explain it, but I just wasn't that threatened by Wilson's call. For one thing, I'd met Wilson, and although he was large and strong, he was also decidedly stupid, and that tends to lessen the level of fear in my mind even when I'm dealing with someone who could rip my arm off if he got mad. For another, I got the distinct impression that Les had been prompting him, which lent less menace to the threats. It's hard to think a guy is frothing at the mouth over the prospect of grinding you into a fine powder when his dad is behind him, telling him what to say.

When the kids came to work, I told them all to be ready for a special meeting at the theatre immediately after school hours on Friday, so they could make plans to come to work early. I told them I'd pay them overtime, and Sophie put her hand to her mouth and guffawed. "Overtime?" she asked. "Is that in our contract?" In addition to being a radical feminist, it was possible Sophie was planning to unionize the Comedy Tonight staff. I'd probably end up joining with them and striking against myself.

The shows that night went off in a routine fashion, and I spent much of the night in my office, paying bills and going over catalogues. But something about Wilson's phone call was nagging at the back of my mind, and I couldn't really identify it. When I realized I hadn't heard from Dutton, I called him again, and was told the chief had left for the night.

I rode home on Bobo's bicycle a little after midnight, and locked the screamingly green door of the town house behind me. I got into bed, knew I was tired, but couldn't for the life of me close my eyes. I thought about playing Lillis's guitar, but then remembered the town houses are connected, which was like having apartment neighbors, who probably wouldn't have appreciated the music at this hour of the morning. Besides, I didn't know how to play the guitar.

Finally, it was all bearing down on me. I got up and went into the living area. Anthony had converted the tape Broeker had delivered to a DVD, and I got it out of the messenger bag I carry on the bike every day.

I don't know why, but I had to see it again. I walked over and loaded it into the DVD player. Avoiding the "sofa," I sat on a director's chair that had been provided for me (with my name on it, like they cared about me) on the set of *Split Personality*. I picked up the remote and started to watch the disc.

After a few minutes, I felt tears rolling down my face. Harry Lillis was dead.

It was hard to fathom, but there it was on DVD in front of me: one of my comic idols was dead, and I was at least partially to blame, as surely as if I'd strangled him myself.

Lillis died, in fact, over and over on my

television in perfect digital clarity. It was enough to make me long for the days of rabbit ears and considerably fewer pixels per square inch.

For someone as given to self-blame as I am, this was a new level of hell. My mind raced until well after four in the morning, coming up with the hundreds of scenarios that would have prevented this from happening: if I hadn't sought Lillis out; if I hadn't used him to promote my theatre; if the advertising hadn't somehow reached all the way to Queens and found Les Townes.

Lillis had died because of meeting me, and I'd have to spend the rest of my life with that knowledge careening around in my head. I might as well turn myself in to the police as an accessory to murder. It's amazing what you can talk yourself into at four in the morning.

I never got to bed again that night. I just kept playing the DVD. It wasn't rational; there was a part of me that wanted to punish myself, and this was certainly the best way to do so. Maybe I just thought that one of the times I watched it, the ending would change.

And then, suddenly, it did.

39

Thursday

Moe Baxter was not happy about lending me a car, but that wasn't at all unusual. I couldn't call Sharon for a ride, clearly. Even if we'd been on good terms, she was at her practice and couldn't take half a day to chauffeur me to Englewood. It was too long a drive to ask Dad again, although he wouldn't complain. Besides, he had to take my mother to her dental appointment; Mom's terrified of the dentist.

Now, I was just driving up to deal with the death of one of our favorite comedians. It wasn't the most enticing thing I could imagine, but I didn't have a choice.

And I wasn't going to ask Sophie to put her Prius at risk again. Besides, she was at school. This is the social circle in which I travel.

Moe and I went through our usual cantankerous ritual, and I ended up with a 1999

Mazda 626 that had needed new brakes. Moe probably hoped that he hadn't done a very good job.

The car radio only seemed to get static, and there was a cassette deck instead of a CD player, so I was forced to deal with the owner's collection, which ran to easy listening. After a sleepless night, easy listening might have served as the equivalent of a faulty brake job, as I could have fallen asleep behind the wheel and ended up in a ditch just the same. Luckily, at the bottom of the pile in the center console was a copy of *Out of the Blue* by the Electric Light Orchestra. Slumming, sure, but it would keep me awake. And besides, who can resist "Sweet Talkin' Woman"?

To tell the truth, though, I didn't hear a lot of the music as I drove. There was too much to think about.

The hour or so passed in a swirl of what-ifs and what-does-this-means that left me feeling frustrated, even if I did have an idea percolating in the back of my head. There were too many loose ends and too many unanswered questions.

I needed to talk face-to-face with some of the personnel at the Booth Actors' Home, and had called Walter Lee ahead of time to make sure it would be all right. Walt did not betray any impatience in his voice, which I considered admirable. If I were in his position, I would have considered this Freed guy one of the chief pests in Western civilization. Which was one of the myriad reasons I wasn't in his position, and he was.

Pulling up to the entrance, I noticed that the burning smell had dissipated; the fire was no longer the first thing a person would think of when approaching the building. I walked through the Ed Herlihy Foyer and tried not to think of Velveeta commercials. I was not successful.

Before she could summon Walt, I asked the woman at the reception desk if she had noticed me wheeling Lillis out of the building the day I'd come to visit. It took her a moment, but she said she did. She also said her name was Linda, and I should use it.

"Had you seen Mr. Lillis walking around before that, Linda?" I asked.

She didn't have to think very long this time. "Yes," she said. "He was up and about quite a bit that day."

"Didn't you think it odd that he was using a wheelchair when you'd seen him walking perfectly well under his own steam before my visit?" I said.

Linda smiled vaguely. "Sure," she said. "But then, I remembered."

"Remembered what?"

"That he was Harry Lillis," Linda answered. "I figured it was part of a joke."

She called Walt, and he appeared almost immediately, the smile on his face no longer as pained as it had been the last time I'd seen him.

"What can I do for you, Mr. Freed?" he asked.

"Elliot. And I'm wondering. May I speak to the doctor who was treating Harry Lillis?"

"Of course, but don't expect her to disclose any confidential information. The doctor-patient relationship remains secure, even after the patient is deceased," Walt said.

Dr. Victoria Spencer was a healthy-looking woman who could have been any age from thirty-four to sixty. I'm very bad at gauging such things, and she obviously took good care of herself. She had a fine bedside manner, which I could discern from the way she kept smiling even as I asked her questions that might have provoked violence in someone less even-tempered.

"Was Mr. Lillis's hip injury so slight that it didn't affect his walking at all?" I asked her.

"His hip injury?" Dr. Spencer repeated. She read through the chart she had in her hands. "I don't see any note of a hip injury."

She glanced at Walt.

Oookaaay . . . "He told me he'd slipped in the common room and did some damage to his hip. That's why he needed the wheelchair," I said.

"I thought he asked for the wheelchair for some scene he was performing in drama therapy," Dr. Spencer said, again looking in Walter Lee's direction.

"That was my understanding," Walt said.

The pattern was starting to make sense, but I didn't want it to. "May I ask, Dr. Spencer: Why was Harry Lillis here? He said it was because he was having trouble 'getting around,' but I was never clear on what that meant."

Spencer exhaled heavily, and looked thoughtful for a long moment. "I really don't know if I'm comfortable saying," she said. "But since Mr. Lillis has passed away . . ." She gave Walt another glance, and he nodded very slightly. "The truth is, Mr. Freed, Harry Lillis had stomach cancer, and he probably would have been dead in six months even if this hadn't happened."

My head was reeling as Walter Lee led me to the front lobby on my way out, and then I remembered the last reason I'd decided to come to Englewood. "But Harry wasn't in the nursing home facility; he was on the as-

374

sisted living side," I said. "If he was that
ill . . ."

"Mr. Lillis didn't require constant care,"
Walt said. "There just wasn't much the doctors could do to help him."

"Walt," I said, "Harry Lillis didn't really
get along all that well with the other residents, did he?"

Walt wasn't going to admit any discord. "I
wouldn't say that, but he did keep to himself, for the most part, except when you
came to visit him. Marion Borello would
talk to him, but Mr. Lillis never sought her
out. He'd be very gregarious with the other
residents when you visited, and I think he
confused some of them. The rest of the
time, though, he'd spend mostly on the
computers."

"The computers?"

"Yes, we have desktop computers and Internet access in some of the common rooms,
and Mr. Lillis was very taken with them.
He spent a lot of hours in there. Seemed
especially interested in Photoshop. I thought
he was getting family photos e-mailed to
him, then I recalled that his file showed no
immediate family at all. But he loved the
computer. It's really a great blessing for
some of our residents, because they can
communicate with people who might not

be able to come visit."

Harry Lillis, webmaster. It was an interesting thought. "I've been feeling awful about something," I told Walt. "Ever since Harry died, I've meant to talk to Mitchell and tell him how badly I feel about it. He seemed so devoted to Harry; this must have hit him very hard. May I see him?"

Walt's eyes went up to his left as he mentally ran through rosters. "I don't remember another patient named Mitchell, Elliot," he said.

"Mitchell's not a patient. He works here."

Walter Lee gave me a blank stare.

"He's an orderly, or a nurse, or something," I tried. "Large African-American guy? Looks like he could lift a Mack truck? He drove Harry to Comedy Tonight the evening of the *Cracked Ice* showing. Mitchell."

"We have a driver who takes any of the residents out whenever they ask," Walt said. "They still like to go to the theatre and remain active. But his name is Ivan."

"No," I insisted, since clearly I knew more about Walt's staff than he did. "This guy was Mitchell. It said so on his white coat."

"I've been working here five years," Walter Lee said, "and I don't recall anyone named Mitchell on staff."

The really sad part was that I'd gotten pretty much every answer I'd expected.

I spent about twenty minutes on the phone in Walt's office, and by the time I reached Jersey City, I had pretty much concluded what I'd find out, but it was necessary to hear it firsthand. And when I found the brownstone and parked, checked the apartment number and rang the bell, I knew the interview I'd set up on the phone would be exactly as I'd expected.

"Actually, my name is Darius," said the man I knew as Mitchell the ambulance attendant. "Mr. Lillis hired me because I'd done some time working for a private medical transport company, but he wasn't looking for a driver; he wanted an actor."

The room was littered with 8×10 images of Darius/Mitchell, in black and white and in full color, with an agency's logo stamped tastefully over the top right corner. The requisite theatrical posters decorated the walls as Darius and I sat in facing armchairs. He offered me coffee, but I wasn't in the mood.

"How did he find you?" I asked.

"How did *you?*" Darius asked.

"It wasn't hard. Once I realized you weren't a real ambulance driver, I figured you must be an actor, and I called Actors' Equity. Gave the union the date and the place of your performance, and they hooked me up with your agent, who was very disappointed I wasn't a producer. Now, how did Harry Lillis get in touch with you?"

"He put an ad in *Daily Variety*," Darius said. "Very specific, had to be a big guy, had to be in the northern New Jersey area. I figured it was for a student film or something, and then I got the call from Harry Lillis. I'd never heard of him, but I looked him up on IMDb, you know." I probably winced at the idea of someone who'd never heard of Harry Lillis.

"Did he tell you what he wanted you to do? How did he explain it?"

Darius smiled. "Said he was playing a gag on a friend. Wanted him to think Harry needed a wheelchair. He'd already rented an ambulance, now he needed someone to drive it and push the chair."

"But the Booth Actors' Home has a driver named Ivan who'll take people wherever they want to go."

"Yeah, I know," Darius answered. "But Harry wanted the drama of an ambulance arrival. So instead, he had Ivan take him to a movie theatre in Englewood, then I came and picked him up in the ambulance. After the show, we drove back to Englewood, and Harry called Ivan to take him home. Told him he'd gone to see a double feature and then met a lady friend for drinks, if you know what I mean."

"But you seemed so concerned," I said. "You kept reminding him that he'd have to leave."

He straightened up with an actor's pride. "That was my motivation," he said. "It was also my responsibility to get a uniform, and the one I found had the name Mitchell embroidered on it, so that became my character's name."

"Weren't you the least bit curious about this elaborate gag, especially after you got to Comedy Tonight and saw what kind of an evening we'd planned?"

Darius shook his head. "I was too deep in the role to worry about inconsistencies," he said.

Actors are crazy.

The drive home was even less memorable than the one coming up. I don't even know if I put the music back on. Jeff Lynne and his cohorts could go on playing songs in the past without me.

Chief Barry Dutton thought it was odd that I was asking about Harry Lillis's remains. Of course, he thought it was odd that I was calling at all, since his detective had never given him my message.

"What *about* Lillis's remains?"

"I'm just curious when the ME released them, because I know the autopsy report took some time." I wanted to approach this delicately, and delicacy is not my best thing.

Dutton sounded like a man whose forehead was wrinkling in puzzlement. "I'd have to check, but the last I heard, the medical examiner had released Lillis's body, but nobody had claimed it. He didn't have any relatives I know about. Do you?"

I'd already checked Internet sites and all the connections I had in the comedy community, so I knew the answer to that one. "No. He didn't have anyone who would have picked him up. But you know, in the Jewish tradition, he's supposed to be buried as soon as possible. What happens if nobody claims the body?"

"After a reasonable period of time, the county will inter the remains in a . . ."

"An unmarked grave. Even if the deceased had enough money to pay for a funeral?" I had to cover all the bases.

"Well, if there was a will, and a provision was made for some service, I'm sure that would be taken into account," Dutton answered. "Even if there wasn't a will in place, the County Surrogate would probably issue an order to garnish the deceased's account."

"There was a will," I told him.

"Then I doubt Bergen County wants to pay for Harry Lillis's funeral if it doesn't have to."

"Well, maybe I can help," I said. "Would they release the remains to me?"

There was dead silence on the phone for some seconds. "You? What's the plot now, Elliot?"

"No plot," I said unconvincingly. "I've decided that there should be a public memorial service for Harry Lillis. Tomorrow. At Comedy Tonight."

40

There's one way to find out if a man is honest: ask him. If he says yes, you know he's crooked.

— GROUCHO MARX

Friday
   It Happened One Night (1934) AND
      Screwball (THIS WEEK)

I had to work fast to get the *Press-Tribune* to work up an ad for Friday's newspaper, but since I was paying half-page rates, roughly eight times the size I normally buy, they were willing to work a little harder. There was no helping the expense: I didn't want to wait for Wilson Townes to come and bend me into a pretzel, and I wanted to make sure the ad wouldn't be missed by Wilson or his father. You can't bury a Jewish man on Saturday anyway, and Sunday we have matinees, so the service had to be Friday, and for my purposes, the ad had to be large.

To make the memorial work into the theatre's schedule and the other meeting I'd already set up, I had to call it for five in the afternoon, not a great time for a movie theatre. Earlier in the day would mean I'd have to staff the whole thing myself (my staff would be in school), and later would mean we'd have to cancel a showing on the night we changed films for the week. Leo Munson would probably stage a coup.

Five o'clock it was.

I spent Friday morning making arrangements: seeing to it that the funeral home had the address and the time right, ordering flowers (you're not supposed to send flowers to a Jewish funeral, but people don't know that and find it strange if there are none), seeing to some finger sandwiches and nonalcoholic drinks. I made some phone calls to people who might miss the ad, like my father, and cleaned up the theatre as best I could. I also alerted local (and some New York City) media on the assumption that the chance to further milk the "mysterious death of a comedy legend" they'd run a week ago might be enough to bring a camera crew and a reporter or two if I gave them enough notice, which I was just barely doing.

By three, I was on a ladder outside the theatre, changing the marquee to read HARRY LILLIS MEMORIAL SERVICE 5 p.m. when Vic Testalone pulled up in his vintage Oldsmobile Cutlass convertible. You could land aircraft on Vic's car, which probably got less than a mile per gallon. He was smoking a cigar as he drove up — just to pollute the atmosphere a little more — and parked a few yards short of the marquee.

It was an hour earlier than I'd expected him. "Vic," I said, coming down from the ladder (I hate heights, so any interruption was welcome). "You're early."

"I was in the neighborhood," he said. "Elliot. Are we okay?"

"You and me?" I asked. "Why wouldn't we be?"

"The last time I saw you, you seemed irritated with me."

I took down the ladder and Vic followed me as I carried it back inside. "You mean because you ratted me out to Anthony and tried to talk him into quitting school? Don't be silly. We're fine. That's just business."

He grinned. "That's what I thought."

We had just made it to the office door. "Go inside," I said. "I'm going to put the ladder away. Be right back."

Vic walked into the office and I went to

the closet to put the ladder back where it belonged. I noticed Sophie as I was walking out. She hadn't exactly reverted to her traditional Goth style, but she was wearing all black. I'd called the staff the night before to let them know about the memorial service, and urged them to dress appropriately. I believe I mentioned something to Jonathan about wearing shoes in which his toes were not visible.

"You all set?" I asked Sophie as I locked the closet door.

"For what?" she asked. "This funeral thing?"

"It's a *memorial service,* if anyone asks, and even if they don't," I told her.

"Yeah, I'm ready," Sophie said. "Why wouldn't I be?"

"I can't think of a reason," I answered.

"Are we selling snacks at the funeral?"

"Memorial service. And no! We're not selling snacks. That would be unbelievably tacky." I started toward the office, and then turned back toward her. "Do you think we could get away with it?"

She pretended the music from her iPod was too loud to hear me, and set about getting the snack bar ready. For the evening showings.

Anthony, in black jeans and a black shirt,

was walking in when I left Sophie. Carla, prim in black slacks and a scoop-neck black top, tried to look properly solemn at his side. He nodded at me, pleasantly (for him), as he walked by. We stopped and looked at each other.

"Anthony," I said, "I didn't steal your movie."

"Okay."

"I *really didn't*," I reiterated.

"I believe you," he said. "I have my own theory of what happened."

Now, that was intriguing. "Come into the auditorium and tell me. If you'll excuse us, Carla." She nodded, looking apprehensive, and stayed put in the lobby. Anthony looked at me strangely, but followed me into the auditorium. I sat down in the last row (row HH) and prepared myself.

"Okay, shoot." I told him.

"I think Carla took it," Anthony said. Over my incredulous expression, he added, "She always feels threatened by my films, and I think when she saw that *Killin' Time* was really good and might take me away from her, she panicked and stole the movie."

"Okay. How'd she do it?" Let's see if he could come up with something plausible, because it didn't make sense at all to me. I was certain by now that Carla hadn't stolen

386

his film.

"While I was talking to my friends from school, and my dad, and you, and your ex-wife . . ."

"I get it. While you were otherwise occupied."

Anthony nodded. "She went up into the projection booth. She knew she couldn't sneak the reels out, so she stashed them in the floor."

"Uh-huh. And how did she get the key to the projection booth? How did she even know there was storage space in the floor under the console? How did she get *back* into the projection booth to remove the reels after Chief Dutton and I found them, but before we were ready to give them back?"

Anthony's lips pouted out as he thought. "Um, I don't know. Maybe it wasn't Carla."

"No, but it's nice to know you two have such a trusting relationship. Look, Anthony, it's none of my business, but Carla is a great girl and she's crazy about you. That doesn't happen very often. You should stop looking for reasons to push her away."

He stood up. "Forgive me, Mr. Freed, but I don't know if I should be taking relationship advice from you. You know, your track record isn't great."

I nodded, although that one stung because it was true. "Your parents have been married for twenty-eight years. What do they think?" I asked.

Anthony didn't answer, and he left the auditorium to get the projector threaded.

I went back to my office, where Vic was sitting with his feet up on my desk. "I've been looking through your Rolodex," he said. "It makes no sense."

"I'm sorry. If I'd realized that casual visitors would be leafing through it, I'd try to organize it more efficiently."

He didn't catch the sarcasm. I saw Sharon walk by the office door, but she avoided looking in. She appeared to be heading for Sophie's station. "It's not even alphabetical," Vic persisted. "How can you tell where anything is?"

"I have my own system, and I don't need to explain it to you." Actually, I *couldn't* explain it, since the system consisted of sticking in a new card wherever the Rolodex happened to be sitting when I got a new phone number to add. It wasn't efficient, but it did help me to review my list of acquaintances on a regular basis. Sometimes it gets slow in a movie theatre. At least, it does in mine.

Luckily, Barry Dutton walked in at that

moment, followed almost immediately by Danton, and then Jonathan. "Good," I said. "We're ready."

"For what?" Vic asked.

"A meeting in the projection booth." I walked out the door, and he followed me. Not that I had actually invited him, or anything.

I called, "Meeting upstairs," as soon as I hit the lobby, and I watched the assembled group: Sophie, Jonathan, Sharon, Dutton, Danton, Anthony, Carla, and Vic, start up the stairs. Sophie turned to me with an expression that indicated she'd just thought of something.

"Why do we have to crowd into the projection booth? Why can't we have the meeting down here, or just sit in the balcony?"

"Good question," I said. "In fact, two good questions. There's a reason, and you'll see once the meeting gets under way."

That didn't satisfy her, but she turned and continued up the stairs, with the group trudging up behind her.

I watched them for a moment, and then retreated to my office. Vic saw me back off, but shook his head at my eccentricity and continued on his way. Nobody'd asked him upstairs anyway.

Inside the office, I quickly threw on a trench coat I'd had in the office since last winter and a fedora I'd borrowed from Dad for a Halloween party eight years ago. Had to get that back to him any day now. I buttoned up the coat, looked at my reflection in the computer screen to adjust the hat, and left the office to climb upstairs.

Anthony had let everyone into the projection booth by the time I got there. I flung the door open and strode into the room as if I owned the place, which I did.

"So," I said. "I suppose you're wondering why I invited you all here."

There was a long pause. Sharon broke the silence with a dry tone that said, "I'll bet you've been waiting your whole life to say that."

"As a matter of fact, I have," I answered. The rest of them stared at my outfit and said nothing. This wasn't as much fun as I'd anticipated, but I went on with it anyway. "I think we all know that a crime was committed in this room some weeks back, and you're here today because I can definitively identify the person who perpetrated it."

"What?" Jonathan asked. I noticed he was still wearing the sandals, but with long pants and black socks. At least you couldn't see his toes. Not clearly.

"He's going to tell us who stole Anthony's movie," Barry Dutton said.

"Good," Vic said. "Maybe I can still make a deal with Monitor Films. Tell us, Elliot: Who took the film, and where is it now?"

"It's someone *in this room*," I intoned, expecting the requisite incriminating glances and beads of sweat on a forehead.

Instead, Sophie said, "Well, *duh*. You wouldn't make this whole show if it was some guy in Utah." Some people just aren't tolerant of high drama.

"You were never really a serious suspect," I told her, doing my best to pace in a room that held five more people than it should. "You were downstairs the first time the film was discovered missing, and couldn't have moved it. Besides, you don't know where the key to the projection booth is kept."

She sputtered her lips into a raspberry and said, "Yeah, right. Like I don't know it's on a hook in your office." Sophie needed a short course in how not to be a suspect.

Still, I knew Sophie hadn't taken the film, so I moved on to Jonathan, who was standing to her side. "And you, young man," I said.

Jonathan, who had been watching Sophie, looked surprised to be included in the conversation. "Me?" he asked.

"Yes, you. You weren't here when the film was first taken, but you *were* here when it disappeared from the storage space. Yet how would you have discovered the film in the first place? Had you stolen the key before?"

"What key?" Jonathan asked.

"So," I said, playing the part to the hilt, "you could have found the film, and then decided to hold it hostage and demand a ransom from Anthony."

"Huh?" said Anthony.

"But no," I continued, trying to ignore them both, "it doesn't add up. There was very little motive, and it still doesn't explain how the film originally vanished. So I eliminated Jonathan as a suspect." I began to wonder why I wasn't using a British accent. That might have sounded more authoritative.

Next in the extremely close line was Carla, who seemed startled that she was being included at all. "Now, you had a motive. If Anthony's film were a huge success, you might lose him to Hollywood. You might not want the movie to come out at all."

Carla's forehead scrunched up like a cross section of a phyllo dough pastry. "I love Anthony," she said. "I want him to be happy. He's not happy with his movie missing. Why would I want that?"

"Suppose you were selfish, and wanted him to stay at school for another two years so he'd depend more on you. Suppose you wanted him to stay close to home." My heart wasn't in it, but I figured I'd play it to the end. How often do you get the spotlight, after all?

"If Anthony loves me, we'll be together," Carla said with great certainty. "If he doesn't, it won't matter where or when. We've *talked* about this, Mr. Freed."

I walked to Anthony (which took roughly two steps), pointed directly into his face, and said, "Marry that girl. You're not going to do better." Carla smiled.

I moved past Anthony, to Danton. "Now, you were very convincing when I inter-rogated you about the missing film. You said you weren't a film major, and therefore harbored no grudge against Anthony about his sudden success."

Danton, who had been trying unsuccess-fully to make eye contact with Sharon, turned to me. "Yeah," he said. "So?"

"But you did have a motive: you wanted to sleep with Anthony's girlfriend, Carla, and she wouldn't succumb to your usual lines. So you decided to make Anthony less attractive to her, by removing his film and his success. Isn't that so?"

"Um, no," Danton said. "Carla's not my type." He turned to Anthony. "No offense, dude," he said.

"No problem," Anthony answered. He turned to me. "I don't think you got that part right, Mr. Freed."

"I was making it up," I admitted. "I don't really believe Danton took the film cans." I sidled past Danton, who shifted his gaze to try for eye contact with Sophie, equally without success. I stood just a few inches from Anthony.

"Now, you," I started. "You were the most elusive of all. Seemingly the victim in this crime, you could actually have been the perpetrator, if there had been an insurance policy taken out on the film. With a studio interested in its distribution, it would have been worth a good deal of money."

"There wasn't any insurance on the film," Anthony said. "I'm still on my parents' policy."

"Yeah," I said, a little deflated. "I found that out. I called your dad. Tell him sorry for me."

"No problem," Anthony said.

Reluctantly, I faced Sharon. "You were the one I didn't want to believe had committed the crime," I told her. "You had the opportunity, as you were out of sight when the film was first discovered missing. You know where I keep the key to the projection booth, and you had a motive, as you were trying that very night to convince Anthony he shouldn't give up his education to pursue a directing career, even if he could find a distributor for his film."

"Oh, Elliot, honestly," Sharon said. "You're being ridiculous."

"Am I?" I asked. "Am I really?"

"Yes."

"You're right," I said. "I am being ridiculous. You didn't have access to the projection booth when the film went missing a second time. You wouldn't put yourself at risk over something that was between a young man and his parents. You're much too good a person to dash his hopes and inflict your will over his. I should have realized that, and I'm sorry."

Her eyes softened a little bit, and she smiled. "Apology accepted," Sharon said. "But I don't understand. That means none of the people you invited stole the film, unless Chief Dutton is a suspect."

Dutton looked at me, amused.

"No, he's not," I told her. "This wasn't so much about naming a thief as it was about returning Anthony's property to him." I walked to the console, dropped down into a crouch, and moved the plywood panel out of the way, having removed the screws before I'd gone outside to do the marquee. "I think some of us underestimated him, and he should be given the chance to make his own decision."

I reached into the storage compartment and in a moment, pulled out a film can marked *Killin' Time.* Then another. I stood up, and offered them to Anthony.

His mouth dropped open. He grabbed at the film cans and pulled them to his chest. "Mr. Freed," he said quietly. "You *did* take the film, after all."

"No," I said. "It was an even bigger softie than me." And I took a few steps toward the door, where Vic Testalone was standing. "Go ahead," I said to Vic. "Tell him."

Vic had an unlit cigar in his mouth, and it was drooping. "Oh, all right," he said. "It was me. I hid the film. But it wasn't to steal it. I just wanted to make sure it was someplace safe."

"You actually listened to me that night," I guessed. "You didn't want to be responsible for Anthony making a rash decision, so when I was talking to Sharon, you grabbed the key from my office, then came up here and stashed the film cans in the storage compartment. You'd been up here enough times to know it was there."

"Yeah, but you couldn't have known," Vic replied. "If you'd seen me coming up or going down, you wouldn't have waited all this time to get the movie back."

"I didn't know," I told him. "It wasn't until Chief Dutton asked me who was here every time the film disappeared that it struck me. *You* were here each time the film 'moved' somewhere, and the second time the movie vanished, you'd just been up here with Anthony. Coincidence? I think not. Were you planning on giving it back to him?"

Anthony, Carla hanging off his arm, looked overwhelmed. Sharon seemed engrossed in the drama taking place in front of her. Sophie was looking away, bored and disgusted with life. Jonathan stared at his sandals, and Danton, having run out of women to impress, was inching toward the door.

"I *was* going to say I'd have a copy made, and then produce the original, so you wouldn't know it was me," Vic said. "But the kid hadn't used digital video, and the idea of striking another print from the negative was too far-fetched. I would have just held out the two weeks you asked me for and then made the movie appear again. Who knew you were going to call in the cops?"

"And then today, when I was talking to Anthony and Sophie, you snuck back up here to put the film back. You had the time; I made sure of it. You really wanted to do right by Anthony, didn't you, Vic?" I asked.

Vic looked directly at Chief Dutton. "I never meant for it to go this far," he said. "I just didn't want to back off the deal, and then have Anthony cash in with somebody else. If I told the Monitor guys they couldn't have the movie because the kid couldn't decide, they'd back off. But if I told them it had been stolen, now they're more interested. See how that works?"

I turned in Dutton's direction. Danton had shrugged and left the booth, and Sophie and Jonathan went to sit on the balcony steps outside the booth door. "Chief," I said, "if I drop the complaint of burglary in my theatre, and the film was never really stolen, has a crime been committed?"

Dutton scratched his head a bit, and sat down on the only available chair in the room. "Only one against logic," he said. "But I don't see a reason to file unless Anthony wants to. The film is his property."

We all turned toward Anthony. His eyes widened a little. "Is the meeting with Monitor Films still available, Mr. Testalone?" he asked.

Vic grinned. "Yeah, kid. I can set it up for early next week."

Anthony looked at Dutton. "I don't think a crime has been committed, Chief," he said.

"Okay," I said. "Anthony, thread up the clip reel, and then get the spotlights in order." He set about the task, but kept the cans of *Killin' Time* where he could see, and if necessary, touch them.

We all started for the door, a relief from the closeness of the crowded room. Sharon walked out just in front of me, and gave me a smile I'd seen only three days before. It was welcome.

We were just passing Sophie and Jonathan on the stairs when I said, "Come on. We've got work to do. People will be here in a little while for a funeral."

"Memorial service," Sophie said as she stood.

41

Before the funeral home delivered the casket containing the body of our fallen comedian to the theatre, I had to make sure the stage was set properly. I had Anthony close the curtains in front of the screen, although during the service they would open for the screening of some of Lillis and Townes's best bits. (Luckily, just such a reel had been compiled for a television retrospective in 1989, and Vic had managed to track down a copy.)

As I stood there, surveying the empty house, I wondered if I had the nerve to pull this event off. There might be a little danger involved; although I'd taken precautions, nothing is foolproof. Take it from the fool himself.

But I was distracted by the sight, far away through the auditorium doors, of Sophie and Danton having a heated conversation. He put his hand on her arm, and she shook it free. I couldn't hear what was being said, but it was clear that Sophie was not pleased.

I stepped down off the stage and headed out of the auditorium into the lobby. But by the time I got there, Danton had dropped his arms, shook his head, and walked out the front doors onto the street. Sophie stood alone, in the middle of the lobby, watching after him, and as I drew near, she turned back toward the snack bar.

She was smiling broadly.

"Now it all makes sense," I said when I reached her. "Until this moment, I'd forgotten that you and Danton were an item a few months ago."

Sophie's amusement was palpable. "An *item?*" she asked.

"What do you call it? 'Hooking up'?"

She made a face as if I'd squirted lemon juice into her mouth. "We never really hooked up," she said. "And I can't tell you how glad I am."

"Let me see if I can guess, based on what I know about you and what I know about Danton. You went out for a while, then he found some other girl he decided to chase, and he told you it was over. How am I doing so far?"

"A typical male behavior pattern," Sophie said. "Attract, conquer, and then move on to a newer breeding ground."

"Don't generalize. We're not all like that. Anyway, his dumping you" (Sophie grimaced at the term) "led to your rejection of all things male, and you started reading up on feminism. It makes sense, if you don't take it as an antimale manifesto, because that's not how it was meant to be read."

"You're oversimplifying," Sophie told me. "A man broke my heart, so I immediately turned against all men? Now who's generalizing?"

"For weeks I've been getting nothing but 'men are pigs' from you, and I'm supposed to think it's more complicated than that?" I asked.

"Maybe I was a little mad," she grinned winningly.

I grinned back. "Get back to work," I said, and returned to the auditorium.

The hearse arrived at about four, and some very nice and very strong men wheeled the casket in through the rear entrance and up onto the stage. Only then did it occur to me that we could have done the same thing with Harry Lillis on the night he came to the theatre in his wheelchair. Opportunity lost.

A half hour later, the press started showing up. The *Press-Tribune* and the *Star-*

Ledger each sent a reporter and a photographer, as did the *Record* and even the *New York Daily News.* Two New York television stations sent crews, and so did one from Philadelphia, as did the local cable access stations. I did a few quick interviews with the print reporters first, because I used to be a writer, and then gave as much time as I could to the TV people, who weren't really that interested in me or Comedy Tonight, but thought they could use my comments as cut-ins between shots of the service.

After the interviews, I changed into the suit I'd brought from home (let the TV people see me in jeans). Sharon opened the office door just as I was putting on the tie.

"You know, you should knock on a door," I said. "I could have had my pants off."

"Nothing I haven't seen before," Sharon answered. "This week, in fact." She saw the trouble I was having with the tie (the bottom part is always too long), and walked over to help.

"What about that?" I asked.

Her eyes widened. "What about it? It's still there, isn't it?"

"You know what I mean."

Her smile dimmed, and she nodded. "Yes, I do. And I don't know. We got up the next morning, and we were the same two people who got divorced. What does that tell us?"

"I don't know. Maybe we need more time to sort it out."

"I think so," she said. "I'll see you out there." She finished with my tie, and of course it was perfect.

Before she reached the door, I said, "Shar," and she stopped.

I looked at her. "Sit in the front where I can see you."

Sharon smiled, and nodded.

At a quarter to five, we started letting people in. The crowd was fairly large, especially considering that there had been very little time to publicize the service. From the wings, I noticed Leo Munson, of course, sitting with his captain's hat in the center of the theatre, and Sharon in the front row, center. Right where I wanted her. My father sat down next to her and patted her on the knee.

The crowd tended toward the not-so-young, of course. A minivan of people from the Booth Actors' Home, including Marion Borello, had arrived, and were seated by a group of attendants who weren't Mitchell/Darius. One tall gentleman with a bushy white moustache that made him look like a grandfather walrus wandered in on his own, looked around as if deciding if he'd ever been to this place before, and eventually took a seat near the back. He closed his eyes and seemed to doze off quickly.

Because of the short notice, not many of Lillis's contemporaries could make it to the service. But I spotted two limousines in front of the theatre before we'd opened the doors, and now, Sid Caesar and Joan Rivers were being seated by a teenage boy in a black shirt, black jeans, and open-toed sandals with black socks. I was awed and humiliated at the same time.

The auditorium was at least two-thirds full (although we had not opened the balcony) when I walked out onstage at about five ten. It made me wish we could have charged admission, and then I was immediately ashamed of the thought. The casket was center stage, with a large photo of Lillis that I'd gotten Vic to bring from Klassic Komedy's archives on an easel. The TV lights came on.

There was, naturally, no applause.

"Good afternoon, and thank you for coming," I began. Yes, it was a solemn occasion, and I was more than a little nervous, but my first thought on reaching the podium was — and I'm not proud of this — *Sid Caesar is watching me!* "Welcome to the memorial service for a true legend of comedy and a remarkable man, Harry Lillis. First of all, please forgive us for the short notice we've given you. I realize it was very difficult for some of you to get here so quickly, but it couldn't be helped, I assure you."

The man with the bushy moustache got up and wobbled out the back door, probably in search of the men's room. Or maybe he was already bored. I saw him head in one direction, then the other. He ended up going the wrong way, toward the balcony stairs. I hoped Jonathan would notice and help him get where he was going.

"I'd like to begin by reading some telegrams that have arrived from some of Mr. Lillis's friends and peers who could not be with us today." The interesting thing is that these days, telegrams come via e-mail. Western Union won't come to your door anymore. I read telegrams from Jerry Lewis, Carl Reiner, Mel Brooks, and Edie Adams. The ones from Brooks and Reiner, especially, got the laughs they intended (I couldn't duplicate Lewis's delivery or Adams's legs), while also expressing sadness at Lillis's passing.

After that, I signaled to Anthony. The curtains opened, and the lights dimmed.

Anthony started the projector, and a fifteen-minute smorgasbord of Lillis and Townes's clips began on the screen.

I couldn't watch.

I went back into the wings, where a chair was waiting, and sat, head in my hands, eyes closed. The idea of seeing the scenes with those two tremendous comedians was just too much for me on this occasion. I listened to the people in the auditorium laugh, and did my best not to think about what they were watching, or what would come next. It was all I could do not to put my fingers in my ears and say "la la la la la la la" until it was time to walk out again.

When the montage finally ended, there was loud applause in the auditorium. Anthony put the lights back on, and shone a spotlight at the podium. I knew I had to walk back out there. But I wasn't sure I could do what would come next.

"I'd like to say just a few quick words, and then we'll ask some people who knew Mr. Lillis for a long time to come up and express their thoughts," I started. "I only knew them in person for a short while, but Harry Lillis and Les Townes were my life-long friends. Harry brought me joy when almost no one else could lift me out of a dark mood. He surprised me over and over, even when I'd seen him in the same film a hundred times. Les reached out from that screen and pulled me along with him, wherever he decided to go. And it was always a wonderful ride."

I looked up into the balcony, because I figured that was about as close to heaven as Comedy Tonight could simulate. "Harry, if you're up there, I want to say thank you. I will never be able to pay the debt I owe; I'll never be able to make you even one-tenth as happy as you've made me in my life. I'm sorry about that."

And then I took a deep breath, and carefully considered what I was about to do. "And I'm sorry, too, that you murdered your partner Les Townes and tried to cover it up as your own death."

There was a loud murmur that swept through the crowd, and I saw a lot of the attendees talking to each other and looking confused. Leo, seated dead center in the audience, went, "Pah!" Nobody else does that like Leo. He sounded delighted, for some reason. The TV reporters, especially, seemed confused: I saw one of them start to read over her notes to see if she'd missed something.

"Come on, Harry," I continued. "I know you couldn't resist coming to your own funeral."

It was at that moment that I first considered how exposed I was in the middle of an empty stage (except for the dead man in the casket, who probably wouldn't be much help). A rifle shot would make mincemeat out of me pretty easily, and with absolutely no warning.

Maybe this hadn't been the best possible plan.

"I saw the videotape, Harry," I went on, talking to the ceiling. "You sent it to me so I would see it. And you re-created the examination scene from *Cracked Ice.* You couldn't resist directing again, even with a static camcorder placed on a dresser.

"It was just like that scene, Harry. You fell to the floor out of that wheelchair you were using — for what, to make it seem less likely you could hurt someone? — and you waited for Mr. Townes to drop out of the frame. You always knew where the camera was and what it could see, didn't you, Harry? And you lit the scene beautifully — no light near the camera, raised up, where it would end up illuminating the floor. You didn't want us to see what was going on there, and you made sure we couldn't. You were a better director than anyone gave you credit for.

"When Mr. Townes leaned over you, you

strangled him. You broke his neck. And then you put on his vest, the one he wore as the barber in the sketch. And you made sure your back was to the camera. You had lit the room so the window wouldn't show your reflection, just the glow from the lamp you'd placed next to it. You spoke a few words in Les Townes's voice. We'd forgotten what a good mimic you are, Harry. You did Townes's voice before, in *Peace and Quiet,* and now you've proved it really was you on that soundtrack."

The spotlight jerked violently to my right, off me and onto the auditorium wall. The TV camera crews started to shift their lights upward, and backward. And from the balcony, where I'd been pointing my comments, came back a voice.

"Thank you, Elliot. Knowing that I've gained your admiration will more than make up for not winning an Oscar." It was Harry Lillis's voice, and the murmur in the audience intensified into a dull roar. Sharon looked up and gasped.

Marion Borello turned white, and fell back in her seat.

It took a few moments for my eyes to adjust to the change from a bright light to darkness. But when they did, I could see what had caused the ruckus.

Harry Lillis was standing in the balcony, next to the spotlight Anthony had been shining on me. He was still wearing the bushy white moustache I'd seen him wearing when he entered.

And he was holding a very efficient-looking knife to Anthony's throat.

42

"I'd really appreciate it if you'd let me walk out of this theatre," Lillis said. "If you try to stop me, I might have to cut this young man's throat, and he seems like a nice enough kid."

Anthony, who had come out of the projection booth to work the spotlight, looked so terrified that he probably wasn't even thinking about how to work this into a screenplay. "Let him go," he gurgled. "Please."

To say that pandemonium broke out would be an understatement. People in the audience, seeing what was going on in the balcony, screamed, stood, and, in some cases, ran for the exits. Assuming you can call what the AARP crowd at the service was doing "running." Apparently they believed that the eighty-year-old man in the cheap seats was going to kill everyone there in his rampage of terror.

Reporters tried to decide whether to cover

the unfolding events, or grab their cell phones to call in for further instructions. It was going about fifty-fifty at the moment.

I was concerned only about Anthony. If Lillis slit his throat, Michael Pagliarulo would probably kill me, and I wouldn't blame him. I didn't want to think about what Carla would do.

Joan Rivers looked up into the balcony and I could clearly make out her lips saying, "It's Lillis."

The best thing was to keep him talking. Maybe I could convince him there was no hope of escape, with all these witnesses. "I don't understand it, Harry," I said. "Why would you kill your partner, and your closest friend?"

Lillis sounded amazed that I'd even ask the question. "He killed Vivian," he said. "Les set that fire and killed her because he knew she was still in love with me."

"No, he didn't, Harry. The fire was an accident. The arson guys confirmed it. And Les was in the studio when it started."

Lillis started backing Anthony up toward the stairs that would take them out of the balcony and down into the lobby. Anthony made a small squeaking sound that indicated he was very frightened, and I certainly could sympathize.

"Didn't you see the records? Les signed out of the studio before the fire. And he was seen taking his best stuff out of the house before the fire started. Didn't you see any of that?" Lillis was disgusted with my lack of investigative skill. "It's on the Internet."

"It's on the Internet because you put it there," I said. "I checked with a friend who understands web hosting, Harry. He did a little research. You owned all the sites that purported to show evidence against Les Townes. Walter Lee said you showed a special interest in Photoshop, to create the fake documents, and they were very good. The studio memo you created, the sign-out sheet you falsified? Excellent. You planted the stuff there because you knew I'd be looking. The records showed you only started the sites a few weeks ago, and contributed to a few existing ones around the same time."

The back auditorium doors were open now, since a number of audience members had bolted the theatre and left them that way. I looked out from the stage, which was where I had the best vantage point of the theatre and Lillis, and saw a few of the older people trying to hurry toward the exit doors with walkers and canes. I wanted to tell them there was no danger, but that would only piss Lillis off, and might actually create some danger.

What worried me was that I couldn't see Jonathan or Sophie.

Lillis had moved Anthony into position almost at the stairs to the lobby. If I couldn't stop his movement, I'd have to get out into the lobby to track him. "The thing I don't understand is, why now, Harry?" I asked. "You've thought that Townes killed Vivian for fifty years. You were wrong, but it was what you thought. So why did you wait so long to get your revenge?"

Lillis stopped walking, and slightly relaxed his grip on Anthony's throat. "Because I'm a coward," he said, his face drooping in shame. "Because I was afraid I'd get caught, and have to spend the rest of my life in jail. Well, now I'm dying, and it doesn't matter anymore. Now I could get justice for Viv and I'll be just as dead in six months, lethal injection or no."

"But you tried back then, didn't you? You called the cops with a tip that Townes was taking his belongings out of the house."

"I thought they'd follow up on that," Lillis said. "But the studio had the cops in their back pocket. They did nothing."

"It's not true, Harry," I told him. "They investigated. But there was nothing to find.

415

So now, when I provided you with the means, you decided to do something. You accepted the invitation to Comedy Tonight because you wanted the publicity. Did you send a copy of the ad to Townes so he'd know to come that night?"

Lillis nodded. If it hadn't been for the lethal weapon in his hand, he'd look like a bent, broken old man. "I couldn't get Les to show up in the same room with me. I told him I had an idea for a comeback movie and he wouldn't even call back, would you believe it? And I couldn't be sure he'd come here that night — he never let me know; he just showed up. So I couldn't do it then. Somebody would see. But this way, it worked. We got all chummy again, and when I asked him to come do one of the old bits with me, he couldn't resist."

His face changed into a pleading mask of pathos as he acted out the part: "Oh please, Les, come on. I don't have any friends here. Let's show them what we can do." Lillis's voice changed back to an angry one. "He loved it. Thought he was doing a real charity for his poor old friend."

My voice was getting hoarse from yelling up into the balcony. "But there never was that first rehearsal, the one you told me about on the phone. That's why Townes was asking all the same questions on the video-tape that you said he'd asked before. And the wheelchair?" I asked. "Was that just to make us think you were too helpless to commit the crime when the moment came?"

Lillis didn't mind showing off how brilliant he'd been. "Who'd suspect a poor little old man in a wheelchair, right? You have to admit, that played pretty well."

After the initial exodus, nobody in the audience had moved. The true-life drama was too riveting, and some of them were simply caught up in the performance Lillis was giving in the balcony.

"It did, I admit it," I told him. "You had me fooled until I did some checking. There wasn't anything wrong with your hip. You'd never fallen in the common room. You hired your own ambulance, and even the orderly was an actor. And you left a pair of dentures with your name in them at the scene of the fire, and took Les Townes's. You wore your spares, didn't you? Every step was planned and thought through. You were putting on a show the whole time, weren't you?"

"Yeah," Lillis said, the steel back in his voice. "And now it's over. Thanks for the help, Elliot." And he pushed Anthony, eyes wide and terrified, into the darkened passage that led to the lobby stairs.

Muffled after they disappeared from view, I heard, "Mr. Freed!"

I jumped from the stage into the main aisle and ran for the back doors to the auditorium. I was aware of Sharon and Dad standing up, possibly to follow me, but I didn't have time to wait. I made it to the lobby as quickly as I think humanly possible. I was milliseconds ahead of the TV crews and the newspaper reporters.

But it just got worse when I made it there. Standing at the bottom of the balcony stairs, holding that goddamn shotgun, was Wilson Townes. And he had the gun pointed at Jonathan, who for his part looked uncomfortable, but not terribly upset. He fidgeted, sitting on the third step, staring at Wilson. When I burst into the lobby, Wilson did not turn and level the gun at me.

"Stop running," he said. "Or I'll shoot him, and not in the ass."

This wasn't part of my plan. I hadn't intended for any of the staff to get involved at all. This was supposed to be between Lillis and me, and while I was relatively sure Wilson would be in the area, I had pictured it as a one-on-one kind of competition. It wasn't turning out that way.

"I don't want anybody to get hurt," I said.

"Good," Wilson replied. "Then you won't

get in the way while we leave."

"How'd he talk you into showing up tonight?" I asked Wilson.

He shrugged, accepting the inevitable. "You listen to what your father says," he said.

"So Harry Lillis really is your father?"

"That's right," Wilson said. "He was having an affair with my mother while she was married to my father. My other father. You know."

"The man you helped him kill," I said. "You helped Lillis drag your father out to the gazebo, you splashed kerosene all over him, and for all I know, you lit the match. Was he still alive when you put him there and incinerated him?"

Wilson's eyes showed anger, but he never got a chance to answer. Harry Lillis appeared at the top of the stairs with Anthony in front of him.

Behind me, at the doors to the auditorium, were Sharon and Dad. I looked around the lobby, and saw Wilson holding the gun on Jonathan; up the stairs, Lillis had the knife to Anthony's throat. I repressed the question that was burning through my brain.

"It would be really good if nobody did anything stupid," Lillis said. "Nobody wants these poor kids to get hurt."

Finally, at the top of the stairs, I saw the salvation I'd been waiting for. But I was crushed when Lillis spoke, because it became obvious he'd seen it, too.

"Those cops behind me had better stay where they are," he said. "Did you have them hiding in the projection booth? Very smart, Elliot."

"Not as smart as you, Harry," I said. "You fooled everybody. I was crushed when I heard you were dead. Distraught. If you're sure you're dying of cancer, why bother to make that tape and send it to me? You could have just gotten away scot-free. You had to know I'd figure it out."

Lillis smiled, and it was a cold, stomach-clenching smile. "I wasn't sure, but I thought there was a chance," he said.

From behind him, I heard Barry Dutton's voice. "Mr. Lillis, just put down the knife. Tell Mr. Townes to put down the gun. You don't want to have any more deaths on your head."

"Is that the best you can do?" Lillis mocked him. "Appeal to the conscience of a man who killed his partner and videotaped it?"

There was movement to my left, but I couldn't identify it. Keep him talking. "The tape, Harry. The tape. Why incriminate yourself?"

"Why shouldn't I get credit for bringing Vivian justice?" he asked. "If I could get Les to admit to killing her on tape, why not leave that behind?"

"But he *didn't* admit to it," Dutton said.

"He *killed her!*" Lillis was weeping, but he didn't loosen his grip on the knife. "He was a murderer, and I showed him justice!"

He was too far gone. There was no point in reiterating that Vivian Reynolds had died in an accidental fire; Lillis refused to believe that. I started walking, very slowly, toward the steps, to get a better look at Lillis's face. "It was more than that," I guessed. "You couldn't stand being anonymous. You couldn't deal with the fact that nobody knew who you were anymore. You were going to get Lillis and Townes back in the headlines."

Lillis's eyes narrowed.

"You could've left it alone. You could've committed the crime and then faded into oblivion." I was almost at the foot of the stairs. "But you kept improvising. You wouldn't stick to the script. You should be thousands of miles from here, but you stuck around, sending Godzilla here" — that would be Wilson — "to threaten me and destroy my property. Because you didn't

421

really want people to think Townes had killed you. You wanted them to know exactly who'd had the last laugh."

"You're smarter than you look, Elliot," Lillis said. "But then, you'd almost have to be."

Barry Dutton loomed up behind Lillis, his weapon drawn, and put the barrel to Lillis's head. "Drop the knife, Mr. Lillis," he said. Behind him, Officer Patel was already in position.

Lillis dropped the knife, and Anthony dropped to the floor, breathing hard. I didn't see any blood, so I assumed Lillis hadn't cut him. Anthony must have been petrified.

And then Harry Lillis, the man who'd made me laugh countless times, said very calmly to Wilson Townes, "Shoot the boy."

It took Wilson a moment to react, and in that moment, I realized there wasn't enough time for Dutton or Patel to train their weapons on Wilson. I also knew that there wasn't any chance at all that I could overpower Wilson. I'm wiry, and he was enormous and muscular. No match. Wilson aimed at Jonathan, who wasn't looking up.

During that moment, however, I was monumentally glad that I'd repressed the question I wanted to ask moments before.

Because if I'd asked Lillis where Sophie was, he would have wondered that himself.

Having crawled out from behind the snack bar, where she must have dropped to the ground when Wilson appeared, Sophie grabbed one of the heavy posts we use to hold up the velvet rope when we cordon off the balcony. With an expression of pure focused fury, she hefted it like a baseball bat and clocked Wilson across the back of the head. I couldn't have lifted it that high. Wilson dropped like a stone, and the shotgun fired into the floor.

"That's brand-new carpet, you bastard," I said to the unconscious Wilson.

Sophie's face had a look of such uncontrolled anger that it was a miracle steam wasn't rising from her nostrils. "Don't you dare hurt my boyfriend!" she told Wilson, although it was a decent bet he couldn't hear her.

"Your . . ." I began. Sophie dropped the post, ran to Jonathan, and hugged him. She started to sob. He looked positively thrilled.

"We're going to have to have a talk," I told them.

Patel began placing cuffs on Lillis, who looked crestfallen at Wilson's failure. "You just can't get good help these days," he said, his voice sounding very far away.

"Is he really your son?" I asked.

Lillis shook his head. "Viv never cheated on Les. But I told him he was, and he believed me."

"And Wilson helped you kill his father."

Lillis almost didn't answer, but then said, "I put his name on my insurance. He gets all Les's money and all of mine. Comes to over six million, when you add it together."

"He couldn't collect as a fugitive, but you figured that, too. Pretty cold," I answered, but Lillis's face was impassive; he seemed to be somewhere else entirely.

With the cuffs on his prisoner, Dutton put his weapon back in his holster and exhaled. "All right, Mr. Lillis, let's go," he said.

But before Patel or Dutton could grab Lillis's arms, the comedian put on a satisfied smile and looked up at an imaginary adoring audience. "Thank you, ladies and gentlemen, and good night," he said in a theatrical voice.

He took a step to the edge of the top stair, and then simply picked both feet up and threw them in front of himself. Lillis landed on his neck, hard, on the top step, and then tumbled all the way down the long staircase, finally landing in a heap at the foot of the stairs.

I rushed to him, but it was obvious from

the angle of his head that there was no helping Harry Lillis now. Dutton and Patel ran
down the stairs, Dutton already calling for
EMS on his cell phone. But everyone in that
room knew rescue workers wouldn't be
anything more than a formality.

Harry Lillis had taken the most perfect,
most graceful, best-planned pratfall of his
career. And the last.

43

You know you've had an interesting day when the highlight is Sid Caesar telling you that you "throw a hell of a funeral." It's a bittersweet experience at best.

The guests had been interrogated and released, the TV crews allowed to leave with ecstasy to return to their home bases, carrying a remarkable story they hadn't expected, and my father, having assessed the carpet damage and declaring it in need of replacement, packed into his truck to go home and tell my mother she really needed to come along with him next time because she didn't know what she was missing.

I sat behind my desk trying to figure out how to get another chair into the office. I'd had a lot of visitors lately, and this was getting tiresome. Anthony stood by my desk, as animated as I'd ever seen him, which normally wouldn't be saying much. But now he was positively electric. He was pale, his hands were still a little shaky, his eyes were wide, and for reasons I couldn't explain on my best day — which this clearly wasn't — he was grinning.

"Mr. Freed," he said for the fifth time. "You saved my life."

"No, I didn't," I reiterated. "Chief Dutton saved your life. Go thank him."

"It was you," Anthony insisted. "You got the police on the balcony to begin with. I'm sorry I ever doubted you, Mr. Freed. You talked Mr. Lillis out of killing me. You're my hero."

This was worse than having him think I was a movie-thieving scoundrel. "Anthony, please. I'm not the person to thank. If anything, I put you in more danger than I could have anticipated. You never should have been that close to Lillis to begin with. I'm sorry, Anthony."

But he just grinned away. "Thank you, Mr. Freed. Thank you. You don't even have to pay me anymore. I'll just come to work for free. Honestly. Thank you."

Eventually, I convinced Anthony that he should go upstairs (apparently going back to the projection booth was not a source of great trauma for him) and get ready to run tonight's movie. He did everything but kiss the hem of my garment on his way out.

Before I could stand, Chief Barry Dutton replaced Anthony in the doorway of the former broom closet and shook his head. "You always have it all figured out, don't you?" he said.

"Obviously not."

"You knew Harry Lillis would come out of the cold if you threw a memorial service."

I rolled my eyes a bit, more at the thought of Lillis than at Dutton. "Anybody who's ever met a comedian would have figured that one out. He'd be here just to see who showed up and who didn't. I just hadn't realized how far over the top he'd gone. I won't sleep tonight thinking about how close Anthony and Jonathan were to . . ." I shuddered.

"Patel and I were in the projection booth," Dutton said. "I'm the one who should have realized Wilson wouldn't be in the balcony. I figured he'd try to pick you off from up there, not that he'd be Lillis's insurance policy downstairs."

"Why doesn't that make me feel better?" I wondered aloud.

"We had a talk with Wilson," Dutton said. "He admitted to sending the 'bomb' to you, as per Harry's directions. It was supposed to scare you, but also to make you want to investigate Vivian's death more closely."

"Harry really thought Townes had killed Vivian Reynolds," I marveled. "You could have laid all the evidence out in front of him, and he still wasn't going to change his mind."

"Think about it, Elliot," Dutton said. "Lillis was in love with Vivian. How long did it take Sharon to convince you that she was better off with Gregory than with you?"

"It would have taken forever," I nodded. "But I believed she'd be *happier,* and that turned out to be wrong, too. Did you see if she's still here? I think she was going to stay for the movie."

Dutton's eyebrows started to orbit his head. "You're going on with the showing tonight?" he asked.

"I let Leo in for free. He'd kill me if I didn't show the movie. But just *It Happened One Night.* After all the police activity, there won't be time for the new one."

Dutton shook his head. "Movie people are crazy," he said. Then a thought occurred to him, and he smiled at me. "You know, C. Francis Jenkins was one of the men credited, along with Thomas Edison, with inventing the motion picture projector."

He had me. "Okay," I said. "Go upstairs and tell Anthony I said it was okay for you to push the start button when it's time for the showing." Dutton turned to leave. "How'd you find that one out?" I asked.

"Ya gotta love Google," Dutton said, and he left, looking like the world's largest seven-year-old about to play with a really cool set of electric trains.

I got up and walked to the snack bar, where Sophie was leaning on the case and talking to Jonathan, staring into his eyes with a rapt attention that I'd never seen her use on anything or anyone before.

"So, how long has this been going on?" I said by way of greeting.

Jonathan grinned the most Cheshire cat–like grin I'd ever seen, and said, "A week or so."

"Five days," Sophie corrected him. She started to move boxes of candy from the floor behind the snack bar to the counter, so she could empty them into the display.

Of course. "You weren't looking for Les Townes's phone number that night in my Rolodex, were you, Jonathan?"

He stared at me as if I'd grown a horn in the middle of my forehead and sprouted hooves. "Of course not," he said. "I didn't want to go out with Mr. Townes."

"Your card must have been next to Les Townes's," I said to Sophie, who looked confused. "I came down one night and found Jonathan looking through my Rolodex. It was open to Townes's card, and I thought Jonathan might have been in on the fake bomb."

Sophie's eyes widened. *"Jonathan?"* she said. "Shame on you, Elliot. My Jonathan wouldn't do such a thing."

"*Your* Jonathan?" Then I recovered. "But that was more than five days ago. It was at least two weeks."

Jonathan stared at his shoes. "It took me a while to work up the nerve," he said.

Sophie actually ruffled his hair. "He's so shy," she said. I wondered if Dutton could bring back his fingerprint kit to make sure she was the same Sophie who rolled her eyes at The Philadelphia Story.

Jonathan reached into his back pocket. "By the way, Mr. Freed," he said. "I forgot I had this." He produced a Rolodex card with Sophie's address and phone number. "Sorry I borrowed it from your office."

I took it from him. It was wrinkled and looked like ketchup had been spilled on it and cleaned off. "Thanks, Jonathan," I said. "The next time you want something, just ask, okay?"

Sophie gave me a sharp look. "You'd give away my phone number to anybody who'd ask?"

"No, but at least I'd know he wasn't a mad bomber." I started away from them to open the front doors for the night's show.

As I did, Jonathan walked behind the counter. "Do you need help with those boxes?" he asked Sophie.

"I can handle it," she said. "Don't be such a *man.*"

On my way to the doors, I noticed Sharon walking out of my office. "I really need to remember to lock that door," I said. "Everybody's walking in and out of there lately."

"I'm just leaving," she said. "Came to say good night, and you weren't there."

"You're not staying for Claudette Colbert and Clark Gable?" I asked. "Mostly Clark Gable?"

"He never did that much for me, I'm sorry to say," my ex-wife told me. "I prefer less oily hair. Something curlier." She put her hand on top of my unruly mop.

"Clark couldn't help it that it was the 1930s," I said.

"I guess, but he could have cut back on the Vitalis."

"Anyway, you're skipping it," I reminded her.

"Yes."

"Thanks for coming today," I told her, running the risk that I could easily start getting far too gushy. "I meant everything I said."

"I know, Elliot." Sharon got close and kissed me lightly. "Let's not make major decisions this week, okay?"

I nodded. "Okay. But eventually, right?"

"We'll see. I think maybe I need to not have a husband for a while."

"How about a boyfriend?"

She lowered her eyebrows and her voice the same amount. "Not this week."

"Okay. I . . ."

The lights in the lobby went out, and then came back on. Sharon looked around.

"Chief Dutton is playing with my equipment," I said.

"Are you sure you *want* a girlfriend?" Before I could answer, she kissed my cheek and started toward the front doors.

44

Wednesday
  Bananas (1971) AND *Guacamole* (THIS
                    WEEK)

Two weeks later, the closeness of my office
(which is similar to the closeness one would
feel stuffed into a shoebox) had overwhelmed me, and it was too cold to go
outside for long — I am a warm-blooded
animal, and should be living in a more
temperate climate — so I set up camp for
the late afternoon in the lobby of Comedy
Tonight, where I could look out onto Edison Avenue and ponder life, since I didn't
actually have anything to do.

Sophie and Jonathan were behind the
snack bar, setting up for the evening and
making each other giggle. Sophie's style had
shifted away from the baggy sweatshirts and
combat boots, and was trying to decide
whether it should return to its Goth roots
or move onto something that allowed for a

color other than black. Right now, she was wearing black pants and ballet slippers (pink, of all things) with a black tuxedo shirt open at the neck. I don't know how, but she pulls it off.

Anthony, still hideously grateful for my almost getting him killed, came in from the street and stopped on his way to the balcony stairs. He held a bag labeled DUNKIN' DO-NUTS, and brought forth from said bag a large coffee with milk and a lo-cal sweetener, which I had not requested.

"Here you go, Mr. Freed," he said. "Anything else I can do for you right now?"

"No, thank you, Anthony. This was really not necessary."

"Don't even think about it. Would you like a doughnut?" he asked.

"No. Thanks."

"I have chocolate-filled." He sounded like my mother did when she was trying to get me to eat more eggs. I was six at the time.

"No, really. Thank you, Anthony."

"No. Thank *you*, Mr. Freed."

I wasn't sure how much more of this I'd be able to take.

After about a half hour of sitting in the lobby, I'd started feeling separation anxiety from my computer, so I went back to the office and began paying some bills online.

Around six, Vic Testalone walked in, no cigar in his mouth or hand. Never a good sign.

"Who shot your dog?" I asked him.

"Worse than that. I have to go up and tell the kid Monitor passed on his film." Vic had been counting on upgrading to a higher-quality polyester on the profits he'd assumed would come from *Killin' Time.* This must have been a blow.

"I'm sorry, Vic," I told him. "What happened?"

"They said Westerns don't sell. Can you imagine? The kid delivers a masterpiece of blood and guts, and they turn it down because they don't like the costumes. Go figure studios."

"Well, it was W. C. Fields who said, 'If at first you don't succeed, try, try again. Then quit. There's no use being a damn fool about it.' " I don't know why, but I felt a little vindicated that the studio had rejected Anthony's film, which made me feel guilty. Of course, almost everything makes me feel guilty. It's my heritage.

"It's not me I'm worried about," Vic lied. "It's the kid. Is he upstairs?"

I nodded. Vic still seemed reluctant to head upstairs and deliver the bad news to Anthony. But I sure as hell wasn't going to volunteer. I'd rather have Anthony overly grateful than sulky again.

"Good luck," I told Vic. "I'm out of here. Be back in an hour or so." And I put on my jacket and headed for the door. Vic didn't follow. "Come on, tiger," I told him. "You need to go upstairs now."

He really looked like a kid who had been summoned to the principal's office. "Can't I just stay here for a minute?" Vic asked.

"Not a chance," I told him. "I lock my office door when I leave." And I showed him the key in my hand.

"Since when?"

I walked to Big Herbs to meet Sharon for an early dinner. We'd decided that this was a reasonable step between our usual lunch at C'est Moi! and a full-fledged date, since I'd be going back to work after we ate. We'd concluded that dating had been ill-advised for us while Sharon was still married to Gregory. Well, *she'd* concluded that, and I'd said I agreed. Like I had a choice.

Belinda waved at me from behind the counter, but this time, I was seated at one of the tables, looking over the menu as if I didn't have it memorized. My polo shirt and khakis were a half step up from the usual grubby T-shirt and jeans, and Belinda smiled knowingly as she approached the table.

"You're expecting a lady," she said as she plunked down the flatware and filled my glass with water from a pitcher.

"Do you read tea leaves as well? Because I'd like to know what the lotto numbers are going to be this week. Powerball, if you've got 'em."

"I have bad news for you, Elliot. She's not coming."

All right, that was odd. "I beg your pardon?" I said.

"Sharon's receptionist called here earlier. She said the doc was dealing with a patient emergency, and to tell you she was sorry, she couldn't make it to dinner tonight." Belinda looked sympathetic, and sat down across from me. "Couldn't be avoided," she added.

"I'm used to it," I told her with a brief sigh. "She was a doctor when we were married, too. But at least in those days she had the guts to call me herself, the coward."

"You don't own a cell phone," Belinda reminded me. She reached into her pocket and produced a small box. "She sent this for you," she said. "If it helps." Then she got up and walked back to the counter, as another customer with a serious veggie craving had entered.

Maybe this was the way it would always be for Sharon and me. Maybe we'd always come close and never really get what we needed from each other. I hoped the medical emergency was a real one, and that she wasn't just ducking out on me to avoid making the same mistake . . . a third time.

At least this time I'd gotten a present. I took off the wrapping paper Sharon had used on the box, which was heavier than you would have expected, and saw a small note she'd stuck inside the flap.

"This isn't a bomb," it read. "I got it for you from my cousin Jane in Colorado Springs. I'll see you soon. Love you. Shar."

Inside the box was a snow globe from Pikes Peak, identical to the one Wilson Townes, now a resident of Bergen County Jail, had crushed in his hand. I shook it, and snickered just a bit.

Belinda sat with me for a few minutes, until I felt a tap on my shoulder. Thinking Sharon might have gotten away after all, I turned with great hope, and saw Marion Borello standing behind me, leaning on a cane.

"What's a gal have to do to get a cup of coffee around here?" she asked.

Marion sat down and Belinda went to find

coffee with, as Marion put it, "extra caffeine." I asked her how she'd found me.

"The girl at your theatre said you'd be here," she said. "She's quite a girl."

"Don't tell her that," I said. "She says she's a woman."

"Hear her roar."

"Precisely," I said.

"You want to know why I'm here?" Marion asked as Belinda placed a cup in front of her and retreated to the counter. (I could be certain she was listening to every word; the distance wasn't fooling me.)

"The question did come to mind," I said. "Was it to tell me how you'd lied for Harry Lillis?"

Marion actually blushed, and made a point of looking at Belinda as she spoke. "Harry asked me to cover for him. Before we came to the theatre that first night, even. He told me the story he was going to tell you about Les and Vivian. He said it was a joke, that he was going to get you to chase around and then tell you how it was all a lie. I knew it was nonsense, but he asked me to back him up. Said you'd ask. I should just agree with whatever he'd told you."

"Why did you go along with it?" I asked. Marion blinked, and I said, "Stupid question. I should have seen it that night at the theatre. You never took your eyes off Harry. You never looked at Les. It was Lillis, not Townes, you were in love with, wasn't it? It was, wasn't it?"

She nodded. "I never had an affair with Les Townes. I barely ever spoke to Les Townes. He was devoted to Vivian, and didn't even look at other girls. But Harry . . . I loved Harry even back then. The ones that make you laugh, you know? I could tell you things about Chico Marx, even at the age he was when I knew him . . ."

"Let's stick to Harry," I suggested. "I can almost understand you corroborating his story, but after you thought he was dead, why keep it up?"

"I'd made him a promise," Marion said. "It seemed like the last thing I could do for him."

"I'm trying to understand Harry," I said. "I can't figure out why, if he was so filled with rage and guilt about Vivian, if he really thought Les killed her, why he'd wait fifty years to do anything about it."

Marion shook her head. "He never said anything to me about it before," she told me. "But when he was diagnosed, and he knew this was the end of the line, that's when Harry had nothing left to lose."

"I suppose he really loved Vivian," I said,

and instantly regretted it. I can fit a pretty big foot inside my mouth, when I give it all my effort.

"I suppose," Marion agreed with a tear in her eye. "I was trying to convince myself that he loved me."

"Maybe he did."

She shook her head again. "That's sweet, Elliot, but no. I just fooled myself. And Harry, he let me do it. I was better than nothing."

"You're a lot better than nothing," I told her honestly. "And Harry was a fool for not noticing."

She smiled. "Thanks," she said.

The evening's showings went off without incident, and after the staff left for the night (Sophie driving Jonathan in her Prius and Anthony heading back to campus, where he assured me he'd stay another year or two), I patted the snow globe on my desk and walked outside. I locked the front doors, then walked around the building into the alley.

I stopped dead in my tracks.

Chained to the pipe, where I'd been expecting Bobo Kaminsky's loaner bike, was my original bicycle, restored to something approximating mint condition. The pipes were straight and beautifully shined; the tires were new, the wheels unbent. The handlebars pointed in their intended directions, rather than in grotesque, splayed positions. And the pellet holes were gone. It was even a gleaming, metallic green, which I'm relatively sure was the color of the bicycle when I'd bought it, used, in another decade.

Speechless, I stood for a few moments, my jaw flapping open and shut a number of times. Finally, I managed to compose myself to the point that I could reach into my jacket pocket and pull out my keys. I unlocked the bike and rolled it, carefully, into the theatre.

In my office, I picked up the phone and dialed Bobo's number. I knew he'd be at the store; it was only eleven thirty.

"Midland Cyclery."

"Bobo, you're a wizard."

The pleasure in his voice was unmistakable. "As if that was ever in question," he said.

"How did you get the old one out and this one in without breaking the chain? Do you have a duplicate key to my bike lock?"

"Don't question the magic, muggle. Just enjoy it."

I thanked him profusely until I started to sound like Anthony, then we hung up.

It was a pleasure to ride home. Even in the autumn chill, I paid more attention to the improvement in my ride than to the wind whipping through my *Split Personality* crew jacket. The suspension system (the shocks) had been strengthened, or more likely replaced, so I didn't feel every pebble in the road. The seat was the same, but had been positioned properly, which I rarely bother to do. The tires, of course, were new and properly inflated. And the shine from the body was evident every time a car's headlights passed on my left. I felt like I'd bought a whole new bike, and it probably cost me only a little more than if I had.

At the remarkably green door of my town house, I was sorry the ride was finished. Already treating my "new" ride better than I had when it was my "old" one, I was very careful about lifting the bicycle properly up the front stairs, and certainly about not scraping it against the doorframe. Inside the hallway, I placed it gently on the floor, using the kickstand instead of merely leaning it against the wall. Then I stood and admired it for a full minute before walking inside.

The ride had exhilarated me; I wasn't tired, and I should have been. But, figuring that I could certainly sleep as late as I liked in the morning, I decided against going straight to bed. I had bought myself a book called *Teach Yourself to Play Guitar,* and tried a few chords quietly, but I was too antsy to pay attention to something I didn't know how to do yet. Besides, I was hungry, so I toasted myself a couple of freezer waffles to compensate for my early dinner, sat down in my director's chair, and pondered which of my thousands of comedy films on VHS or DVD to watch.

I'd been avoiding it for a while, but I couldn't put it off forever, no matter what. I put the disc in the player, got myself a beer from the fridge, set up a snack table, and picked up the remote control to hit Play.

On the screen, the opening credits to *Cracked Ice* showed up on the flat screen, and I braced myself. After all that had happened, all that I knew about the men involved and where their lives would go from that moment, would the wondrous comedy that had sustained me through my adolescence and my young adulthood still be as perfect as it had been? Would I become depressed at the sight of them, distraught at the part I'd played in both their deaths? Was it possible that Lillis and Townes could still take me to the place that had meant so much to me with all the extra baggage my mind had accumulated?

I took a long swig from the beer and let out a deep breath. And I felt a knot in my stomach as the caveman sequence with Les Townes, which opens the film, began. I couldn't help seeing in that face, with the pasted-on beard and the "caveman" hair that was obviously from the studio's wig department, the look he'd had when he was bending over his partner, more than fifty years later, in a residence for elderly show business veterans moments before he died. It was hard to shake.

But within ten minutes, maybe four scenes into the movie, my dread had dissipated. I was caught up in the beauty of Harry Lillis's delivery, Les Townes's natural ability to set up the punch lines, and the amazing, dexterous slapstick each of them could perform. I heard myself laugh once, then again, and by the time fifteen minutes were showing on the DVD's counter, I was totally engrossed and roaring with delight.

Damn, they were funny.

FURTHER FUNNY FILM FACTS FOR FANATICS

Cracked Ice (1956)

Okay, you got me. There is no movie called *Cracked Ice,* although there almost was. All of the Lillis and Townes movie titles were alternative working titles for Marx Brothers films. *Cracked Ice* became *Duck Soup* (1933); *Step This Way* and *Bargain Basement* were working titles for *The Big Store* (1941); and *Peace and Quiet* was the title of an early draft of *A Day at the Races* (1937). As for the Lillis and Townes stage show *You're Making It Up,* well, I . . . made it up.

While Lillis and Townes are meant to belong in the same strata as other great comedy teams — such as Abbott & Costello, Burns & Allen, Laurel & Hardy, and Martin & Lewis — they are in no way based on any real-life comedians (at least not consciously); with the one notable exception that I swiped their names from a pretty well-known comedy duo: Harry Lillis

"Bing" Crosby and Leslie Townes "Bob" Hope.

My Man Godfrey (1936)

Directed by Gregory LaCava, screenplay by Morrie Ryskind and Eric Hatch, based on the novel by Hatch. Starring William Powell, Carole Lombard, and Eugene Pallette.

- Powell plays a "forgotten man," another name for a homeless victim of the Great Depression, who is acquired by Lombard as part of a scavenger hunt and made a butler in her somewhat dizzy home. But there's more to him than meets the eye.
- Morrie Ryskind, who wrote the screenplay from Eric Hatch's novel, also co-wrote *Animal Crackers* (1930) and *A Night at the Opera* (1935) for the Marx Brothers, with George S. Kaufman.
- In a very small role, one can find Jane Wyman, who later married (and divorced) Ronald Reagan.

Never Give a Sucker an Even Break (1941)

Directed by Edward F. Cline, screenplay by Prescott Chaplin, W. C. Fields, and John T. Neville, story by Otis Criblecoblis. Starring W. C. Fields, Gloria Jean, Leon Errol, and

Margaret Dumont.

- In case anyone was wondering, Otis Criblecoblis was actually W. C. Fields.
- The film blends reality and fantasy as Fields plays himself, trying to sell a story to Esoteric Pictures. It then moves back and forth into Fields's story and his trying to sell it. It was Fields's final starring role.
- Mrs. Hemoglobin is played by Margaret Dumont, apparently on leave from playing straight man to Groucho Marx.

The Ghost Breakers (1940)

Directed by George Marshall, screenplay by Walter DeLeon, based on a play by Paul Dickey and Charles W. Goddard. Starring Bob Hope, Paulette Goddard, Anthony Quinn, and Willie Best.

- Willie Best eventually played the elevator operator on the fifties TV show *My Little Margie.* He also wrote the song "I Love You for Sentimental Reasons."
- Not in any way related to *Ghostbusters* (1984), this film stars Hope as a somewhat disreputable radio reporter who tags along with Goddard when she

inherits a supposedly haunted mansion. The film was actually a quick follow-up to the hit *The Cat and the Canary* (1939), with the same stars and director.

- Another bit part: Robert Ryan (*The Wild Bunch, The Dirty Dozen, The Longest Day*).

It Happened One Night (1934)

Directed by Frank Capra, screenplay by Robert Riskin, story by Samuel Hopkins Adams. Starring Clark Gable, Claudette Colbert, Walter Connolly, and Alan Hale.

- Yes, Alan Hale is the father of the Skipper (Alan Hale, Jr.) on *Gilligan's Island.*
- This was the first movie to sweep the "big" Academy Awards: Best Picture, Best Director, Best Actor, Best Actress, and Best Adapted Screenplay. The leading roles were originally offered to Robert Montgomery and Myrna Loy, both of whom turned the movie down. Colbert originally didn't want the role, either, but agreed to take the part when her salary was increased. Gable allegedly told a friend after filming, "I just finished the worst picture in the

world."

- The working title, from the short story it was based on, was *Night Bus.* Thank goodness I didn't have to come up with a pun for *that.*
- Director Capra tricked Colbert into doing the famous "skirt lift" hitchhiking scene, which she initially refused to do, by bringing in a body double with legs Colbert found unattractive.

Bananas (1971)

Directed by Woody Allen, screenplay by Woody Allen and Mickey Rose. Starring Woody Allen, Louise Lasser, Carlos Montalban, David Ortiz, Rene Enriquez, and Howard Cosell.

- No, that isn't the David Ortiz who now plays for the Boston Red Sox. But Carlos Montalban was Ricardo's older brother, and also played El Exigente in coffee commercials, and Rene Enriquez played Lieutenant Caetano on *Hill Street Blues.*
- One of Woody Allen's earlier, funnier movies, *Bananas* features Woody as Fielding Mellish, a timid New Yorker who becomes involved in a South American revolution to impress his

girlfriend. Sportscaster Howard Cosell gives play-by-play of both a dictator's assassination and Fielding's wedding night.

- Watch for a brief scene in which a young punk terrorizes Woody on the subway. The punk was played by Sylvester Stallone.

ACKNOWLEDGMENTS

It might take a village to raise a child (where are the villagers when you have to pay for college?), but it definitely takes a small army to get me through the writing process. Without a selfless and generous group of individuals, I would have to go out and get a real job, and who would *that* help, exactly?

In order for Harry and Les to seem like real classic comedians (did anybody notice the reference to them in *Some Like It Hot-Buttered*?), I relied on a number of sources, including my Marx Brothers bible, *Groucho, Harpo, Chico and Sometimes Zeppo,* by Joe Adamson. If you can find a copy, more power to ya. I have two.

Special thanks to everyone at the Lillian Booth Actors' Home in Englewood, especially Jordan Strohl, the administrator of the Home, and Lynne Hoppe, the director of communications for the Actors Fund. I am a proud member of the Fund, largely because of these two extremely accommodating, helpful, and cheerful people. I hope the Actors' Home is presented in the most positive way possible herein, because it really is a special place.

Thanks to Ivan Van Laningham, who contacted me through the DorothyL Listserv (here's a shout-out to the intrepid moderators there), for educating me on the subject of dentures and how they're marked. It might not have seemed like a big point to you, but I couldn't have gotten past that page without Ivan.

Invaluable help to the Double Feature Mysteries overall has come from many kind souls who seem bound and determined to help me succeed. My sincere gratitude to Victoria Hugo-Vidal and all of Team Pepperoni, who don't realize they have better things to do than promote my work (so don't tell them); Victoria's dad, Ross; her mom, Julia Spencer-Fleming; and her brother, Spencer, are all on the team, and I think a lot of people wouldn't have heard about these books without their tireless, generous work. I can't thank them enough.

Thanks of course to Linda Ellerbee for being a good sport and a true friend. Thanks to Tom Straw, Joe Stinson, Matt Kaufhold, and Chris Grabenstein for saying nice things when I really needed nice things to be said — and none of them knew it.

At Berkley Prime Crime: Thanks to Tom Haushalter for putting up with my incessant questions and goofy schemes, and to the incomparable Shannon Jamieson Vazquez, who forced me against my will to have the book make sense, and even braved the wilds of New Jersey to attend a popcorn party. Sure, other editors will correct your grammar, but how many are willing to take New Jersey Transit?

To Christina Hogrebe and the gang at the Jane Rotrosen Agency, thank you for dealing with all the stuff I couldn't possibly understand, which is anything that doesn't involve writing the book itself. What a relief to have a wonderful agent in your corner!

All that effort would be for naught, however, if it weren't for terrific booksellers, like Marilyn and Lisa at Moonstone in Flemington, New Jersey; Dianne and Craig at Borders in Fairfield, Connecticut (they should put on a seminar in author events for other bookstores); and the irreplaceable Bonnie and Joe at Black Orchid, whom I won't miss, because they're still around, but whose store was so friendly and welcoming, and isn't there any more. Dammit.

But more than anyone, thank you to my

astonishing family: my mother; my brother, Charlie; my inspiring son, Josh (as he approaches college!); my *awesome* daughter, Eve; and especially my incredibly understanding wife, Jessica, who has supported my writing habit for twenty-one years and hasn't complained once. Now, *that's* inspiration.

ABOUT THE AUTHOR

Jeffrey Cohen grew up in the same town as Jerry Lewis and Queen Latifah (different years). He is a freelance writer for the *New York Times, USA Weekend, Premiere, TV Guide,* and the *Newark Star-Ledger,* among many others. He's also written more than 20 feature-length screenplays, and his work has been developed by Jim Henson Productions, CBS, and Gross-Weston Productions. He is the author of four previous novels and two non-fiction books, and lives in New Jersey with his wife and children, who have been sworn to secrecy.

We hope you have enjoyed this Large Print book. Other Thorndike, Wheeler, and Chivers Press Large Print books are available at your library or directly from the publishers.

For information about current and upcoming titles, please call or write, without obligation, to:

Publisher
Thorndike Press
295 Kennedy Memorial Drive
Waterville, ME 04901
Tel. (800) 223-1244

or visit our Web site at:

http://gale.cengage.com/thorndike

OR

Chivers Large Print
published by BBC Audiobooks Ltd
St James House, The Square
Lower Bristol Road
Bath BA2 3SB
England
Tel. +44(0) 800 136919
email: bbcaudiobooks@bbc.co.uk
www.bbcaudiobooks.co.uk

All our Large Print titles are designed for easy reading, and all our books are made to last.

MB 7-09

PMath 1-12

NJ 2-13

WMV 1-15
MME 7-15

FN 1-14